Pierre Maël, Elisabeth Luther Cary

The Land of Tawny Beasts

Pierre Maël, Elisabeth Luther Cary

The Land of Tawny Beasts

ISBN/EAN: 9783743386280

Manufactured in Europe, USA, Canada, Australia, Japa

Cover: Foto ©Andreas Hilbeck / pixelio.de

Manufactured and distributed by brebook publishing software (www.brebook.com)

Pierre Maël, Elisabeth Luther Cary

The Land of Tawny Beasts

CICELY CAME THIRD.

THE LAND OF TAWNY BEASTS

By Pierre Maël

TRANSLATED BY
Elizabeth Luther Cary

With fifty-two illustrations by A. Paris

NEW YORK
FREDERICK A. STOKES COMPANY
PUBLISHERS

TO MY FRIEND

MAURICE DUBAREL,

INSPECTOR GENERAL OF THE COLONIES, IN CHARGE OF
THE INSPECTION SERVICE.

VERY AFFECTIONATELY,

P. M.

CONTENTS.

LIST OF ILLUSTRATIONS.

THE NEWCOMER DRAINED THE GLASS AT A SINGLE DRAUGHT.

THE LAND OF TAWNY BEASTS.

I.

A SCIENTIFIC FLURRY.

THE landlord of Great Tower Inn, one of the best hotels of Srinagar, was literally worn out.

That morning, the 15th of March, 1890, he had been obliged since daybreak hastily to prepare his rooms—which numbered forty—to receive an influx of travelers such as he had never before seen. The previous night he had received, one after another, the two following dispatches :

"Mr. Cecil Weldon begs Mr. Jackson of the Great Tower Inn, to keep six rooms for five gentlemen and himself."

"Keep an apartment for the R. H. Major Plumptre and six persons of his attendance."

The first of these dispatches came from Bombay, the second from Calcutta.

The excellent Jackson had thus disposed of thirteen rooms. Twenty-six others had been retained on that same 15th of March, by divers travelers, all of different nationalities. Of the number, fifteen were English, which goes without saying, three were German, two Belgian, two Russian, two Italian. The remaining two were highly educated Hindus, speaking several languages, and educated in various English schools, Dr. Lall-Sing-Catterjee and his young disciple, Madar-Goun, physician of the University of Paris.

There remained a twenty-seventh room, which the honest Mr. Jackson was reserving, with all sorts of scruples, for a traveler long since announced and expected.

He did not know his guests present and to come. One of them, however, bore a reputation. This was the Right Honorable Major Plumptre, a Scotchman from the Highlands, the youngest son of a noble family, one of the most brilliant officers of the Indian Army, and, moreover, already celebrated by his remarkable ascents of Hindu Kush and the Himálayas.

What then was the motive that drew such a crowd into the capital of Kashmír? Was it the commencement of the heated term in Bengal and the Deccan? No, for sojourners in those countries found nearer at hand summer resorts in which they could seek coolness, in the Nilgiris for the people of the south, for those of Calcutta at Dárjiling.

The explanation of this eagerness could only be furnished by reading the English newspapers. Three days before, in fact, the *Morning Post* had published this news, which had stirred the scientific world, and which the Indian gazettes had immediately copied.

"In all probability the French traveler, Jean Merrien, whose departure from Batúm by the Trans-Caspian Railroad, for the purpose of repeating the adventurous passage across the Pamirs accomplished by Messrs. Bonvalot, Capus, and Pepin, we announced three months ago, will presently arrive at the gates of India, according to reports sent to the authorities of the frontier by the Governor of Balkh."

How and why had this simple notice had the power to move scholars and to attract to Srinagar such a concourse of the curious?

The reason was that, three months previous, Jean Merrien had made known his intention of entering India by way of land. But this feat would not have sufficed to provoke such excitement, M. Gabriel Bonvalot having already successfully accomplished it, if Merrien had not betrayed, at the same time, his intention of scaling the giant of the Himálayas, the peak Gaurisankar, called Mt. Everest by the English, and reputed the highest of the formidable chain of which Kinchinjinga, Sihsour, and Dhaulágiri, rival one another in height.

To scale Gaurisankar! What height of audacity! And a Frenchman, too! A Frenchman come from France, one of those barbarians whom it is customary to make fun of nowadays, since the great humiliation of France in 1870. Only the serious people of England value him more highly than does France. They credit him with a history of sixteen centuries. They know that what a Frenchman resolutely undertakes he accomplishes—witness this same Bonvalot and his prodigious passage across the Pamirs.

Thus the excitement, though great, was justified.

At Calcutta, among other cities of the British Empire,

numerous projects had been formed. It had not for an instant entered the minds of our trusty adversaries to hinder the bold traveler in his attempt. On the other hand, they had said with one accord: "We must not permit this Frenchman to be the only one to perform his exploit. An Englishman must precede him, and the day that he sets foot upon the inviolate crest of the peak, he shall find there the flag of Great Britain planted by English hands."

This was the general sentiment, and this sentiment found special echo in the soul of Major George Plumptre, the most valiant of the adopted sons of Albion, since Scotland is only sister by adoption to England.

The brave officer at once made his arrangements for the campaign that he was about to undertake.

Duly authorized by his superiors, provided with an unlimited leave of absence, he prepared his equipment, the arms and utensils necessary to this perilous expedition. He called together two of his friends, a Dr. William Randolph, and Captain James MacKinnon. Each of these was accompanied by a Hindu domestic. The major on his part retained two, one of whom, Bardwar by name, was an Afghan of Chitrál, a mountaineer of unusual vigor and audacity. The seven men landed together on the morning of the 15th of March at Srinagar.

During the day there arrived at the Great Tower Inn Mr. Cecil Weldon and his five companions.

Jackson remarked, not without some surprise, that, among the five "gentlemen" announced, was a woman of a certain age, wearing the appearance of a stewardess or housekeeper. He was struck, moreover, by the extreme youth, the frail and delicate aspect, and the gentle voice of Cecil Weldon himself.

"Jupiter!" said he to Mrs. Jackson, an exclamation

habitual to him, " this young man has all the appearance of a young woman in disguise ! "

But the ease with which Cecil Weldon wore his masculine costume subdued all his doubts. Furthermore, the pseudo young woman was accompanied by four fine fellows, of herculean build, who spoke to him as soldiers to a superior. Mrs. Jackson was the first to say to her husband :

" I do not know where your wits are, Bob. This young gentleman is certainly one of the very prettiest boys I have ever seen in my life. He is too pretty a man to be an ugly girl."

And with this observation, worthy of the great Frenchman La Palisse, the good landlady went to look to her ovens. She wished to do honor to the distinguished guests that Providence had sent.

The two groups met in the evening at the *table d'hôte*. The major and his friends were forewarned. And already their British pride had taken alarm. Their thoughts were no longer occupied by the imprudent Frenchman alone. They had just learned that this Mr. Weldon and his party were Americans, who had crossed from New York to London, from London to France, and from France, by the *Messageries Maritimes,* to Bombay, where they had taken the train which had brought them by way of Múltán, Lahore, and Ráwal Pindí, to Srínagar, where they arrived toward three o'clock in the afternoon.

Of course conversation opened promptly. The major did not like to find himself confronted with strangers. Had he not been seen, in the last English expedition into Afghánistán, to advance alone, helmet in hand, to meet a hostile column, and after a ceremonious salute, to cry to the officer who commanded the detachment :

" Sir, I beg your pardon. Tell me, please, your name."

And the Afghán who, luckily, spoke English, had laughed gallantly at this sally of the adventurous Scotchman. He had given his name and first name, after which he had, not less politely, invited the " Inglis " to return and defend himself. Plumptre, satisfied, retraced his steps and said to his companions in arms :

" Decidedly these Patháns have been calumniated. They know very well how to behave."

Such was the man who found himself seated opposite the young American Weldon at the great central table of the Grand Tower Hotel. From the moment Jackson's guests had taken their places at dinner, they had not ceased their observation of one another.

The major appealed directly to Cecil Weldon.

" Sir," he commenced, " you come from New York, I am told."

The frail Yankee, with the feminine ring to his voice, responded :

" You have been correctly informed, sir. We come from New York, my companions and I."

" Ah ! " said the officer. " As for me, I come from Calcutta, which is a good deal nearer. But perhaps our aim is the same, and we are rivals without knowing it ? "

Mr. Cecil Weldon had a charming smile, which aroused the same doubts in the major's mind that it had excited in the less distinguished brain of the excellent Bob Jackson. He replied :

" Sir, I cannot say if we are rivals. I have come with my friends to attempt the ascent of Mount Gauri-sankar, which a Frenchman, they say, is preparing to climb. I have thought, with all my fellow-citizens of New York, that this would cast shame upon the most advanced people of the world——"

The officer here interrupted with a certain vivacity:

"Young man, the most advanced people of the world are certainly the English people."

Mr. Weldon smiled suggestively. He saluted British susceptibility with a shade of irony.

"Upon the road to Gaurisankar, assuredly, sir, since Calcutta is nearer to it than New York; while, to tell the truth, at the present moment New York and Calcutta are together at Kashmir."

"Upon every road, sir!" cried the fuming Englishman.

The young Yankee, not wishing to enter upon a discussion of this subject, parried him courteously:

"It will be very easy for us to sustain our flags upon the summits of the Himálayas."

"What!" cried Plumptre, "you intend to attempt the ascent?"

"That is, indeed, my intention, sir."

"But, my good fellow, you have no suspicion of the dangers of this undertaking!"

A light gleamed in the steel-blue eyes of the young man. His voice was cutting as a sword-blade, when, looking fearlessly into the face of his haughty interlocutor, he responded:

"Major Plumptre, I have accomplished in the course of my existence things quite as difficult. I have been among the ices of the North Pole, as far as the encampments of Greely and Nares. I have climbed Chimborazo, Cotopaxi, the giants of the Andes, and the Kilimanjaro in Africa. I have crossed Niagara, and the Zambezi at the very brink of their cataracts. You see that I may attempt the scaling of Gaurisankar."

The Englishman stretched a large and loyal hand across the table to the proud youth.

"All right. You are worthy of me. Let us make a compact between ourselves, as becomes Saxon brothers. We will prevent the miserable Frenchman from being the first to arrive."

The honest major forgot that he was Saxon only by annexation, being descended from the Scots and Picts of old Caledonia. No matter! He believed his honor concerned in the defeat of France.

The Yankee responded with energy to the hand-clasp; but he added:

"Each for himself, major. I intend to beat not only France, but Old England as well. Hurrah for Young America!"

The other travelers around them kept silence, listening with interest. The two Hindu physicians, in particular, showed close attention. The major was doubtless about to say something in reply to the provoking frankness of his frail antagonist, when suddenly a clear and vibrant voice rang out, saying in good French: "France is not yet beaten, gentlemen! She salutes her trusty adversaries, and drinks to their health."

At the same time a man crossed the room, came directly to the table, where he filled a glass of champagne, and, raising it to the level of his head:

"To Young America, whom France aided at Pittsburg and at Yorktown; to Old England, whom France succored at Inkermann!"

The newcomer drained the glass at a single draught. He was a man of stature a trifle above the medium, of athletic build. His face, with its refined though clearly marked features, revealed indomitable energy.

A single cry broke from the lips of all, amid universal astonishment :

"Jean Merrien ! Jean Merrien !"

The stranger proudly saluted the assembled company.

"Yes, gentlemen, Jean Merrien, himself, alive in the flesh, who has just crossed the Pamirs after Bonvalot, and who will set out again to-morrow—with you, if that please you ; if not, without you—for the mountains of Karakoram."

There was a fresh exclamation. The rivals of the bold Frenchman failed to comprehend.

"But isn't it Gaurisankar that you purpose climbing ?" asked Cecil Weldon.

"Precisely so, monsieur. It is indeed Gaurisankar."

"You spoke, just now, of Karakoram : the Gaurisankar road does not lie in that direction."

The French explorer regarded his interlocutor with a suspicion of disdain.

"My young sir, it must be believed that Americans are badly informed as to Asiatic geography. If you had come, as I did, by the north, you would know that Gaurisankar is climbed only by the north ; the roads of the south are closed."

"Ah ! And why are they closed ?" asked Major Plumptre, with curiosity.

"Because the 15th of March is here, when the snows of the southern slope commence to melt, and the flooded streams render the Tarái impassable. But that is not the true reason for so long a detour. If I ascend by the north it is simply because the frontiers of Nepál and those of Bhután are rigorously interdicted to Europeans who have not a direct commission from the English Government."

These words produced profound astonishment and great dismay among those present.

Young Weldon, in particular, appeared a prey to lively annoyance.

But Major Plumptre, as a good servant of Her Gracious Majesty, protested then and there.

"Mr. Frenchman," he cried, "it is permissible for you to retrace your steps and take the northern road. Nevertheless, if you trust me, you will take my advice. I will take the train back to Calcutta. I will see the Lord-Governor, and I will undertake to bring back a double commission, opening the gates of Nepál to us—one for you and one for me."

"And I, major," implored Cecil Weldon: "are you going to leave me here?"

The officer shook his head and gave two or three sonorous "humphs!"

"Three commissions, my dear fellow, may be a good deal to ask. No matter! I will make the attempt. If necessary, you can pass as one of our party."

The Frenchman and the Yankee simultaneously extended their hands to the generous Scotchman.

"Bravo, Major Plumptre! and thanks for this proof of good faith."

The entire room gave three cheers for the officer. He thanked the company graciously, and went at once to his room methodically to repack his valise. When he came down again, ready to take the evening train, he went directly to his future companions of the ascent.

"Well!" said he, "I have reflected. It would be much quicker for you to come with me. Instead of crossing the Tarái at the west, we will approach the chain by the passes of Bhután to the north of Dárjíling. In this way, we will have the best of the road, and we shall encounter, into the bargain, three of the good brothers or sisters of Gaurisankar upon the way : Kinchinjinga, Chumalari, and Kinchinjaou."

Jean Merrien thanked the Englishman warmly for his proposition. Then he said with a smile :

"Major, your idea is inviting. But I will hold to my programme. It will be just as satisfactory to us. We will go to Gaurisankar by Dhaulágiri. And we shall at the same time admire Morchiadi, Barathor, Yassa, Dáyábang, and Deorali. Furthermore," he added, "there is nothing to prevent our coming down again into India by the road you just now mentioned, unless we have time and strength to proceed to the discovery of the source of the Brahmaputra."

"You are right, Mr. Merrien," gravely replied the Scotchman. "The French have the reputation of hesitating at nothing. You nobly sustain that reputation. But by Heaven. Old England will not yield to you at any point. We will do all these things together, Mr. Frenchman."

"And Young America will be first at the summit !" cried the enthusiastic Weldon.

Thereupon, as night had come on, and the train must not be missed, a parting punch was drunk, and the Europeans conducted Major Plumptre to the station.

Hardly had they quitted the hotel when the two Hindu physicians rose simultaneously.

"You have heard ?" asked Lall-Sing-Catterjee to Madar-Gown.

"Yes," replied the other.

"Thus," resumed the elder of the two men, "bit by bit, inch by inch, our land is becoming the prey of the foreigner. When it is not in the name of humanity, it is in the name of science that they come. Humanity! Ah, yes! England loves it, on condition that she makes of it a great herd of slaves. And as to their 'science,' we know it— you and I. We have studied upon the benches of their most famous universities. What have they then to teach us that we do not already know?"

He paused, and clenched his fists with a gesture of savage energy.

"Their science? How does it serve them. We have won their diplomas, we have the right to practice medicine even in their own countries. And when my European colleagues come here, among us, into this Hindustan that draws them and infatuates them, they do not know what use to make of their knowledge of words and books. They have nothing with which to heal the bite of a cobra or the cerebral congestion caused by our sun. Do they even discover the remedy for cholera or the marsh fevers, when our humblest fakirs obtain astonishing cures? Ah, Madar-Goun! my blood boils at this thought. India is only a land of conquest for the whites, and the misfortune is, that she is becoming accustomed to her servitude!"

The young doctor raised his head. A light flashed in his eyes.

"Is it you who speak thus, master? You, Lall-Sing- .Catterjee, who have vowed to battle all your life for the freedom of our land? Do you then doubt the sentiment which still reigns in the heart of the various countries of our soil, which animates our pundits, which guides these very fakirs of whom you spoke just now? Do you not know that there is not a district of the peninsula in which there do not beat hearts aflame with the fire of Independence? And we ourselves, are we not faithful servants of the 'Great Family,' jealous to free our land from its European oppressors?"

Lall-Sing let his arms fall in discouragement.

"I would fain have your faith, my friend, your indomitable confidence. Alas! the obstacle is always present to my view, What can we do against these men? What means do we command? We are not a single people with our two hundred million of inhabitants. As you have just said, a hundred different races live in common upon this triangle which reaches from the Indus and the Ganges to the point of Ceylon. A handful of Englishmen holds this multitude under the yoke. Since Tippu-Sahib, what useless efforts, what attempts drowned in blood! England no longer fears since the day when Nâna of Bithûr mysteriously disappeared, and our still independent rajahs contend for the honor of figuring in the train of the Empress-Queen. Our secret societies are no longer anything more than gatherings of fanatics performing abominable crimes without aim or reason. Moreover, the British police hunt them like wild beasts, and the Thugs survive only in legend."

The brows of Madar-Goun were knit. He made an angry gesture.

"Ha! what are you saying! Stigmatizing with the name of 'crimes' acts inspired by a patriotism as sincere as it is cruel? Is it for us, who dream of the emancipation of our country, to check ourselves with such narrow prejudices? What matter the means, provided they render to the oppressed their liberty!"

Lall-Sing was less savage than his young interlocutor. He sighed:

"Ah, my friend! you touch precisely the weak point in my will. I doubt. I hesitate. Is it indeed true that all means are legitimate? Is it a cause noble enough,

pure enough, to justify serving it at the cost of violence?
And to redeem a people who themselves subscribe to their
dethronement, has one the right to spill innocent blood, as
our brothers so many times have done?"

The young doctor gave an ugly laugh.

"Ah, master! you have too long sojourned in Europe.
Humanitarian sophisms have troubled your mind and softened your heart. For me, who, like yourself, and even
being your pupil here, have studied at the great scientific
centers of the white continent, the question was long since
decided. I make no scruple in closing the road by all possible means to the 'pioneers of civilization,' as our adversaries call themselves, and I care so little for their lives that
I have, since morning, notified the 'Great Family' to hold
itself in readiness to receive our communications."

"You have done that, Madar-Goun?" asked Catterjee,
with an accent of reproach.

The young man rapidly passed his arm under that of the
"Master," and drawing him out of doors upon the Jhelum
road, said to him, with the same mocking laugh:

"You shall see what I have done!"

They paused at the brink of the river, and approached
one of the seven wooden bridges which connected the two
banks. Under the radiant light of the moon, the river and
its quays, with their houses of brick, stone, and wood,
took on a fairy-like aspect. From time to time some distant melody, from an English harp or an Hindu instrument,
broke the dense silence of the sleeping city. A fresh,
pure breeze—a spring breeze descending from the southern
chain of the Panjàl Mountains, through the snowy pass of
Zóji—saturated the atmosphere with perfumes gathered
upon its way in the lovely Vale of Roses. At times there
was also heard the plash of oars bringing a late gondola

MADAR-GOUN CALLED GENTLY.

from the balmy depths of the Dal Lake, into one of the twenty-two canals of the Indian Venice.

The two men crossed the bridge, and approached the lake. A bark with a sharp prow swung near a large *ghat*, whose marble steps dipped into the water. Innumerable gardens stretched in various directions, filling the air with the odors of plant and flower. A man was lying in the boat, and seemed to be sleeping heavily.

Madar-Goun went to the edge of the water, and called gently : "Pandári!"

The sleeper bounded to his feet, and, recognizing who it was speaking to him, leaped ashore. Then he approached humbly, with hands extended in front of his forehead in salutation to receive the young physician's message.

"Are you rested? Are you ready?" inquired the latter.

"You may speak, sahib," replied the Hindu. "I am ready. Is it time to go?"

"Yes, immediately. You will not stop until you reach Drás, to give the watchword to the brother who will replace you."

"Very well, sahib. And when must I be at Drás?"

The doctor reflected, and counted aloud. Then, with haughty brevity, he gave his orders :

"It is eighty-two miles from here to Drás by the Zóji pass. The roads are bad, but we have the start. It will be in time if you arrive day after to-morrow."

"I will be there. Have you a writing to give me?"

"No. This is what you are to say to the brother : 'The white men will number about ten in passing the boundary. They will doubtless go by Simla, and will have English permits. Let the brothers of the Three Ganges keep watch!'"

And extending his hand over the bowed head of the man, as in benediction, Dr. Madar-Goun turned away without a word more, drawing Lall-Sing with him toward Jhelum, while the messenger detached the boat, which glided over the silvery waters of the lake.

AT THEIR HEAD WALKED A TALL OLD MAN.

II.

DEVOTEES OF THE FIRE GOD.

To the north of Simla, in the high valley of the Sutlej, rise the first terraces of the western Himálayas.

There, peaks of lesser elevation shoot up abruptly, whose average altitude equals, however, that of Mont Blanc, of Maladetta, or the Pic du Midi. Narrow ravines such as the passes of Bhabar, of Manirung, of Dal, and of Bahbeh, give access to the Indian cities of Chipki and Sultánpur.

Below, on one of the first buttresses of the chain, rises the wholly English city of Simla, which might be called the second capital of the Indo-British Empire, a sanitarium and pleasure resort which, during the great heat, becomes the seat of government itself, for the viceroy, his household, and the principal civil and military functionaries, move to these cool slopes, in this belt of hill-country commanding from a height of some seven thousand feet the double valley of the Sutlej, and the Jumna ; and covered with other pleasure resorts and military stations such as Jaitak with its formidable batteries, Dagshai, Sabáthu, and Kálka.

Below Simla is found Masúri, and higher up the stream of Taoungsa, the half Indian city of Chakrata.

This is the Garhwál district, the original country, it is believed, of the Sikhs, those redoubtable warriors who issued thence to conquer the Punjab, and whose last king, Ranjit Singh, the "Lion of the Five Rivers," surrounded by French generals such as Allard, Ventura, Avitabile, and De Facien, was able to make himself respected by the English to the day of his death. To Garhwál belong the healthy, picturesque, and fantastically inhabited regions of Kullu and Seoráj, with their Tibetan, Rajpút, Paharan, and Hindustáni populations. Sultánpur is the capital of Kullu, and is connected with Mandi by a very pretty road.

Now on the 15th day of March, 1890, an eager crowd of three or four thousand travelers climbed the crests of Sikanda-Kadar, "Mount Alexander," directing their course from Suket toward Mandi, along the steep banks of the Biás. Men, women, and children, some on foot, some on asses and mules, appeared hastening toward their destination. The sun was already touching the southern peaks which hide Pilaspur, and violet shadows lengthened on the lower ranges, while the rapid fall of the temperature gave reason to fear that night would surprise the pilgrims in the narrow, cold defile.

At their head walked a tall old man, who was constrained by the increasing chilliness to wrap himself in a mantle of white wool. On his forehead, the lower por-

tion of which was uncovered, were three scars crossed
and painted red. He was a Brahmin by caste but not in
office. Those who followed him seemed to profess for
him respect, mingled with superstitious fear. From time
to time the band separated, falling back upon the slopes or
the sides of the road, to make way for some cavalier, an
English officer in white undress uniform, his linen helmet
on his head, his clanking sabre at the back of his saddle,
followed by a native soldier, clad in European dress with
the exception of the head-dress, which still consisted of
the turban in knotted folds of the mingled colors of the
different regiments, according to native custom.

Before the white man the crowd showed great humility,
and lavished their salaams upon the insolent conquerer,
who pushed through the press with that haughty swagger
peculiar to the Saxon race ; his left hand upon his hip, his
right hand indifferently letting the reins fall on the neck
of the horse, a costly animal imported from England or
brought down from Persia by the passes of Afghanistan
or the Pamirs. And the pilgrims no longer wondered that
a horse should risk itself where mules would hardly venture. They knew, from having all too often heard it said,
that the "blond men" excel in all bodily exercises, and
take pleasure in all such feats of strength and daring, in
open defiance of common sense.

But after the white man had passed, the travelers turned
and sent after him, along the slope of the frightful precipice, looks filled with execration.

Meanwhile darkness was descending upon the valley,
the waters of the Biás became shadowy, and all the sides
of Sikanda-Kadar disappeared under ragged clouds of mist
drifting obliquely across them. Alone in the eastern horizon the summits of the Babah pass retained a golden and

purple light upon their carpet of melting snow. Eagles
flew with hoarse cries above the cedars, the firs, the
teaks, the cypresses and larches covering the sides of the
mountains. From time to time a sound, strident yet sonorous because of the depth of the echoes, hastened the
footsteps of the crowd. They well knew that the *Kala
bágh*, the black tiger of the Tarái, ventures among these
great altitudes where sheep abound. Abruptly, at a bend
in the road, a sort of platform of three or four square
kilometers revealed itself to the eyes of the travelers upon
their left. Abandoning the bed of the Biás upon its right,
the crowd precipitately followed the Brahmin in the direction of certain ruins of rather vague aspect. This brought
them to the foot of shapeless monuments, some formed of
monoliths of considerable dimensions, others of a quantity
of stones in ruins.

The Brahmin threw himself on his knees before the
highest of these time-defaced constructions. He put his
face against the earth and prayed in an ecstasy of fervor.
The following words were heard in his guttural voice,
speaking with monotonous rhythm :

" Principle of sacred fire and of the force which
destroys in order to renew; august brother of Vishnu
whom thou combatest, Sivá, God of Death, who reignest
upon the peaks of the Dhaulágiri, upon the triple tooth
of Trikotá; thou who hast created these rocks and these
mountains in order to arrest the steps of impure men,
receive our adorations, and give unto us the light of thy
breath."

The night had shut down completely. Nothing was
now to be heard but the rustling of branches upon the
slopes of Sikanda-Kadar. The Brahmin rose and commanded :

"Withdraw the women and children. Let them take shelter under the altars of the east."

Women and children obeyed with docility. The crowd divided itself into two unequal masses, one of which took its way toward the shapeless constructions situated at the east of the narrow valley, while the other, that consisting of the men alone, grouped itself in a solid body about the religious Hindu, who then sent up a new form of invocation :

"Sivá, principle of sacred Fire, Parvái, immortal spouse of living death, we adore you in this place that you have filled with signs of your power. It is here that the first man from the West, come for conquest, was checked : it is here that Maha-Sikandar, before taking his way to the white countries, raised these altars to your glory, Ô Pá˘-vái, Ô Sivá, Mahádevi of holy Fire, Mahádevi of Death, which transfigures. May the earth open under our feet, in order that we may celebrate our sacrifices at the feet of your divine images ! "

Upon finishing this speech, the Siváite priest approached the " altar of Alexander," a square structure, without ornament, quite like the megaliths of Brittany, and formed of a collection of twelve regular blocks, covered over with a thirteenth like a ceiling, after the fashion of a " dolman."

The Brahmin extended his arms, and, seizing one of the stones with a peculiar movement, without effort made it whirl in its socket.

An opening was disclosed, large enough to permit a man to pass through, and the mysterious personage entered it, followed by the crowd of the faithful.

These went through, one by one, and the long chain of men, engulfed in the silence beyond the narrow opening, threaded their way like a procession of phantoms.

THE BRAHMIN EXTENDED HIS ARMS.

This was one of the subterranean temples of which
India possesses so many. The revolving stone set free a
slab, and this, swinging into a perpendicular, exposed
the gaping orifice of a stairway of forty steps, giving access to a vast pillared room, at the back of which rose two
monsters with three heads and six arms, effigies in gilded
bronze of the Deva of Death, and his celestial companion
the redoubtable Párváti, called also, according to the custom of the different cults, Durgá, or Káli.

The Hindus, led by the Siváite Brahmin, all entered
this cavern, which was perpetually lighted by the flame of
ten golden lamps filled each night by one of the faithful
with the holy oil indispensable to the maintenance of this
sacred light.

The crowd prostrated itself before the hideous idols, and
after a series of invocations chanted in alternate verses, the
ceremonies of the sect commenced.

From the shadowy recesses of the cave sprang creatures
of incredible emaciation : old men with long white beards,
youths whose young bodies were reduced to skin and
bone, even children, veritable skeletons, hardly able to
crawl. Some women were among the number, belonging
to the class of *devadassis* or dancing priestesses, dedicated
to the decorative pomp of open or secret festivals.

All this class of fanatics were devoted to the practice
of fakirism, that strange and inexplicable custom of the
Brahminic code ; the meaning and reason of which the
researches of contemporaneous science have not yet been
able to discover. Men, women, and children gave themselves up to frightful macerations, to impossible fasts, and
submitted to atrocious mutilations, such as those of which
the public had a glimpse in the unbridled saturnalia of
Durgá Pujah.

Some pierced their tongues with a stiletto of steel or with bars of iron heated red hot; others passed these bars over the entire surface of their bodies, and the scorched flesh could be heard shriveling while the features of the sufferers betrayed not the least pain.

They were seen to whirl continuously, faster and faster, until, crazed, they threw themselves upon the ground foaming at the mouth and at the point of death.

A number wound about their bare limbs frightful serpents—the hooded cobras, whose single bite brings death in less than half an hour.

Suddenly the religious transports ceased, and the voice of the pontiff rose:

"Principle of renewing fire," cried he, "manifest thy presence!"

Then took place a natural phenomenon well calculated to impress all these minds, weakened by the degrading practices of a worship as sanguinary as it is superstitious. All at once the rocks behind the idols of Sivá and Párváti appeared to cleave asunder. A fissure, previously invisible, extended the full height of the subterranean temple, and rings of acrid and nauseous smoke, indicating the presence of numerous carburates of hydrogen, rose toward the vaulted ceiling. At the same time, from various holes made in the wall, water commenced to fall in cascades into basins of marble arranged along the foot of the wall. Obeying some cleverly concealed inner mechanism, the two monstrous statues turned away from each other, melting, so to speak, into the opaque shadow of the side passages. And, suddenly, from the enlarged fissure rose a bluish flame which, developing into a sheet of light, put out the golden lamps and filled the entire cave with a strange light and at the same time with insupportable heat. A deathlike silence reigned in the sanctuary. Then, through the thick vapor of the suffocating atmosphere, the guttural voice of the priest was again heard, saying:

"Glory be to Sivá and to Párváti, in the unity of the Fire God!"

The illusive phenomenon lasted about a quarter of an hour, after which the flame, diminished in intensity and volume, appeared to re-enter the orifice from which it came, then went altogether out, leaving behind some puffs of vapor, traces of its passage as they had been forerunners of its appearance. Then these also diminished and disappeared, at the same time that the streams of water at the infernal heat of 194° ceased to run.

The gasping mass of demoniacs rose little by little, and when the faithful, exhausted with their ritualistic practices, had recovered enough strength and intelligence to listen to the exhortations of their priest, he went and stood erect at the feet of the idols, which had returned to their respective places, and harangued the multitude:

"Very holy brothers, it is not by prayer alone that the Mahádevas are honored. It is by sacrifices that are peculiarly agreeable to them. You know what they are."

"Yes," clamored the crowd, "the sacrifice that pleases God greatly is the blood of the impious and those who profane."

"Brother Ramu," said the priest, addressing one who had spoken, "how many victims hast thou offered up for the repast of the great goddess?"

The man, a young Hindu, vigorously built. rose and responded:

"Holy Priest, since our last assemblage these hands have offered to our gods twelve victims. Seven were of the cursed race of the invaders: one man, three women, and three children. The five others were of our race, but they were criminals, since they had made themselves servants of the accursed English."

A clamor of enthusiasm greeted the avowal of these execrable crimes.

After Ramu, other Indians followed in their turn to relate their abominable exploits. Then when the account had been made up of the murders accomplished during the previous year, consisting of twenty-seven European victims and sixty Indians from among the Mussulmans and the Buddhists, as well as from among the innumerable sects of Brahminism ; when the faithful who had caused death without drawing blood, as is agreeable to the heart of Párváti, had been praised for so doing, and those had been blamed who had made use of other arms than the cord or the handkerchief, which prevents Sivá from pre-senting the sacrifice to his over-sensitive spouse, the pontiff summoned all the zeal of the sect to new acts of faith.

"At this very moment," he said, "ten white men and ten Indians are preparing to violate our sacred boundaries. They come by the Mandi road, that which we are on, and will go up as far as Sultánpur. Their sacrilegious intention is to invade the sacred mountain, and push their footsteps even so far as the inviolate snow of the thrones on which sit Sivá and Párváti. These men, who do not believe in our doctrines, who blaspheme our divinities, are especially formidable. One of them is that Scotch officer who made himself so terribly con-spicuous in the English expedition upon the frontiers of Afghánistán, and who, later, with thirty cavalrymen, went up from Mandalay as far as the boundaries of Assam, pitilessly sabering the Burman Dacoits."

"Major Plumptre!" wailed the group, stricken with terror.

"Another," continued the priest, "is a young American whom some of our brothers have seen at Bombay and Srinagar. Gun in hand, he is invincible. His ball cuts a needle in two at eighty meters, and will kill a Bengal bird on the fly."

A shudder of fear shook the crowd. Some of them found voice to ask the name of this terrible adversary.

"Cecil Weldon," responded the Brahmin. And, pursuing his address:

"The third is more to be feared. He is a Frenchman; that is to say, he belongs to that extraordinary race which is daunted by nothing. He is stronger than Major Plumptre, and has even repeated the prodigies of the other Frenchman, Bonvalot. Moreover, the Christian's demon cares for him, for he seems guarded by invisible protection. Ten times already our brothers of Persia, Afghánistán, and Chitrál, have tried to arrest his progress. The accursed Frenchman has broken all their nets, overcome all their witchcraft, and it is our brothers who have perished or who have been made to suffer. He is called Jean Merrien."

A silence full of trembling followed this address. Finally, the panting and agitated crowd broke into eager questioning.

"What can be done? What can be done, Holy Pontiff?"

The Brahmin meditated for an instant and appeared to enter into communication with the inspiring god.

"Brothers," he resumed finally, "these men are doubtless formidable, but what cannot the will of one of the faithful do? They are twenty, enough assuredly, since each one of them, of the white men at all events, is as good as ten. Their plan, which they do not in any way conceal, is to enter the holy mountain by these ranges where we now are, in order to mount to the highest summits by way of Jamnotri and Nanda-Devi. If they only wished to see Dhaulágiri we would not need to agitate ourselves. The Mountain of the Son of Man belongs to the faithful of Vishnu-Rama. It is for them to defend it, but Nanda-Devi is the throne of Párváti, and only the faithful have the right to offer up goats to the goddess. But further than this, the blasphemers wish to follow the entire chain, and their final aim is to attain to the supreme throne, the holy Tchango Pamari, which the Nepális call Gaurísankar."

An explosion of ferocious cries broke forth. Arms waved, eyes filled with hatred.

"Brothers, these men must not pass the waters of our Sutlej. The snows of Nanda-Devi must not be polluted by the foot of one of them. It is already too much that heretofore one white man has been able to penetrate thus far protected by the safe conduct of the princes of Khátmandú. These others must die upon the frontier of Nepál, even though all human laws protect them."

"Yes, yes, yes!" howled the excited crowd. "They must die! Glory be to Sivá! The laws of man cannot check the fulfillment of the will of the gods."

There was then for some moments an indescribable tumult. A thousand projects crossed each other. An immense disorder reigned ; and the devotees of the Fire-God moved amid incredible confusion.

Silence, however, was re-established and the Brahmin

profited by it to distribute orders apportioning the troop
of assassins along the mountain road from Sultanpur to
the frontiers of Tibet.

Accordingly, as the old man pronounced the name of
a man and the station designed for this murderous campaign, he to whom the order was directed mounted the
staircase and started immediately upon the road across
the country, by night, in order to occupy his post the
sooner.

Thus the mob dispersed, and at the hour of mid-
night there remained only half a score of the faithful
about the Brahmin, chosen as among the most trusty
and able. Of this number Ramu was one.

"For thee," the old man said to him, "I have
reserved the most difficult, but also the most honorable
post. Thou wilt go to join the white men. Thou wilt
attach thyself to their persons, as their guide, or as their
servant. Not only wilt thou be able to offer the sacrifice
to Mahádeva in person, but thou canst also advise our
brothers, in order that they may accomplish that which
thou wilt not be able to execute. Go, then, and may the
strength of Sivá be in thy arms : the smile of Párváti on
thy lips."

The Hindu prostrated himself before the old man,
whose right foot he took and placed upon his head,
but at the moment when he prepared to mount the
staircase in his turn, a man in European costume
descended it precipitately. Pushing aside those present,
in spite of menaces of death and poniards raised against
his breast, in two or three rapid bounds he had joined
the Brahmin. Then he was recognized, and a profound
stupor succeeded the anger with which the entrance of
the unholy one had been received. He was in fact not

one of the unholy ; he was a brother, and of the most zealous : the Dr. Madar-Goun. He began to explain even before they questioned him.

"I do not come too late," he cried, "since you are still here. It is necessary to advise immediately as to new measures. The accursed Frenchman and his companions will not pass by the Kulla nor the Garhwál."

"Ah !" cried his hearers, much disappointed by his news.

The physician proceeded, having finally overcome the breathlessness caused by his haste :

"I have come at full speed from Simla, for I only knew this yesterday afternoon. Major Plumptre re-entered Calcutta day before yesterday in the afternoon. He waited for the government to advise him of the instructions expected from Khátmandú, but they were not known till a late hour. The maharájá has fixed the road which the travelers must follow. It appears that the Governor of Calcutta has spoken threateningly, and the king has been afraid that the redcoats would profit by a refusal on his part to take from him the countries to the north of Dárjiling bordering on Sikkim. He has therefore granted them right of way, but on condition that the explorers do not wander from the road designated, at least until they reach the level of the Great Chain. Once in the mountains, since he is no longer responsible for their lives, he troubles himself no further about their path."

The Brahmin, interested by this communication, asked :

"Then, once in the mountains, the king and the governor are indifferent to their existence ?"

"Yes," answered the physician, "but once in the mountains they have on their side the worshipers of

Vishnu, they have the snow and the cold. The men of the South will not be able to pursue them."

"Then they must die before they have left the chain of Chiriya-ghâti," said Ramu, in a hollow voice.

The physician gave a little silent laugh: "In Tarai Death is forever on the watch. She has many names and aspects. The tiger and the panther, the elephant and the rhinoceros, the cobra di capello, and the black serpent, rather than the Hindus, will prefer to kill the white man."

The Brahmin extended his hand and imposed silence upon his few companions, who were commencing to murmur:

"Brother," he said, "we must first know what we are going to do, and how we shall proceed. You have forgotten to tell us the road imposed upon the travelers by the maharâjâ.

Madar-Goun made a gesture of manifest annoyance.

"That is what I do not know," he replied. "The white men have kept their instructions secret. We shall have to guess the itinerary they will be apt to follow, for I know that the Frenchman expects to commence his excursion with the Dhaulâgiri."

The Indians looked at one another in much confusion. It was evident that their too limited ideas of geography would hardly permit of their establishing a base of operations. The physician, educated in Europe, and thus familiarized with the processes of contemporaneous science, extricated them from their embarrassment.

"The road that they will be almost certain to follow is that from Jamla to Rawni. It is there that we must seek them."

There was a heavy silence among the group. The

faithful of the Fire-God were doubtless reflecting upon the course they should take.

Then, when their meditations had come to an end, the Brahmin chief, speaking last, announced :

" Ramu will take the mountain road. He will remain at Jamla until the travelers arrive. There he will do as I have said. Nothing is changed but the road of the white men. But that road passes over the land of our gods. The profane ones must be chastised. So shall it be ! "

Then, one by one, the worshipers of the God of Death left the cave and joined the encampment of women.

The physician remounted his horse, which he had tied to an iron hook fixed at one of the angles of the altar of Alexander, and addressing Ramu, who was about to set out. on the same road as himself : " Brother," he said, " mount behind me. You will thus gain a part of the way."

The Hindu did not wait to be urged, and the next moment the animal's hoofs were resounding on the horse-road, well covered with broken stone, owing to the diligence of the English administration, as they rode through a cold night resplendent with stars.

THEY SET OUT UPON THEIR WAY.

III.

THE TARÁI.

Dr. Madar-Goun and his fanatical companions were mistaken.

It was not by way of Jamla and Rawni that the explorers were going to commence their dangerous ascent.

At the moment of leaving Srínagar they had taken counsel together, compelled as they were to submit to the conditions imposed by the King of Nepál. But these conditions left them the choice of two ways of entering: that of Jamla and Rawni the most direct certainly, but also the most subject to control, that is to say, to the innumerable annoyances of local authorities, and that of from Milam to Taklagar, nearly unknown, bristling with natural obstacles, but offering this advantage, that the travelers would find themselves at once in the mountains, and would thus escape the vexations of the Nepalese and Tibetan custom-house.

The ill-will of the maharájá was manifest. While appearing to make a friendly concession to the Lord-Governor, the sovereign had hoped that in going directly across his states the travelers would promptly become discouraged. There, where Montgomery had failed, where Adolph von Schlagintweit had succeeded in passing only by means of stratagems and ruses, it was not possible that a column of twenty men could find an egress.

Thus the road to Dhaulágiri was to all appearances closed. Therefore, in a moment of ill-humor, easy enough to justify, Major Plumptre had reproached Merrien with not having embraced his suggestion when he had proposed to approach the base of Gaurisankar by the east.

"At least," he said, "the greater part of the journey would lie through Sikhim, that is to say, upon English ground, and we should at the same time have had the view of the four highest peaks of the chain."

Merrien had replied laughingly to the Scotchman's ill-temper :

"Let us see, major ; difficulties will not stop you, I fancy. Very well, even if you should refuse to face them, I have made up my mind. I shall take the longest road, that of Milam. I will do even better ; I will see the sources of the Ganges in their own sanctuary at Gangotri."

An exclamation of astonishment greeted this totally unexpected declaration.

"But you wish then to give a year to it," cried young Weldon. "That takes us very far from Gaurisankar !"

"What matter !" replied the Frenchman. "Do delays trouble us ? I shall say with Mazarin, if necessary,

'Time and I,' and I shall add," he concluded with careless challenge : "'Who loves me, follows me !'"

"I shall follow you !" cried Cecil Weldon sturdily. "I also, by G——," added the major. "Besides, I know something of the road, and it will give me a chance to kill some tigers and panthers on the way."

"Bravo, then ! We are all in it ! There will be the fun of hunting !"

The young Yankee uttered these last words with his delicate, slender hands raised.

The agreement being thus clenched they decided that they would take the next train, and that they would stop at the station of Hardwár, to start from there directly for the mountains.

Major Plumptre took with him his four companions, these not having decided, however, that they would take the complete trip. Cecil Weldon was escorted by the two robust Yankees who had accompanied him to the Great Tower Inn. As to Merrien he kept by him only one servant, almost a confidant, Yves, or rather Euzen Graec'h, an old sailor, a Breton, of almost supernatural stature and vigor.

To this athlete was added a Hindu, Goulab, a man of thirty-five or thereabouts, of the Brahmin caste, *Shikari*, that is to say, professional hunter ; long, thin, and supple as a reed in his ample vestments of white cotton cloth.

The five Englishmen had, on their part, retained a *personnel* of eight native domestics, chosen somewhat at hazard from all castes, and distinguished rather by their employments than by their social rank. One of them, Salem-Bun, a Mussulman of the Sikh race, occupied the important post of *baburji*, or cook. Finally, young Weldon had attached to himself a Madrasi boy of fifteen—a Christian child with fine and delicate features lighted by beautiful black eyes, sparkling with intelligence. The sojourn at Hardwár could not be of long duration. The travelers stopped there just long enough to take a meal, and recruit the wagons and the beasts of burden necessary to the journey.

Mules and buffaloes were put to the four main wagons, one of which was occupied by Cecil Weldon, the second by Merrien and his two attendants, the third by the major and his companions. The fourth was used in common by the eight Hindus of the suite. Two other vehicles carried the equipment of the English officers and the American. Jean Merrien had reduced his own baggage to a bag buckled across his shoulders, and the Breton, Euzen Graec'h, had conscientiously imitated him.

They set out upon their way, crossing the Ganges at Kirksampur, then they followed the course of the Mundakni or Alaknanda.

They reached the cool valley of Dehra-Dun formed by the Ganges and the Jumna, the Tempe of northern India, inclosed between the Siwalik Mountains and the outer ranges of the Himálaya. Upon these slopes the English had established their sanitariums, and cantons at Landaur and Masúrí. Further to the north the climbers admired the famous stone of Calsi at the confluence of the Tongsa and the Jumna, upon which the early Buddhists engraved, two centuries before Christ, the figure of an elephant and the tables of their laws ; but they were in haste to get to the heights, for each passing day rendered access to the Great Chain more difficult. The melting of the snows would swell the torrents and transform the lower slopes

into marshes; by what they had been able to see at
Dehra-Dún, it was easy to guess what the state of the
Tarái would be; and by whatever side one approached
the Great Chain, one would have to undergo the
passage across the Tarái.

The plan of campaign had been heedlessly drawn
up. Upon the representation of one of the Hindus,
the Europeans had nourished the hope that they would
be able to go up the Ganges east of Landaur.

At the very outset it was necessary to renounce this
project, and recross the divine river this side of Siwálik.
The marshes which they had wished to avoid at Fáizabad,
they found again at Bodalleth, and at Pinnath.

This time the major, exasperated by the delay of eight
days, declared that he would cross in spite of all obstacles.
It is needless to say that no one wished to abandon him.

"It is an ill wind that blows nobody good," says
the proverb. This rejection of the eastern road rendered
the travelers the service of bringing them near to the
Nepál frontier, while at the same time it led them into
a part of the Tarái where human industry had made
veritable conquest over the jungle and the desert.

In India the name Tarái, or Taryáni, is given to that
warm and humid zone which lies at the base of the
Himálaya along the entire length of the chain, some
three thousand kilometers from the Passes of Kashmír
to the vales of Assam. This girdle, very unhealthy
because of the pestilences hidden within its marvelous forests, very dangerous through the presence of innumerable
wild beasts, seems to have been placed there by nature to
forbid human access to the giant lands, the two arms of
which, Himálaya and Kuenluen, embrace the mysterious
unexplored region called Tibet.

Thus it is necessary to cross the Tarai to reach the first terraces of the Himalaya.

" Now, where are we ? " asked Cecil Weldon of Plumptre and Merrien, when, after having passed a thick wood, the travelers found themselves to their great surprise upon a beautiful road, well kept, stretching like a long ribbon in the direction of the Chain, whose snowy domes and gilded peaks could be seen sparkling.

It was Dr. MacGregor, a friend of Plumptre's, who took upon himself to furnish his young companion with the desired explanation. He amiably constituted himself cicerone of the company.

"Gentlemen," said he, "this portion of northern India is *par excellence* holy ground. It is the domain proper to the Hindu-trimorti. When India had in some sort abdicated from sovereign power, Brahma, born of the sacred lotus, or of the eggs of Baohani, created this land, to conserve and to devastate which was the mission of Vishnu and Siva. That is why the Hindus force themselves every year to accomplish the great pilgrimage, the most meritorious of all, that of the Sanctuary of Gangotri, that we are to undertake ourselves, but in the role of the merely curious. Very few bring it to a successful end, for the difficulties are formidable, and we cannot guarantee that we shall be more fortunate than the natives in this dangerous attempt."

" We shall be, MacGregor," rang out the very positive voice of Major Plumptre.

They resumed their march. Forests alternated with cultivated ground laboriously reclaimed from the jungle. Toward evening, however, they found themselves in the middle of a thicket. The road was extremely difficult.

" Does not some one of our men know the region ? "

asked Merrien of the cook Salem-Bun, when he was setting
up the tents for the night. Questioned one by one, the
natives avowed complete ignorance of the road. The
embarrassment was at its height when Cecil Weldon's
little Madrasi servant, who answered to the name of Christi,
given at baptism by the Fathers who had Christianized
him, timidly approached his master, and spoke to him in
a low voice.

The American then said : " Gentlemen, Christi has
assured me that there must be near here a Catholic mission,
founded by the Capuchins. The Doums, in fact, almost all
belong to this religion, which they have embraced through
hatred of their old tyrants, the Gúrkhas. The boy will
undertake to reconnoiter the neighborhood."

The major broke in with a word of caution : " The boy
will make his excursion to-morrow. There is too much
danger in attempting it this evening."

" Danger ? " cried Weldon and the two Frenchmen
simultaneously.

The officer smiled somewhat conceitedly, then he
resumed seriously :

" I know, my dear comrades, that you fear nothing.
But take the word of a man who had some experience of
the country. We are here in the Taräi, and the Taräi is
not an ordinary place. We shall very likely realize that
this very night. Just now, in crossing a clear space, I discovered unmistakable traces of the great flesh-eating
animals : tigers, panthers, and chitas."

" But, then," observed young Weldon, " we are very
badly situated in the event of a night attack. We should
be wiser to seek some village which might furnish us a
shelter."

Everyone approved this advice, which was dictated by

prudence. There was, in fact, no refuge other than the
wagons drawn by buffaloes and mules. The very presence
of these animals indeed, might attract wild beasts, so, as
the night had not yet settled down, they decided to take up
their march as soon as the meal was finished, and to stop
at the first hamlet which they encountered. The smoke
which drifted across the openings of the forest led them to
suspect that some poor huts were close at hand.

Half an hour later they had reached one of those
Hindu villages built of earth and thatch, miserable dwellings lacking not only luxury, but even the most elementary comfort. Their very aspect caused the young Yankee
to recoil in disgust, his delicacy, excessive for an explorer,
somewhat astonishing his companions.

However, at the end of a moment, this repugnance was
shared by Major Plumptre, Dr. MacGregor, and all their
compatriots, and in order to cut short the discussions sure
to be provoked by the choice of a lodging among the
repulsive huts, Merrien expressed the general sentiment in
proposing to sleep in the wagons after having established
them in the village.

This last proposition somewhat startled Cecil Weldon,
and his hesitation again awakened the surprise of the other
travelers. But it was quite necessary for him to resign
himself; there was no choice of hostelry, and the nearest
*bungalow** was still no less than two miles away.

They decided, therefore, to accept Merrien's advice, and
the vehicles were brought into the village into the midst of
a population of Mehras, whose extreme timidity rendered
them very shy. It was with extreme difficulty and at the
cost of numerous *paissas* distributed right and left, that

* Halting-place or station.

some of these savages could be brought to consent to fill
the offices of *bhistis*, that is to say, of water-carriers.

Only two of them decided to do so, and on the condition that the white men accompany them with arms
and lanterns. The spring was under cover of the wood,
and everything was fearsome at this hour of dead night :
the watering-place was surrounded by flesh-eating animals
lying in wait for antelopes and deer.

The major at once demanded to be one of the escort.
Jean Merrien accompanied him as well as Euzen Graec'h
and the Indian Goulab, the special mission of the latter
being the surveillance of the two Mehras.

But there was no occasion to fear treason on the part of
these men. The Mehras, are, in fact, together with the
Doums, the most ancient people of the India peninsula :
at least, in the cis-Gangetic portion. Successively conquered and brought under subjection by innumerable
incursions of invaders, enslaved for centuries, they owe
their liberty only to the coming of the English, who have
delivered them from the Gúrkhas, those terrible mountaineers from among whom the government of Her
Britannic Majesty recruits the best foot-soldiers of the
Indian army, the most substantial soldiers of the Sepoy
regiments.

But the Mehras, of Aryan race, have kept a wild
independence which has degenerated into savagery, while
the Doums, black of skin, with woolly hair, represent
in *l'Inde Ulotrique*, or that part of India where the
natives have crisped hair, a negro race, expelled in an
immemorial past, the nearest approach to which is found
in the hideous and cannibal population of the Andaman
Islands. The Doums, laborious, sober, accord marvelously
with the whites, and it is thanks to their arms that civili-

zation encroaches each day upon the domain of the
Tarai jungles.

The spring from which the water was to be brought
was situated at quite a distance, nearly a mile in the
forest. Through the darkness, and in spite of the reflection of the torches, the march was difficult.

The village in the center of which the travelers had
placed their wagons was laid out, after the fashion of
its kind, over the entire extent of this narrow territory.
The Doums had come first. They had attacked the
outskirts of the forest with fire, and with the ax.
Then, the place once cleared, they had planted the
nutritious and sheltering mango tree in place of the
useless palms, turpentine trees of strong species, flora,
similar to that of Europe, but among which appeared,
with its peculiar individuality, the astonishing banyan
tree, that giant which multiplies itself: which, like
Antæus, acquires new strength each time that it touches
the earth, since each of its branches, provided with
adventitious roots, is transformed into a new tree, and
becomes the pillar of an arch which extends in all
directions around the primitive trunk, procreator of a
veritable forest in itself.

Then the Doums, their work of clearing finished to a
nicety, passed on to other labor, urged further by the
English, who pay them for their valiant toil. Then came
the Mehras, and even other races, some of whom emi-
grated from the valley of the Sutlej, or the banks of the
Jumna and the Gogra. These last are the ones who
build pitiful dwellings, a species of sordid hut, and
create wretched villages under the shade of the mango
trees. If the race be industrious, it surrounds the
territory thus conquered with all the resources necessary

to combat the pestilence of the climate, and the perpetual menace of terrible famine. Then arise breadtrees, butter-trees, cocoanut trees, the mhowa, that strange tree whose flower, of an insipid and resinous odor resembling that of the mango, is a veritable manna for persons living in the most cruel scarcity.

The two Mehras gave loud cries, and Goulab imitated them, counseling the two Europeans to do the same. It was a measure of prevention to disperse noxious beasts, and more especially the serpents asleep in the heaps of decayed foliage, or in the hollows of fallen trees.

Every moment a rustling of the branches, a murmur in the thicket, warned the travelers that they had disturbed some living creature in its repose, or in the performance of some nocturnal task. From time to time a hoarse growl revealed the departure of some tiger or panther, or small-sized ape.

In proportion as they neared the watering place, the cries of the Hindus redoubled in intensity and frequency. The watering place is the classic ambush of the great slayers, because it is the common rendezvous of all the animal tribes. Suddenly a startled bellowing rose some hundred feet from the little path. The Mehras stopped, giving signs of violent terror.

"Attention!" said Jean Merrien, quickly bringing his rifle to the shoulder.

"Well!" replied the Englishman; "I know what that is. That is only a spotted deer coming to drink."

Goulab shook his head, and said in a low voice to the fearless major:

"Sahib, it is only a deer, but this deer leads his herd. It is not us that he has discovered, for the wind comes from his direction. There must be some other enemy behind him, more formidable perhaps, and more disquieting."

"And what may it be?" asked the Scotchman.

"It may be the *seigneur* tiger, unless it is a panther."

The group had paused; the three white men and Goulab, armed with rifles, had rapidly made a square in the center of which they placed the two Mehras. These had laid their empty bottles on the ground, and had taken the two extra torches from the hands of their protectors. With their two arms raised, they held these torches above their heads, sending a fantastic light into the dense shadows of the surrounding forest. But at that very moment the wind, shifting unexpectedly, swept away the clouds, and revealed the full disk of the moon. An intense radiance illumined the heavens, and such a light streamed down upon the landscape as is only seen under tropical skies. The spring appeared, spread with silver, pouring out of a large fissure in the rock upon a basin of transparent pebbles of that marvelously colored quartz that the Ganges draws from its bed, and that the people utilize in the ornamentation of those exquisite boxes of precious wood, those elegant sandal-wood cabinets, charming in appearance, and of delightful fragrance.

Then an agitating scene was enacted under the eyes of the explorers.

An entire herd of spotted deer, seven does and four fawns, appeared upon the banks of the stream. The animals did not drink. They pricked up their ears, and turned their heads, with visible anxiety in their beautiful black eyes. Ten paces in advance the male, a superb

stag of ten, with proud, intelligent eyes, sniffed the air
in the direction of the wind. It was he who had, for
the purpose of warning the others of danger, given the
cry just heard. He was suddenly seen to stretch out
his powerful neck. A second wailing cry, pitiful this
time, a true call of alarm, broke from the hollows of
his deep chest, and the entire troop fled at a gallop,
running wildly into the depths of the forest. He himself, after providing for the safety of his family, thought
of his own means of escape. Lying close to the ground,
effacing himself, so to speak, among the trees, he examined the surrounding openings. One alone was large
enough for his majestic horns, that by which the
explorers and the two Mehras had come.

Plumptre, suiting the action to the word, said to
his companions : "Let us stand aside to let him pass,
otherwise he will force the sentry. Moreover, he will
not attack us. The enemy is certainly behind him. That
is the one we must receive at the muzzle of the gun."

He had not finished speaking when the stag, crouching on his hind legs, bent for a spring, rose with a
prodigious bound, and passed the little troop in two
gigantic leaps.

"Brave animal!" exclaimed the Scotchman.   "Did
you observe his maneuver?   He attracted the advancing
tiger to himself, in order to let the females and the little
ones reach the center of their herd. I should like to do
something for him."

"We too, major," said Jean Merrien, smiling.

The four rifles were raised at the same time, ready to
aim, and the appearance of the wild animal was awaited.
He was not long in showing himself. The underbrush on
the bank of the stream suddenly moved, the tall grasses

THE STAG SNIFFED THE WIND.

parted abruptly, and made way for a magnificent beast with a supple and sinuous body, and a yellowish-gray coat spotted with circles of black velvet. It was not a tiger, but one of the leopards very common in Central and Southern Asia. European naturalists call it *guepard*, but the Indians designate it by the name of *chita*.

The chita is susceptible of education to such a degree that the hunters of Persia, of Turkestan, of India, and of China, train it to hunt with more facility than the dog. It thus becomes the valuable aid, and the faithful companion of the horseman, who takes it behind him and lets it loose upon the prey designated. The one which had just come into view was of great size. It came, attracted by the trail of the herd, and was counting on choosing from among it a morsel of ample dimensions. It prepared to bound off in pursuit of the buck along the very road that he had taken, when the sight of the six men, illumined by their torches, stopped him short, halting between fear and the cravings of his stomach. One or two guttural notes issued from his bronze chest. The formidable beast was hesitating, not daring to disregard the counsels of prudence.

"We haven't the leisure to parley with this pretty fellow," said the major, in an undertone.

"What a pity that he cannot be taken alive!" sighed Goulab, the Indian.

"Why so?" asked the Breton sailor, much mystified by this regret. The shikári explained the puzzle in his words:

"You do not know, then, sahib, that the chita is easily tamed, and becomes an excellent companion for him who loves the chase?"

"Doubtless," replied Major Plumptre, "but this one

does not appear to be precisely in the humor to confide to us the responsibility of his education. Furthermore, we are a little pressed for time. And then the fate of this brave deer interests me."

During this short dialogue, the *guepard* had, on his part, reflected, and the inclinations that he presently showed were entirely hostile. He had come around the pond, and, flattened against the ground, was moving his rump and his tail, and scratching the earth with his claws.

It was in this position that he was surprised by the major's shot. The ball penetrated the point of the shoulder and prostrated the magnificent beast, while the noise of the report reverberated through the black depths of the forest. The chita turned over two or three times with convulsive movements, and died.

Then the two Mehras ran to the stream, promptly filled their bottles, and rejoined the group, while Euzen Graec'h, putting his enormous strength to good use, lifted the body of the *guepard*, still warm and palpitating, upon his shoulders, and carried it triumphantly back into camp.

The noise of the shooting had caused the whole company great excitement, and everyone ran to look at the superb game and compliment Major Plumptre on the happy beginning of his hunting in the Tarái. Some of the Mehras themselves came out of their cabins and approached the wagons.

The two brave *bhistis* who had given proof of real courage were royally rewarded, and they departed from their habitual speechlessness warmly to thank the generous donors.

After which the wagons were disposed in a circle, in the center of which were placed the mules and the buffaloes. Two Danish dogs of great size watched at the spaces left open by the angles of the wagons. Then the men wished one another a cordial good-night, very desirable after so momentous an evening as they had just passed, and each group shut itself into the wheeled house assigned to it.

The day once at hand, it was necessary to think of returning to the mountain road, in spite of the very marked opposition of Major Plumptre and Dr. MacGregor.

"My dear comrades," cried the officer, "mountains after all are only mountains. Whoever has seen one, has seen all. It is not so of the Tarai, which is a place unique in the whole world, the land of promise for the hunter. The experience of yesterday evening has given you a chance to judge of the numerous delights that a sojourn in this fortunate region would procure for us. We should all return with at least ten skins apiece. I ask, then, that we give ourselves ten days' grace worthily to accomplish our huntsman's task."

Jean Merrien commenced to laugh at this proposition. He answered the officer gayly :

"Parbleu ! major, that is what comes of praising your cynegetic tastes, and if Mr. Weldon and your friends see no inconvenience in it, we can very well dedicate a week to the massacre of tigers, panthers, bears, and other injurious creatures of the region. But let me remind you that I have come with but one end in view, the climbing of Gaurisankar, which you call Mount Everest. You must also recall that you all swore to carry off this palm from the Frenchman. What have you done, then, with your beautiful ardor of Srinigar ?"

And he added by way of conclusion :

"Hurrah, then, for a week or ten days of amuse-

ment in the forests of the Tarái! But, this delay once
over with, come what may, I will pause for no leave-
taking, but will return to the Gangotri road. It will be
the worse for those who will have been overcome by
the exhalations of the neighborhood, and who will have
contracted the marsh fever."

"Well!" returned the Scotchman, "those who are
sick can return to the Dun road. Ladour and Masúri
are not far distant, and, if necessary, they could be sent
on to Simla, where they would be able to recover."

"Hurrah, then, for the hunt! But let us take measures to have our days well filled. It would be too
humiliating to be left in the lurch after having made
such a loop in our itinerary."

"Mr. Merrien," said Cecil Weldon gently, "we shall
not be left in the lurch. And furthermore, supposing
that the beasts of prey all steal away from us, the
mountains will not escape us, I think, and Gaurisankar
will remain in its place."

Upon this sensible conclusion they held a veritable
council of war, and decided to follow the forest, without,
however, departing from the northern route and the
Nepál frontier.

THE MONK DESIGNATED RAMU.

IV.

VARIETIES OF MONSTERS.

THAT very day, Christi, the little Madrasi, carried out
the project he had formed the previous evening, of
putting himself into communication with the Christian
Doums in order to procure some guide from out their
ranks.

The boy set out, accompanied by one of the Hindus
in the service of the five Englishmen, and plunged
through the forest the sooner to gain the clearing.
There he knew he should find those laborious negroes
who have been indefatigable aids to English civilization.

Christi and his companion, a Pahári of Rohilkhand,
were nearly three hours in reaching the first of the Doum
settlements. These were veritable cantons. Directed by
a Capuchin father, several black tribes, men, women,
and children, had raised their portable barracks furnished

52

by a European company of Calcutta, as were the wooden convoys and wagons. Houses of boards erected upon trestles of iron, with floors and roofs of sheet iron to avoid contact with the earth and the invasion of insects or serpents, offered an itinerant home to these troops of benevolent workers, content with little, supporting themselves upon the moderate remuneration accorded them.

Christi at once sought the *padre*, an old Portuguese monk, who had lived for thirty years among these people, so remote from all civilization.

He made known to him his desire; and the padre hastened to call to him two men who were working some distance away.

One of the two was a pure-blooded Doum, small and stocky, black of skin, and woolly-haired; the other did not belong to the race. He was a large, fine youth, superbly set up, with smooth hair and olive complexion. Naked to the waist, where was knotted a large *pagne*, the folds of which fell over the legs, he presented the aspect of great strength joined to real intelligence.

The monk especially pointed out this latter to the two emissaries of the white men.

"Ramu," said he, "I believe this is your affair. You are looking for work. There happen to be very near here some Europeans who are asking for a guide. Would you like to go? That is, if you know the country?"

The Hindu made a sign of acquiescence with his head.

Then the padre, quitting his flock for the moment, took the road to the encampment in company with the three Indians.

He was received with respect. Although he spoke English with great incorrectness, the use that he made of

this language permitted him to explain himself sufficiently
to the travelers.   He told them that Ramu was a Dogra
of Jumna, that is to say a Rájpút, not a Mussulman,
who had been sent to him by a young physician, Madar-
Goun, who had been educated in Europe.   He added
that the Dogra had only arrived the evening before, but
that the recommendation of Dr. Madar-Goun was in his
eyes the best of all guarantees.

The white men could not desire better reference than
that of Father Antonio, the name of the Portuguese
monk.   Consequently they engaged Ramu in the capacity
of guide, and begged him to enter upon his duties from
that very day.

He spoke several languages, English among them,
with infinitely more facility than the good monk who
had brought him there.   He explained laughingly to
the travelers that his duties would be very easy, as
it was the month of March, and at that time pilgrimages abound, the more daring for Gangotri, but the
greater number for Hardwár, Badarináth, and Kedárnáth.

"Furthermore," he added, smiling, "this region is very
improperly called Tariyáni.   It is hardly more than the
advance guard of the forest.   The true Tarái is still
some fifty kilometers from the place where we are,
and it would only have been necessary for you to
ascend the Mundakni as far as Kedárnáth to choose
between the Gangotri road and that of Niti Liti."

Major Plumptre, who had not taken his eyes off the
Hindu while he was speaking, replied in a somewhat
testy tone of voice :

"Very well, my boy.   We are charmed that you possess such geographical knowledge of the country.   For
the moment what we ask of you is that you lead us

as conveniently as possible into the forest between the
frontiers of Nepál and those of Tibet. We are to the
north of Ránikhet, and Almora, but we are to the south
of the Himálayas. It is for you to acquaint us with
the best hunting territory. You can even make a map
of it, if that will give you any pleasure. *À bon entendeur,
salut!*" (A word to the wise is sufficient.)

The officer let fall this very French phrase, emphasiz-
ing it in such a way that Jean Merrien laughingly
applauded him.

When he found himself again among friends, the
major could not disguise his sentiments :

" My dear Merrien, I will tell you at once that the
face of this Dogra does not greatly please me."

" To be as frank as yourself, my dear major, I can
make the same confession without difficulty."

" And you, Weldon ? " asked the two Europeans
simultaneously.

" Frankly, gentlemen," replied the young Yankee, " I
admit that I had not received the same impression as
you. This Rajpút seemed to me very intelligent, and ·
I believe him to be active and courageous."

They exchanged no further opinions upon the subject.
In order to preserve perfect harmony Weldon proposed
to attach the guide to his own *personnel*. In that way
he would be placed, he declared, under the strict surveillance of his two companions, Davis Morley and
Hermann Knebel, the latter of German descent.

That very day Ramu gave his companions a high
idea of his capacity. After some very natural hesitation,
he came to announce to the caravan that if they wished
to swerve a little further to the west, they would find
game in abundance. The wagons accordingly plunged

into the forest, and in less than three hours all trace
of habitations had been lost sight of.

The ground rose rapidly, but the thick curtain of
the trees did not admit of any glimpse of the horizons
of the Great Chain. In spite of the elevation of the land
the temperature remained heavy and suffocating. Furthermore, the soil, deeply channeled, and covered with alluvial
deposits of all sorts of detritus, rendered walking very
difficult. It was necessary to encamp toward the middle
of the day, and they installed themselves in a sort of
clearing, where the perpendicular rays of the sun barely
succeeded in making some spots of light upon the damp
grass.

"A pretty place to contract all sorts of known and
unknown fevers!" cried Dr. MacGregor.

The doctor was in a very bad humor. He declared
that if they lingered only two days in that altitude, half
their force would be on their backs.

"Bah!" joked the major. "We are at the same
altitude as Simla, as Naini-Tál, as Ránikhet."

"With this difference," retorted the physician, "that
Ránikhet, Naini, and Simla are on exposed slopes, down
whose sides the water has drained, and which receive
the winds direct from the mountains."

"Let us not think of that," cried Merrien, "and since
we have agreed upon a week of shooting, out with the
guns."

This was the great compensation for sojourning in
these unhealthful regions.

For dinner that evening they had only game to eat.
The hunt had been miraculous. The major and his four
companions contributed sixty white partridges, eight
pheasants, and two grouse. Merrien, Graec'h, and Goulab

the shikari, preferred the four-footed game. Their portion was seven hares and sixteen Guinea pigs. But the triumph of the day went to the Americans. Weldon had brought down a male *nilgau* close to the muzzle, at the very moment when the antelope, brought to bay, leveled his horns and charged impetuously upon the bold hunter.

His two companions had brought down two beautiful fawns of the same herd.

That did not keep the major from sighing over what he called a sorry result.

" We have only had small game to-day," he said.

Occasion to modify his judgment was not slow in coming.

Toward the second half of the afternoon, just as the English, faithful to their goodly custom of *tiffin*, that is to say lunch, had laid the cover in the shelter of a group of mango-trees, at the foot of which the ground was perfectly dry, cries of distress rang out, coming from the very edge of the forest, less than five hundred yards from the wagons.

Everyone seized arms, and ran in the direction of the outcry.

A frightful spectacle met their sight. A sort of marsh lay beneath the nearer trees. From the stagnant water four or five hideous reptile heads had started up, darting their forked tongues with horrible hissing. They were of that particular species called *daboia*, water serpents, of gigantic size, uniting to the strength of the boa the fatal venom of the cobra, which kills in less than half an hour.

A man belonging to the escort, one of those in the service of the English, was writhing from many wounds inflicted by poisoned fangs, a prey to the last convul-

sions of the death agony. Some steps distant, a second
Hindu of the same troop, bound to a tree by the deadly
embrace of an ophidian, was yelling with pain. His
were the cries that had given the alarm.

To rescue him it would be necessary to pass over the
bodies of five threatening daboias.

Goulab made this useful though little comforting
observation :

"It is neither a *naga* nor a daboia which is holding him ;
it has no fangs. It is a python."

But whether the poor boy must be crushed to death or
poisoned mattered little. The essential thing was that he
should not die. But the embrace of the constrictor tightened, making the limbs of the poor wretch crack.
Shooting could not be thought of. Besides the chance
that the ball might glance harmless from the scales of
the serpent, there were ten chances to one of killing the
unfortunate being held in his entwining grasp.

Fortunately, Jean Merrien was a man of resource.
He had foreseen such an emergency, and was provided
with special arms of his own invention.

With a gesture he indicated to Graec'h the ax that he
wore at his belt, and cried to him :

"To the man ! extricate him. I will take care of these
villainous water beasts."

Then he was seen to draw from a sort of quiver
that hung at his waist a syringe terminating in a rose
like that of a watering-pot. He rapidly filled it half full
from the stagnant pool, then he poured into it some
drops from a flask which he drew from his game pouch.
Then he marched resolutely against the daboias, who, far
from avoiding him, raised themselves in increased fury
in front of him.

The syringe did its work. It threw upon the ophidians a large jet of the corrosive liquid that it contained. The effect was immediate. Struck on the points of their viscous rings, the hideous creatures showed by their quicker hissing, and by their convulsive movements, that the vitriol was burning their skins and penetrating deep into their flesh.

Without pausing, Merrien quickened the terrible sprinkling, and in a few moments the five dying reptiles fell back into the muddy water of the marsh, showing the scales of their bellies, after the manner of dead fish.

The way was clear. The Breton leaped with a bound to the succor of the unfortunate Hindu, whom the python was lacerating with cruel wounds while endeavoring to strangle him. The herculean hand of Euzen Graec'h had torn the head of the ophidian from the shoulder of its victim in which it had buried its fangs, and pressed it against the trunk of the tree.

A single blow of the ax decapitated the creature, whose rings at once relaxed, letting the enormous body fall inert, still shaken by the spasms of death.

They drew the swooning Indian from its embrace, and hastened to lavish on him the care that his condition demanded. Happily the daboias had not touched him, and he had had the truly extraordinary fortune to be picked out by the python. They had, therefore, only to wash and then to cauterize his wounds. As to his companion, all efforts in his behalf were henceforth useless. Already swollen and distended, his body covered with green blotches, his tongue tumefied, his wounds—he had received more than twenty bites—purulent and bluish, the Hindu could not be long in succumbing. He expired, indeed, at the end of some moments, literally asphyxiated by the poison, and with nerves agitated by tetanic convulsions.

This event sobered all hearts. The major himself, ordinarily so bravely care-free, could not repress his sadness.

The man who had just died was an old servant who had been over fifteen years in his service, and who possessed his entire confidence.

In the midst of the comments provoked by this catastrophe, Goulab the shikári, whose brows were knit, put in his word, which was anything but reassuring.

"One thing astonishes me in all this," he said. "Among the innumerable varieties of serpents which infect Indian territory, there is hardly one who dares attack a man except the cobra-di-capello. Even then the man must surprise it, and disturb its sleep. As to the boas and daboias, they are reptiles whose first movement is of flight, and who only defend themselves in the last extremity. I am utterly surprised by what has just taken place. I find it so very strange that I dare not yet express an opinion on the subject."

"What do you mean?" questioned Merrien. "What are you concealing under this reticence?"

The shikári shook his head, and contented himself with responding enigmatically:

"Sahib, when the wounded man is able to speak to you, ask him simply how his accident occurred, how the thing was done. I have no right to say more at present." And urge as they might, the Indian refused to throw off his reserve.

"Truly," said young Weldon, who appeared strongly moved by the incident, "there is good reason for say-

A SINGLE BLOW OF THE AX DECAPITATED THE CREATURE.

ing that India is the land of mysteries. I come from a country where serpents certainly are not lacking; where they are as formidable as these. But our trigonocephales, our rattlesnakes, would not venture thus imprudently to approach the neighborhood of man. You have just heard, moreover, the reflections of this shikari. He also finds it strange, even inexplicable. I should like to know, I admit, the hypothesis that he has conceived."

"Meanwhile," grumbled the major, "I have just lost in a single instant my poor old Gourap-Sing. I cannot be reconciled to it."

He was sincere. The cruel fate of his faithful *behra* caused him violent grief, and had he been able to vent his sorrow, aggravated by the mysterious words of Goulab, he would have pitilessly killed the man or the animals whose imprudence or stupidity had led to this terrible catastrophe. Naturally, the day ended in gloom. They dined rather early on an excellent curry made by Salem-Bun out of white meat.

Then, night having fallen, they stockaded the wagons, and lighted six fires, to guard which they stationed some Doums recruited in the neighborhood, over whom the travelers kept watch two by two, in turn. This was not a useless precaution, as they were soon in a position to recognize.

Indeed, darkness had hardly closed down before the noises of the forest broke forth, discordant at first, but soon united and blended in an immense concert, to which every beast in creation contributed his note. It commenced by the yelping of jackals, and the mournful notes of the great horned owls, to which were soon added the bellowings of those enormous frogs, sisters of the American *pipas*, which people all the marshes of

India. Then this prelude gradually died down, as if the murmur of the overture had given way to the virtuosos, to the great chief performers. To the cries of the wide-mouthed frogs succeeded the bellowing of the true rumi-nants, such as the formidable *gáial*, with a head maned like that of the yak, the bison, and the buffalo of the swamps, the most terrible, perhaps, of the wild inhab-itants of the jungle, the only one, which, like the rhi-noceros, every day growing more rare, always attacks the white man, for whom it seems to feel a furious hatred.

Soon afterward troops of wild elephants started the echoes with their cries like the jangle of a bronze rattle, and the travelers trembled at the mere thought that a band of these gigantic animals might surprise their encamp-ment. They knew well that the gangs of *gandas*, or tusked elephants, are never under a dozen individuals, composing two or three families. What could they do in the way of defense, in the presence of such formidable adversaries. They did not breathe easily until the noise of the voices was lost in the depths of the forest.

But then a new voice arose, which at once imposed silence upon the bellowings and wailings. A long shudder was heard to run through the thick under-brush—the sound of animals fleeing or crowding close together, to avoid the pursuit of the great wanderer of the night, the frightful huntsman thirsting for warm blood, starving for palpitating flesh. The *bagh-sahib*, the *seigneur* tiger was prowling in the woods, in quest of his repast.

The tiger has no cry. It is an imitative play of sound that has given birth to the word *feulement*, because of that particular sound which comes from the animal's throat at the moment when the muscles of its face contract in a grin of defiance. One clearly distinguishes the letter *f* or *v* lengthening into a yawn, that terminates in the growl of a double-bass roughened by an unskillful stroke of the bow.

When the day had finally dawned, after long terrors, Merrien gathered together his companions.

"Gentlemen," he said to them, "I shall, perhaps, greatly astonish you by speaking the language of prudence. But I have always considered, and I judge that you are all of you of my opinion, that courage does not consist in throwing one's self heedlessly into the midst of danger.

"Now let me say to you that we have acted with absolute heedlessness, and it is a veritable miracle that we have not been crushed or devoured during the past night by the multitude of mischievous creatures which have surrounded us. If I may believe the testimony of Goulab, an expert in these matters, buffaloes and gáials have approached our camp by hundreds. The shikari, moreover, counted tigers to the number of five, and elephants to the number of eighteen or twenty."

"It is certain," said Cecil Weldon, with emphasis, "that I have not felt very tranquil."

"Consequently," pursued the Frenchman, "I propose that we ascend some miles to the west, in order to insure ourselves a better shelter than that of our wooden wagons, which would not form a sufficient rampart against beasts of the size of gandas and buffaloes."

"All right!" concluded the major. "You speak wisely, Mr. Merrien, and your advice will be particularly acceptable to the doctor, who fears nothing so much as the miasma of these marshes."

Camp was therefore broken, and, after a glance at the map, they decided to approach Kedárnáth, from which they were separated by a distance of not more than thirty kilometers. Certainly they could not fail to come across one of those bungalows placed by the order of the English administration on all the lost roads of India, and at which no traveler can remain more than one day, unless provided with a special permit according him a longer period of subsistence.

At the moment of departure they called the roll. Only the unfortunate Gourap-Sing was missing, whom they had buried the evening before, heaping upon the grave the heaviest stones that they could find, to guard the remains from the profanation of hyenas and jackals.

Merrien remarked that Goulab was at that moment stealthily watching Ramu, the guide.

Without saying a word, the shikári had approached the Dogra, and had put his finger on the arm of the Rájpút, indicating a scratch an inch or two in length, which formed a swelling on the forearm.

Master as he was of himself, the Siváite zealot could not restrain a start.

"Serpent's tooth," said the Sikh finally, speaking laconically in his own language.

"Yes," confessed the Dogra, "I have been bitten, but I have washed the wound."

The incident had drawn all the travelers about the guide, who could not repress a movement of impatience.

The look which he cast at the shikari was filled with ferocious hatred. But, without otherwise moving, the latter again indicated with his finger a flexible malacca reed half lost in the floating folds of the pagne which surrounded the Rájpút's waist.

"Excellent for cutting the little ones in two, insufficient for the big ones," said he.

He articulated these words clearly, with a little guttural laugh full of insinuation.

Merrien knew his servant well. He guessed at once that Goulab had suspicions. But he said to himself at the same time that the faithful shikari would not impart them until they had been subjected to scrupulous verification.

Nevertheless, Goulab profited by a moment when the guide had gone to the head of the column, to approach Jean, and give him this tolerably enigmatic advice :

"Sahib, recommend the doctor not to lose sight of the man who was wounded yesterday, and to question him as soon as possible, that is, as soon as the man is in a condition to speak."

All this sufficiently obscure language was not reassuring to the explorer. He refrained, however, from communicating his apprehensions to his companions. During the short time that he had been in his company, he had gained sufficient knowledge of the major's character to be persuaded that he would not scruple to break the guide's head in spite of his presentation by Father Antonio, and the excellent references from the physician Madar-Goun.

The march through the forest was accomplished with difficulty. The principal reason for this was that one must climb the gently sloping plane of the Taräi, and animals as well as people slipped on this declivity, completely coated as it was with a vegetable mold which was constantly enriched by the leaves and branches, rotting in the water that trickled down from the mountain.

It was, moreover, necessary narrowly to watch the

line of wagons, because from the tree-trunks as well as from the stagnant pools of water there might at any instant leap the most formidable of adversaries, those hideous serpents, the recognition of whose presence in these dangerous parts had been only too well enforced by the accident of the day before. By means of such precautions as giving loud cries, and beating or setting on fire the underbrush, this perilous encounter was avoided.

It was otherwise with other wild creatures.

Before reaching the first encampment for the day the travelers had to undergo a regular battle.

By a lucky chance, however, they had time to fortify themselves against this terrible onslaught, by inclosing themselves in an old cattle park, built there, some years before, by some Tibetan shepherds who were bringing to Ratmando their sheep and their goats previously shorn at Hardwár.

The event was as frightful as it was unexpected.

Cecil Weldon, who had placed himself in the vanguard with his two Yankee companions and young Christi, suddenly informed the rest of the troop that he had just discovered traces of a considerable herd of large ruminants !

Little acquainted with the habits of these savage beasts, and full of confidence, moreover, in the effect of his glance seconded by his incomparable skill as a marksman, the young American walked straight up to the first individuals of the herd that he met on his way. In this place the trees, after having opened for a very defectively marked path, suddenly cleared upon a space of three or four square kilometers. They had reached one of the lower terraces of the Himálayas, and water, draining from the slopes or oozing from the cracks of the rocks, formed an immense marsh hidden by reeds, bamboos, and tall grasses under a thick carpet of vegetation. There, in that morass inaccessible to all other quadrupeds, splashed and pastured at their ease a score of gaurs (wild oxen) with sharp horns, and quite as many black buffaloes with enormous foreheads, protected by inordinately large horns expanding on either side in frightfully threatening curves.

The buffalo of India has the disquieting peculiarity of making spontaneous attacks, above all, when the enemy upon which he charges is a European. He offers, furthermore, to the inexperienced hunter the disagreeable surprise of presenting a skull that is impervious to balls, unless the balls are conical and provided with steel tips.

The imprudent Weldon had plenty of steel-tipped balls, but he had neglected to put them in his hunting belt. It was, therefore, only with ordinary leaden bullets that he went forth to the battle.

THEY DREW CECIL WELDON, ALMOST SWOONING, FROM UNDER THE BUFFALO'S BODY.

V.

THE GUARDIANS OF THE HOLY GANGES.

WHILE the rest of the column were, with great difficulty, extricating themselves from the embarrassments of the road, which was nearly obliterated by landslides due to the constant undermining of the earth by the rains, the three Yankees had already reached the verdant terrace in the center of which gamboled buffaloes and gaurs.

"Major," the audacious young man cried from a distance, "you have desired a hunting trip. You are marvelously gratified, and I shall be most happy presently to offer you some roast-beef such, I imagine, as you can eat neither in London nor in Calcutta." The breeze blowing from the hills carried his voice. Unfortunately it beat back that of his companions, who immediately gathered together to call to him with violent gestures to

retrace his steps at once, before he had been perceived
by the formidable ruminants.

Thus Cecil Weldon heard not a word of the wise
cautions given him by his friends.

He advanced upon the species of causeway, or rather
upon the pier of rocks which Nature herself had built
across the enormous marsh, without paying attention
to the tumultuous movements caused among the agitated herd of wild oxen by the apparition of three
white-clad men.

But there was no time for long remarks on the
subject.

Abruptly one of the gaurs started from the grass
with a bellow of anger, shaking his mane that dripped
fetid mire, and Weldon, whatever his courage, could not
repress a shudder at the sight of the formidable animal
which, lowering its horns, spouting foam and vapor at
the mouth and nostrils, advanced toward him with blood-
shot eyes, at a steadily increasing pace. He could not
mistake the hostile intentions of the beast, which must
be stopped without loss of time.

Cecil Weldon did not hesitate. Rapidly raising his
rifle to his shoulder, and aiming between the gaur's
eyes, he pulled the trigger. The animal, struck down,
fell headlong on the jetty, while the echoes of the swamp
repeated the report with such force that the tumult was
increased a hundred-fold by the neighboring buttresses of
rock.

But, at the same time, this unusual noise, instead of
terrifying the herd, only excited their rage. In an instant
the terrible animals, advancing by groups of four or five,
precipitated themselves upon the jetty of stones.

The situation became truly critical.

The young American was too adventurous. Although he had not proceeded more than a hundred steps upon this natural road, which might have been cut by the strange gods of Hindu mythology, in those fabulous times when Rama made alliance with Hanuman, King of the Apes, Cecil ran great risk of being outflanked, and having all retreat cut off by the aggression of his implacable adversaries. He turned, after having retreated some fifteen meters, and his alarm was great at perceiving two gigantic buffaloes charging upon the causeway. A cry of distress naturally rose to his lips. He called : " Help, Morley, Knebel, help ! Shoot ! Shoot ! or we are lost ! "

The two Yankees fired simultaneously. One of the buffaloes fell into the mud ' of the swamp. The other, confused for a moment, stopped short on the first steps of the rocks, and set up a frightful bellowing. Knebel, the American of German extraction, seemed suddenly struck with terror, and fled as fast as his legs could take him, without pausing for the furious imprecations of his comrade or the reiterated appeals from Weldon.

Meanwhile, two other beasts had set foot upon the causeway. Now the two men were facing three assailants. Never had greater peril confronted them.

Happily the convoy hastened up. Merrien, Euzen Graec'h, the shikári, and the five Englishmen flew rather than ran. Three shots again rang out. Two of the ruminants fell. The third in spite of his rage recoiled before the number of the new-comers, and plunged into the marsh.

Cecil Weldon profited by this short respite to beat a precipitate retreat. But he had not yet gained the extremity of the causeway when six buffaloes of great size threw themselves forward in attack.

But one of the recently fallen beasts lay across the road. At the moment that Weldon, carried away by his haste, with his eyes turned toward his assailants, reached the body, his foot struck the enormous mass sharply, and he fell upon the yet warm remains of the wild ox.

Behind him the irritated animals were coming at the top of their speed.

The fall he had just had saved the young American. Stunned by the shock, he lay quiet for some seconds. This short delay sufficed to avert danger. The thin, trembling voice of little Christi reached Weldon's ears.

" Don't budge, Sahib ; do not rise ! Put yourself under the animal's belly."

Weldon crouched as best he could between the feet of the carcass. During this time, the buffaloes, hindered by the narrowness of the causeway, became entangled one with another, and stumbled with all the impetuosity of their chase over the dead body. The shock the young man sustained was a rude one, but it gave him the advantage of covering himself almost entirely with the enormous prostrate mass. He thus at least escaped the violence of the assault.

At the same moment Merrien and his companions, running to the rescue, fired simultaneously upon the thick, living barrier of entangled ruminants. This time the balls were steel-tipped. Five buffaloes fell, pierced in skull or flank. This made nine bodies, a more than sufficient obstacle temporarily to check all new demonstrations from these stupidly headstrong beasts.

They ran at once to poor Cecil, whom they drew, almost swooning, from under the carcass, the weight of which was stifling him. There was no thought of too bitterly reproaching Knebel for his recent shameful flight.

Furthermore, this had been but a passing weakness on his part. The Yankee had returned bravely to the charge. He excused himself later, alleging a sudden irresistible giving out, the effect of which had been physical, causing the nervous system to be thrown into a perturbation that he himself could not explain.

There was, moreover, no time to lose in recriminations. Frightful bellowings, rising from the marsh, announced, beyond the possibility of doubt, that the entire troop, with an *esprit du corps* as ferocious as it was obstinate, was about to return to the charge.

They beat a retreat in all haste toward the wagons, and they all experienced a lively satisfaction in finding that Ramu, the guide, had already placed the wagons and the animals within the shelter of the stockaded inclosure of an old abandoned park.

Alas! it was but a very uncertain shelter. The badly joined palings, of a height scarcely sufficient to keep the beasts without from leaping them, were worm-eaten besides, and worn by remaining long in the stagnant water of the heavy rains. It was necessary at once to make additional strategic arrangements by placing the various wagons in such a way as to form a second inclosure. The marksmen were placed according to their skill, at posts necessary to the defense. Merrien, Plumptre, Goulab, and the American Morley stood in front of the palisade, while the four Englishmen, Graec'h, and the seven Indians of the escort installed themselves at the windows of the dock-carriages. The second of the two Yankees and the little Madrasi had enough to do in attending to Cecil Weldon.

The besieged had barely time to make their preparations for combat. Twenty buffaloes and ten gaurs

advanced in one compact mass, necks extended, horns
menacing, scanning the marsh with rhythmical and sonorous bellowings. And it was an astonishing spectacle,
that of this strange army marching to the attack like a
well-drilled regiment to the sound of trumpets and bugles.
It had been decided that the major should have the
direction of operations, and in order to obtain more unity,
and more effective results, they were to shoot only at his
command. He ordered them to aim particularly at the
buffaloes, the gaurs being of a less aggressive and tena-
cious disposition. They commanded sixteen rifles, and,
said the major, it would be entirely inexcusable for
them to be conquered by a troop of oxen.

"Attention!" he cried, "the tide is rising. Aim well,
without haste."

He waited until the attacking line of the troop had
come within sixty paces of the palisade. Then, placing
his rifle quietly against the palings, he counted with his
hands :

"One! two! three! Fire!" The discharge struck
the assailants like a tempest. All the shots had told.
Fifteen shaggy, muddy bodies lay on the reddened grass.

Plumptre, laughing, amused himself by bringing down
the sixteenth.

But such was the obstinacy of these stupid creatures,
that, closing their ranks on the spot, the survivors
rushed upon the kraal with such speed that the besieged,
taken by surprise, had no time to anticipate the second
attack. Three or four isolated shots alone rang out. A
single gaur was struck. The rest of the troop rushed
against the palings with frightful impetuosity. The stock-
ade yielded under the pressure, and one of the buffaloes,
carried away by the impetus of his onslaught, upset

"THE BUFFALOES AND THE GAURS RUSHED UPON THE KRAAL."

Goulab, and entangled his horns in the wheels of the first wagon. The breach was made, the whole herd were about to invade the encampment. Suddenly, the band stopped short and pricked up their ears. Then, renouncing their attack upon the travelers, the formidable animals retreated some paces, and, with hollow bellow-ings, gathered together back to back, in the manner of bulls protecting their families against wolves. With a furious wrench which shook the vehicle, the buffalo whose horn was caught between the spokes extricated himself, and rejoined his fellows.

"Ho, ho!" said Jean Merrien. "It occurs to me that we shall be better off inside the wagons. Something new is certainly up, and from our windows we shall be in the best possible position to see, and to interfere, if necessary."

The prediction was too well founded, and the counsel too wise to be neglected.

They, therefore, replaced their wagons, and shut themselves in, not without serious apprehensions as to the fate of the mules and the domestic buffaloes inclosed within the kraal. What was about to happen? No one could guess precisely, but everyone understood that the savage inhabitants of the swamp had so unexpectedly given up their attack because they feared to be them-selves attacked. Furthermore, their attitude, their tactics of common resistance, would have revealed to the most ignorant eye that they were preparing for combat.

The travelers were promptly enlightened, and shut within their wagons, they could not help, in spite of their anxiety, contemplating, as passionately interested spectators, the most stirring drama that it was ever given to human eye to witness. The scene was worthy of the epic tableaux given in the great amphitheaters of Rome.

While twelve or thirteen united animals presented to the still invisible enemy a cluster of menacing horns, uttering from time to time deep murmurs, suggesting the first rumblings of thunder, the neighboring underbrush was agitated by the coming of the wild beasts whose presence the buffaloes had got wind of.

Suddenly, almost simultaneously, they showed themselves at four different points in the clearing. Three tigers and two tigresses appeared under a stream of sunlight on the carpet of high grasses.

They were marvelous animals, in all the splendor of their golden fur striated with black velvet, in all the elegance of their light, nervous carriage. They belonged to that Bengal race which prevails over the species of Indo-China and the Sunda Isles, just as the lion of the Atlas prevails over its conquerors of Senegal or the Cape of Good Hope. They deserve their name of "royal tiger." Much taller than their brothers of the other parts of Asia, ten or eleven feet long from the muzzle to the end of the tail, with the face framed in large cheeks with silky white whiskers, the terrible felines justify the terror which their prodigious force and startling beauty inspire, not only in men but in all living creatures.

They approached as by a preconcerted signal, and prefaced with movements full of undulating grace the strategic maneuvers which they were about to put in practice.

At the windows of the camp wagons the explorers stood motionless and panting. Each had his rifle in his hand, and his cartridges ready.

Cecil Weldon, in spite of the bruises he had received, had obstinately refused the assistance of his companions. While still pale enough he had desired to be present at the spectacle, and rejoined his colleagues in Jean Merrien's wagon, where they had chosen their place.

"We are going to assist at a drama entirely unique of its kind," cried Major Plumptre.

"God grant," added Dr. MacGregor, a little crustily, "that we may be spectators only."

There was very little leisure for further reflection. The curtain had risen, the first act of the drama was about to begin. The five tigers had commenced to prowl about the circle of buffaloes.

This formidable rampart of horns, this fortress of powerful spines buttressed against one another, whose shaggy convexity hid the cruppers from sight, were very well qualified to inspire the felines with the sentiment of prudence. They understood that all their suppleness, all their lightness, would not serve them either against these enormous heads capable of grinding them upon the ground and crushing them against the trunks of trees, or against the pointed tusks, a single well-directed blow from which would suffice to disembowel them.

It was necessary for them to use strategy in their attempt to break the line by drawing one of the formidable creatures outside of the ranks. Invincible as a fort, taken in the aggregate, the buffaloes and gaurs would promptly lose their advantage when their line of battle suffered any break. For then it would be mere play for the tigers to take them from behind, seize them by their cruppers, or grapple with them in the way a bulldog grapples a wild boar. In order to attain this result

the five tawny beasts set about fascinating their adversaries by confusing their vision with the rapidity and
multiplicity of their movements. Slowly, at first, and
with apparent indifference they paced about the clearing
with great steps, then, accelerating their pace, they dropped
imperceptibly into a sort of undulating trot of such gracious sprightliness that, in the wagon of the Europeans,
Euzen Graec'h made the picturesque remark :

"Hullo ! I wonder how long they mean to dance that
quadrille ? "

To which Merrien on his side added the no less just
reflection, founded on the peculiar capriciousness of
tigers :

"Unless it occurs to them to leave these wild buffaloes in the lurch to come and eat ours."

The question of the French traveler was a most
natural one. He was obliged, however, to content himself with the approximate answer with which Goulab
the shikari furnished him. The latter explained, in
effect, that the tiger is an animal whose sense of smell
is but moderately developed, and that these perhaps had
not distinguished the trail of the wild beasts from that
of the others. These last being placed between them and
the corral, the felines had judged it to be better tactics
to clear the ground to the profit of their insatiable
ferocity.

Now the wild beasts, hastening their pace, varying
their feints, gave themselves up to unrestrained leaps,
crossing their ellipses, springing to great heights to fall
again lightly upon the grass, where they stretched themselves, twisting and rolling like kittens, and striving
more and more to induce a break in the skillful order of
their enemies.

But the latter did not quit their defensive position ; like those Saxons of Hastings, invincible behind their stockades, who did not succumb until they were forced to descend into the plain in pursuit of the astute Normans.

Suddenly the tigers, weary perhaps with too long effort, risked an assault from the front. Two of them, rising in a concentric spring, passed over the heads of the buffaloes and fell upon the mass of crowded rumps. They did not remain there long. Two giant horns received the first one on the fly, and like a gigantic racket sent him violently outside the circle.

The other had not time to plant his claws in the backs on which he had fallen. These separated, and the tiger falling into the opening, found himself immediately crushed with such force that his sides cracked. Then when, with a more energetic wrench, the animals had let him fall at their feet, they trampled and mangled him with fury.

In vain the tiger tried to strike his terrible blow right and left, the victory remained with the well-drilled ruminants, and in the twinkling of an eye the superb furry coat was spotted and defiled, and the supple body twisted and crushed among the mass of the assailants, and the beautiful, imprudent animal, pierced by many horns, with broken bones and crushed paws, was finally rejected by the hostile line, or rather thrown back, dying, to his brothers, where he expired in a few swift convulsions. The felines recoiled, rendered prudent by this grave check, while the buffaloes celebrated their victory by a long bellow.

But the tigers responded in concert with hoarse growls. Evidently they did not confess themselves vanquished.

Pretending to give up the struggle, they appeared to

content themselves with the bodies felled by the balls
of the explorers. Consequently they approached the
heap of carcasses with considerable indifference, and
crouched to lick off the blood, without, however, showing
much appetite for it, for the remains, cold already, were
little to their taste.

Nevertheless, this stratagem changed in an instant
the repective situations of the combatants.

The buffaloes proceeded to assume the offensive.
Breaking their circle of resistance, they drew up in a
single line of attack, and set up a frightful clamor of war.
The ground trembled under their onset. They charged
straight for the tigers, swinging their enormous heads
from right to left, and striving to gain by the shortest
road the marsh, where they would find shelter.

The felines did not await the attack. They fled on
either side to make way for the onslaught, comprehend-
ing that the victory would finally be theirs. And while
the ranks of the ruminants, forcibly hindered by the
prostrate bodies, broke up into several parts, the tigers,
turning the enemy's flank, and taking them in the rear,
precipitated themselves upon the troop in a concentrated
attack, and instantly put them to rout.

It was the gaurs, less robust and less swift, who
had to bear the greater penalties of the combat.
Three among them were seized and stricken down by
the three uninjured tigers. As to the fourth, the one
whose imprudent aggression had been so rudely
repulsed by the buffaloes, he avenged himself by seizing the throat of a young female, whose warm blood
and tenderer flesh permitted him to recuperate the
forces that had sustained so severe a trial. Thus the
combat ended.

But that was not any more encouraging for the travelers. Plumptre, whose fingers clutched the barrel of his rifle, made a bold proposition, the logic of which, however, convinced the entire company.

"Gentlemen," said he, "you are aware that the seigneur bagh is a glutton of the first order, who does not eat the half of what he tears to pieces, and that, in consequence, after having tasted their breakfast, the four consumers confronting us are entirely capable of coming to continue their repast to the detriment of our poor servants and ourselves. I am, then, wholly of the opinion that, in place of losing time in watching them eat, which would retard our progress, and detain us beyond reason in these manifestly unhealthy parts, we should interrupt this feast by one good handsome fusillade, which will procure us four superb skins, while giving us the freedom of the neighborhood. Furthermore, our sixteen cattle are worth the trouble with which we have obtained them. They will furnish us a superabundance of that roast beef of which Mr. Weldon so generously offered me his share, and which had just missed costing us so dear."

The young American took the raillery gayly.

"Major," he said, "I have learned the lesson so much the better for having paid for it." And, turning toward Merrien, he added with a charming smile :

"*Monsieur le Français,* your inimitable La Fontaine has written a fable that I may apply to myself. I have just proven this truth at my own expense, that one must never sell buffalo fillet before the animal is down."

Having made this witty observation, he seized his rifle, and urging his companions on, "Forward, gentlemen !" he cried, "it shall not be said, surely, that we have shot these charming animals from the height of a block-house. On foot, face to face, and each for the honor of his native land."

He said no more, and, without giving his companions time to make any comment, he threw himself out of the wagon, rifle in hand ; Merrien, Plumptre, Dr. Mac-Gregor, Graec'h the Breton, followed him immediately in spite of the danger of the adventure.

The tigers, warned by the noise, rose, abandoning their prey. They had scented the presence of man, king of creation, conqueror of plagues and monsters. With bloody mouths and flaming eyes, they paused to defend themselves, and to attack, if necessary.

Cecil Weldon, always imprudent, marched resolutely toward the one nearest him, the one vanquished by the male buffaloes, but vanquisher of the female buffalo. At the very moment when the superb animal, more astonished than frightened, flattened himself along the ground, preparing for a spring, the Yankee's ball struck him between the eyes. The beast did not even stir. He turned upon his side with a swift convulsion, and died upon the spot. Then, instead of justifying their reputation for boldness, the three other tigers gave a growl of mingled fear and anger, and with a backward bound plunged into the underbrush, where they disappeared, followed by some useless shots.

As the astonished Europeans dared not believe their eyes, Goulab again came in with his explanation of this anomaly.

The animals just encountered were certainly young tigers, having never yet tasted human flesh, and never having seen Europeans. The noise of fire-arms, the unexpected apparition of unknown creatures, had sufficed to terrify them. They had fled, never to return.

The explorers nevertheless set rapidly to work. While the Hindus skinned the dead buffaloes, detaching the best bits, among which must be counted the dorsal hump, Cecil Weldon, aided by Merrien, Plumptre, and the Breton, took the tiger skin, a magnificent bedside rug for future use.

"A very pretty shot, truly," said the Englishman with sincere admiration. "You fired like a hunter of the first order, my young comrade. It is a royal shot, and if there is a paradise for tigers, this one must bless you for having hurried him into it without suffering, according him a hero's death : right between the eyes! Ah, well!" he added, a little spitefully, "the luck is all on your side. Since the beginning of our trip, all the brilliant shots have fallen to you. You have just brought down a tiger—a true tiger—while I, an old professional hunter, can only boast of a miserable chita."

He said that with a grimace, making his tongue clack with an expression that sent the other travelers into shouts of laughter.

"You will soon take your revenge, my dear major," replied Weldon lightly.

"I hope so indeed, young man. Without that hope, I believe I should leave you all in the lurch to seek good fortune elsewhere."

"And the sources of the Ganges, major? And Gaurisankar?"

"My dear friend," replied Plumptre, "I repeat that Gaurisankar can wait for me. As to the sources of the Ganges, they seem to me to be frightfully well guarded by the inhabitants of the Tarái. It is for us to exterminate these noxious creatures, and then we shall have realized the myths of Hercules, Theseus, and Belerophon, slayers of monsters."

This dialogue did not hinder their departure at a later hour. The plans and itinerary were definitely fixed ; they would make no more halts before getting out of the forest, at least unless the difficulties of the journey obliged them to encamp for the night. The major part of the company, contrary to the advice of the Scotchman, wished to have done with the dangerous gloom of Tarái as soon as possible. They would have all the leisure for hunting that they desired when they had cleared the Nepál frontier.

Their progress was thus accomplished without relaxation or respite. Fortunately the boundaries of the wooded lands were near at hand, and the only difficulty upon which it was necessary henceforth to count was the painful ascent of the first slopes of the Himálayas. These were perceived immediately upon their arrival at Kedárnáth. Of the seventy thousand pilgrims who come every year as far as Hardwár, barely three thousand have undertaken to finish the sacred journey ; more than two thousand remained this side of Badarináth ; certainly not more than a fiftieth would continue to Gangotri. But the ascent of the lower ranges suddenly became very rough. A new council was necessary. In fact, the cattle wagons were of no further use. The travelers then paid their drivers and dismissed them. Furthermore, an accident diminished their number by depriving them of one of their companions. Captain MacKinnon had so serious a fall that he broke his right leg, and was constrained to remain at the dak-bungalow at Kedárnáth. He bade adieu to the rest of the company, and decided to wait in the care of his

Indian servant until the removal of the splints adjusted by Dr. MacGregor should permit him to return to Masúrí and Simla.

The travelers had thus suffered three losses in less than ten days: that of the Hindu Gourap-Sing, dead from the bite of the daboias; of Captain MacKinnon, invalided by the fracture of his leg, and of his servant. Their number now consisted of nine whites and eight natives, among whom was the poor devil who had escaped death from the mortal embrace of the python, and who had been so valiantly rescued by the ax of Euzen Graec'h.

THE BOHEMIANS HAD IN THEIR TRAIN AN IMMENSE FLOCK OF SHEEP.

VI.

THE SACRED RIVER.

THE company of tourists still comprised eighteen
men, counting the guide Ramu, whose conduct, since
the incident of the forest, had given no cause for
criticism or even for suspicion.

Upon his advice they decided to join the first
group of pilgrims whom they should meet on the
mountain.

This first group of fifty-five people, two of whom
were women, was not long in appearing. From the first
encounter, which was moreover full of reserve, Merrien
believed that he observed a shadow on Goulab's brow.

This time the Frenchman did not care to keep silence,
and hastened to question his servant. The shikári, as
prudent as he was upright, but moderate in his expres-
sions, only revealed a part of his apprehensions.

"Sahib," said he, "I would not wish to alarm your mind with chimerical fears. But I do not hesitate to tell you that it will be henceforth necessary to take great precautions. Many disquieting things have taken place, and are still taking place around us."

Then he explained to the young explorer that he had found the incident of the forest in which the unfortunate Gourap-Sing had met his death, a very strange one—the simultaneous appearance of serpents that are never found together. It was on this very account that he had recommended to Merrien to have the wounded man questioned by Dr. MacGregor. This insistence on the part of the shikari decided Jean to confer anew with the physician. The latter profited by an improvement in the condition of the wounded man, still stretched out in one of the mule-wagons, to question him. The man's response confirmed Goulab's statement, and increased their suspicions. He recounted that at the time he had been surprised by the boa he was in the company of Gourap-Sing. The Dogra guide who was with them at first had separated from them for a moment. The two men advanced without suspicion, and were suddenly surprised to hear, some distance off, soft notes like those that the snake-charmers draw from the reed flutes that they carry with them, and it was while they were seeking to divine the origin of this melody in this desert place, that they were attacked by these reptiles.

The words of the wounded man explained to Merrien the meaning of the raillery that Goulab had addressed to Ramu in joking him about the reed with which he was furnished : "excellent to cut serpents with." The shikari, without going so far as to accuse the guide formally,

suspected him of not being unconnected with the
appearance of the venomous creatures. To the direct
question that the traveler put to him, the faithful
Hindu responded very clearly this time that such indeed
was his thought.

By mutual agreement they decided not to let their
suspicions be perceived. Prudence itself counseled this
determination, for they had just quitted the beaten track
which, in spite of its defects, had permitted up to that
time a sufficiently rapid ascent of the cliffs. They had
before them now only extremely steep paths on which
the mules and asses, the only beasts of burden that
one could utilize in such regions, could scarcely keep
their footing. Here and there gorges appeared, announc-
ing still narrower defiles and more frightful *cluses*.
The road was hidden between enormous perpendicular
walls overhanging the way, from the height of which a
handful of men would have sufficed to destroy an army.
Then the passage widened, the road became practicable
again, and, the difficult point passed, they breathed easily
once more, still trembling with the terrors which had
excited the imagination so violently impressed by the
grand and terrible picture of the abysses skirted and the
dangers escaped.

Each step which the tourists took brought them
nearer to the sanctuary of the Brahman worship. Was
it not in these savage places that the divine Ganges
was born from springs flowing direct from heaven?
Was it not here that the three streams of water which
contend for precedence, the Bághirathí, the Mundakni,
and the Ram-Ganga, run nearly parallel, tempestuous
streams before their currents unite beyond the Tarái in
mighty confluents, such as Hardwár and Almora?

Already the travelers discerned on the horizon the high terraces where stand the temple of Gangotri and its convents of Brahmans at three thousand meters' altitude. Beyond, the cleft rocks scaled the sky, and the somber and lofty sides of the gorges of Nilang were visible, from which Bághirathí, together with its first tributary, the Jahnavi, sprang.

It was necessary to ascend to that point if one wished to see the cradle of the divine river born under the trident of Sivá, under the five peaks of the Káilas. The column ascended resolutely, but the increasing obstacles had already caused some of the Hindu pilgrims to retreat. At the entrance to the first ravine five hundred of them could barely drag themselves painfully along the rough road, which was full of cracks as sharp and cutting as the points of a hunter's trap. The feet of the unfortunate people were bleeding, and they were shaken by violent chills whenever at nightfall, after the torrid rays of the sun upon the bare rocks, the mountain wind came to freeze their limbs shivering under their *dhotis* of cotton cloth, white or striped with gay colors.

Such, however, was the power of belief, the sway of religious sentiment, that the exhausted troop pursued the pilgrimage to them the most hallowing of all. They had come from all parts of India, these " Faithful of the God Yama," "the guide of death," these *anivarttina*, or "travelers who do not turn back." And when they should have attained the summit, when they should have kissed the holy stones of Gangotri, how many would die on the banks of the Bághirathí of destitution and exhaustion ; happy, however, to enter into immortality on the very threshold of the divinity.

The spectacle was calculated to touch feeling hearts.

Of all the Europeans who followed that steep ascent, and scandalized the zealots by the presence of their mules, as if one had any right to ascend to God's sanctuary by the aid of animals, Cecil Weldon appeared the most moved. A number of times, constrained by pity, he had offered the unfortunate pilgrims the relief of the supplies that the white men carried with them. Generally he was met with refusal by the devotees, who practiced a more rigorous fast in proportion as they approached nearer to the temple. Nevertheless, he had been fortunate enough to be able to succor and relieve some of the miserable creatures falling from starvation by the way. At other times, aided by his companions, who were won over by the example of his generosity, he had made a part of the journey on foot, after putting those who were sickest on mule-back.

At the same time that unfavorable suspicions of the Rájput guide sprang up in Jean Merrien's mind, doubts of an entirely different nature concerning his young American companion haunted him.

On many occasions he had been struck by the extreme reserve of this young man, by his modesty, his bashfulness even, which had sometimes seemed exaggerated even to the major, a rigid Puritan in spite of his soldierly license.

Cecil Weldon had never consented to share a room occupied by others of the travelers. Moreover, Cecil had a very strange aspect for a man. In spite of the energy and courage of which he had always given proof, his constitution was frail and delicate. His voice was too sweet, his skin too fine for a man, and the beauty of his features would have been remarked even had he been in woman's dress.

Merrien could not refrain from suspicions analogous to those which had brought upon the worthy Jackson, land-lord of the Great Tower Inn at Srinagar, the vehement objurgations of Mrs. Jackson, his spouse.

The ascent became more and more painful. On reaching the high village of Ahosinath, the explorers esti-mated that a hundred pilgrims at the most followed the road to Gangotri in their company. Merrien noticed that the face of Goulab, which had been very solemn up to this time, brightened. He questioned him.

"Sahib," responded the shikari, "I will not conceal from you that I was very anxious. The major part of these people were devotees of Siva and of Káli. Happily the fatigue of the journey has discouraged many of them, and now a large proportion of those who will keep on are of the same religion as myself, the faithful of Vishnu, the preserver. Nevertheless, my fears are not all dissipated, and we will do well to redouble our caution ; above all when we shall be within some miles of the sanctuary."

Following the advice that he had received from his faithful servant, Merrien gathered together his com-panions and informed them of his misgivings. They, then, accepted the part of prudence, and as the mules themselves seemed to refuse to travel by night, they raised the tents of their camp under the starry skies of the Himálayas.

Cecil Weldon's attitude still gave the Frenchman food for reflection. The Yankee isolated himself entirely from the rest of the troop, and appeared disagreeably surprised that they had not waited to gain some village of the mountains before making a halt. There, miser-able though the huts might be, he would have been able to undress, and taste repose.

But this was only a beginning of the fatigues and troubles inherent to all enterprises of this kind.

So remarked Major Plumptre, who joked the American with some liveliness.

"My dear Weldon, what will you say, then, when we get into the upper ravines? Though you are as brave as anyone, your education leaves something to be desired for an explorer. You are as soft as a woman."

"Major," retorted Cecil quickly enough, "I confess my weakness for sleep, which is indispensable to my nature, and I reserve my epigrams until the Right Honorable Plumptre shall be constrained to make but one meal a day."

The officer took this retort in very good part. He burst out laughing as he replied :

"Then, my good fellow, I shall not have occasion to applaud your spirit of raillery. Keep this in your mind : Major Plumptre is a mortal like other human beings, but with the protection of God, and the aid of his rifle, he will always find enough to eat were it in the very domains of the devil, and as I was born generous this will be a guarantee to you that you will never suffer hunger."

"In that case, my dear major," cried the other, in the same tone, "I am entirely reassured. Eating when hungry I shall sleep my full, if it be only during the leisure that you afford me in provisioning the larder."

This exchange of repartee enlivened the evening. Then they snatched a little slumber during the latter hours of the night.

Alas! when morning dawned a double catastrophe appalled the travelers. The Hindu who had escaped from the embrace of the boa had been able to regain his

strength, thanks to the intelligent care of Dr. MacGregor.
The wounds which the bite of the terrible ophidian had
left were closed, and in a fair way to heal, so that the
poor boy had been able to continue following on mule-
back the Englishman by whom his services were
engaged.

But it happened that morning as they folded the
tents for departure the little Madrasi came running,
terror depicted upon his face, to announce to Dr. Mac-
Gregor that Ali, the name of the wounded man, who
was a Mussulman, writhed upon his couch, a prey to
intolerable agony, and that his wounds had opened again
and presented an ugly aspect. The child's eyes filled
with tears while relating this.

Everyone ran to the tent where Ali lay. They found
him dying, shaken by convulsive movements, foam coming out of the corners of his mouth, and green and
fetid pus showing from the wounds left by the teeth of
the python. It was manifest that the sick man had grown
worse suddenly, and this in contradiction to the opti-
mistic expectation of the doctor. The latter could not
refrain from a grimace on seeing the wounded man.

"There is nothing to do," he said to his companions. "We are in the presence of a disease as
grave as it is rare — of spontaneous septicæmia. The
man is lost. It is a purulent general infection."

Goulab also had bent his brows. He contented
himself with saying to the physician :

"This man has been poisoned during the night."

"Hey!" cried Dr. MacGregor, "what do you
say?"

"I say," replied the shikári, very positively this
time, "that a criminal hand has poured upon such

wounds of this unfortunate man as remained open
some of the tincture of euphorbia."

"Is it, possible?" questioned the doctor. "But then
who is the criminal, do you think?"

The shikári extended his right hand with solemnity,
and placing his left upon his heart, said:

"The Mahadera knows that I never accused one
of my brothers vainly, but I accuse of this murder,
and of Gourap-Sing's, Ramu your guide, the Rajpút
Dogra."

A shiver ran over all present. Plumptre seized his
rifle with fury.

"Ah! the rascal!" roared he. "I will kill him like a
dog!"

"If you find him," said Goulab, shaking his head
ironically. "I have sinned through prudence, sahibs; I
should have spoken yesterday. The assassin should
have been gotten rid of yesterday."

"Truly, Goulab," agreed the doctor, "you have been
too reticent."

They were not long in deciding upon their plan of
campaign. It was necessary to overtake the murderer
as soon as possible. He must be with the pilgrims,
and they were a whole night in advance.

They set out immediately when they had decided
that the unfortunate Ali was lost, and that Ramu had
deserted his post of guide. A tribe of nomadic Ban-
jaras engaged, in consideration of a compensation, to
take to Hardwár the body of the poor Mohammedan
who had begged earnestly to be delivered to his brethren. His last prayer was granted. The Bohemians had
with them an immense flock of sheep which had
come down from Tibet, as well as planks of teak-

wood and pine all ready for the southern industry. Four of these planks sufficed to furnish Ali with his last vehicle, and with tears in their eyes, the Europeans bade adieu to the body of their unfortunate servant.

But then came a fresh torture, and a new cause for grief and indignation. They counted one member too few in the column : the little Madrasi who was attached to Cecil Weldon had disappeared.

"Ah ! the unhappy boy !" cried the young American, whose eyes filled with tears. "If they only have not killed him also ! This Dogra deserves no pity, if we find him again !"

It was difficult to repress the exasperation of the different members of the little troop ; and if the infamous Ramu had fallen into their hands at that moment, "they would not have left him to languish," in the picturesque language of Euzen Graec'h.

"As for me," cried the Breton, "I only ask to have him for a moment in my hands. And I should have no need of arms to do the business for him," he added, with a movement full of expression.

There were, then, two new gaps in the ranks of the little column. There were but eight members left. It was necessary to redouble their vigilance, and, especially since they had entered the bad passes of the mountain, to manage to keep elbow to elbow, in order that each of the explorers should be security for his companions.

But just as they were about to enter the high closes of the water courses, young Cecil Weldon assembled his companions of the journey and made them a confession which, stupefying as it was, did not astonish them. They had had a presentiment of it.

"Gentlemen," said the young traveler, with blushing

confusion, "I owe you a confession, and I have a request
to make of you."

"A request?" cried Plumptre gallantly. "Let us call
it granted in advance."

"Bah!" replied Cecil, with a mischievous grimace,
"you don't know what you are bargaining for,
major."

And before the officer could protest, the American
explained himself clearly:

"The request that I make of you all without distinction, gentlemen, for you are all my friends, is a little
cruel. If our expedition should incur too formidable
trials, if we should be exposed to dangers which left
us no resource, no hope, swear to me that the last
survivor among you will kill me, if I have not preceded him in death."

"Oh! oh!" said Dr. MacGregor, smiling, "that is
indeed a strange request, young man, and you were
right just now in reproaching Plumptre for pledging
himself too rashly."

"During the crusade of St. Louis in Egypt," said
Merrien gravely, "the Queen of France, a prisoner of
the infidels, exacted a similar promise from the old
chevalier appointed for her defense."

The young American wore a melancholy smile. Then
he said, with great sweetness:

"It is for the same reason, gentlemen, that I entreat
you. I am a woman, but for others than you I must
always be Cecil, not Cicely Weldon."

All bowed respectfully before the intrepid young
girl, and Merrien added, with a kind of gayety:

"That is all right, miss. But calm yourself: all the
Dogras, all the Rájputs, all the Siváites in the world

cannot prevent people like ourselves from bringing their enterprise to a fortunate conclusion."

And, though a little embarrassed by this secret, the brave men did not permit themselves to show the feeling.

All precautions had now been taken. The column divided itself into three groups : a vanguard, the body of the troop, and the rear guard.

Merrien, Graec'h, Plumptre, and the doctor, and one of the Americans in rotation, and the faithful Goulab relieved one another at the difficult posts, that is to say, at the head and at the rear of the procession.

Thirty kilometers from Gangotri, at the last bungalow established by the English company, the travelers were constrained to part with their animals. They must henceforth depend upon themselves to overcome all obstacles. These were numerous and varied. Never in the entire universe was a pilgrimage made more deserving of credit than that of the faithful Brahman to the cradle of the divine Ganga.

There were at every step frightful precipices five hundred and six hundred meters in height, opening from the edges of the bad road clinging *en corniche* to the buttresses of the prodigious chain ; plateaus calcined by the sun by day, and swept by night by the sharp wind from the snowy regions ; and valleys so deep and so narrow that daylight scarcely ever penetrates to them.

Finally, after a day of unspeakable effort, the column arrived at the holy place. As they had no concern with the neighborhood of the Brahman convent which surrounds the middle pagoda, they at once took the most frequented way, that on which they were sure to find the greatest number of pilgrims of the two orders of Vishnu and Sivá.

It was natural that a pious man like Goulab should profit by the opportunity which was offered him of sanctifying himself by contact with the sacred spring. So he solicited and obtained permission from his companions to accomplish the prescriptions of the religious law, which orders the ceremonial of the pilgrimages with great particularity.

They had arrived at the boundary of the consecrated territory at the confluence of the Bághirathí and the Jahnavi.

The shikari completely divested himself of his clothes, and took his place in a line of some forty Hindus as naked as himself. One after another, each of the men plunged into the swift, icy waters of the river, and came out shivering. On the bank a Bráhman clad in white, attended by two children filling the office of acolytes, murmured a benediction upon the heads of the purified. Then the latter, before dressing themselves again, received from one of the children a sheaf of flowers and fragrant herbs, rich in color, which they threw into the current of the river, after which the Bráhman, with a new formula, took from a little basket carried by the other child an oval biscuit, and gave it to the penitent, who, fasting and exhausted in all probability, made haste to bite into it vigorously.

The shikári complied with all these forms with the rigorous piety that characterizes the people of the Orient. But the prescriptions did not stop there. From the sacred confluent to the sanctuary the distance was not excessive. On the other hand the road bristled with difficulties of every kind, and even though having no concern with the religious exercises, the European travelers were none the less subjected to the same trials.

For henceforth the word "road" could be used only in antiphrasis. It was an irony which mocked the energy of the explorers at every step, threatening, even, to discourage them. So that Graec'h the Breton, a seaman, and used to scaling the yards, could not help thinking the mountains fatiguing.

"If it is like this at the beginning, before coming to the real climbing, what will it be when we are on Gaurisankar?"

"Bah!" retorted Merrien gayly, "when we are on Gaurisankar, we shall only have a thousand or fifteen hundred meters more to climb. Ibi-Gamin, which we can see from here, is very nearly eight kilometers in the air. We shall long before have acquired the habit of ascent."

"There is still another habit which one acquires even more easily," joked the Breton. "It is that of dying."

While Goulab lifted himself by the strength of his wrists from rock to rock until he reached the level of the sanctuary which covers the spring of the Baghirathi-Ganga, his European companions resolutely entered the frightful gorge where the holy river falls tempestuously in cascade after cascade.

A perpendicular wall, three hundred meters in height, rose before them. They were barely able to climb the first terrace with the aid of some steps cut in the wall.

Above that, a frightful staircase presented itself, formed of shelves of iron sunk in the perpendicular wall at a distance of about a foot one from the other. It was by this dizzy ladder that the travelers must attain to the upper platform.

At sight of this unexpected difficulty, young Weldon, or rather Miss Cicely Weldon, since she was henceforth known to her companions by her true name, could not repress a shudder of fear.

One may perhaps brave man and beast, and look calmly upon the most cruel death, but here one was in the presence of another kind of danger, a trial directed to man's physical resistance, and to which the nervous system of a woman, especially, must offer still less resistance. Everything contributed to terrify the eyes and to disturb the *sang-froid* indispensable at such moments, and the fear of vertigo was added to the horror of the place. One could not, however, pause by the way. It was necessary, at any cost, to get out of the terrible cluse.

As a measure of prudence they decided that the Hindus should go first in the ascent. But this produced an unexpected defection.

Of the seven natives who had remained with the travelers, four were men of the plains, whose good will and devotion had been already seriously shaken by the difficulties of the ascent. This last test found them insensible to all exhortations, to all promises of remuneration. They absolutely refused to carry the experience any further. Merrien and Plumptre did not, however, insist beyond reason. When the poor devils were brought to the foot of this "monkey-ladder," as Graec'h called it, they were seized with violent trembling, their teeth chattered, their legs failed them. It was manifest that the poor creatures could not climb fifty meters without accident.

Unde· such conditions, humanity as well as prudence obliged the explorers to dismiss these useless and even embarrassing servants.

Merrien settled up all accounts, and each of the behras came in turn to kiss the feet of the masters whom they had so poorly seconded. It was apparent, nevertheless, that they were ashamed and disconsolate at their faint-heartedness.

"There is as much superstition as there is nervousness in their case," said Dr. MacGregor. "They are persuaded that we are going to our death, and they by no means pride themselves on their heroism. Let us not forget that above Gangotri is the 'Mouth of the Cow,' to the south of the glacier of Nilang. To the west is Trikánta, to the east Nanda-Parváti. When we arrive there we shall be divine beings to some, abominable profaners to the others."

In order not to linger in these perilous gorges, they at once undertook the scaling of the iron steps. The two Hindus who had remained faithful went first. Then Merrien and Graec'h thought of a way practically to aid their group in the weird ascent. They knotted about their shoulders two cords of unequal length, the other ends of which they fastened to the shoulders and about the body of the young girl. That done, the Breton, whose incredible strength was seconded by his habit of climbing yards, and who feared no vertigo, leaped in his turn upon the frightful ladder. Merrien followed him, and Cicely came third, helping herself so energetically with her hands and her feet that she rendered the provisional aid of her two companions unnecessary. After them came Dr. MacGregor and the Americans. The brave major brought up the rear.

CICELY CAME THIRD.

Fortunately this dizzy staircase did not extend further than a hundred meters. The wall was again broken away at the summit, and natural notches, with sharp edges, gave easier foothold.

Finally the upper plateau was reached. They had before them the slopes of the nearer ranges, and the horizon disclosed enormous distances with marvelous perspectives.

To the south were the valleys they had just crossed, the Hindu Tarái ; to the north the source of the Ganges appeared springing from the glaciers of the Káilas. To the left stretched the vanishing chain of which Dehra-Dún, and the Siwálik mountains are only the stairways ; to the right extended the parallel lines of the Chiriya-gháti, gigantic propylæa of the principal mass, or rather of the succession of the prodigious masses which commence at Chumalari on the frontiers of Bhután. Nepál was at their feet ; the central Himálayas. lay open to their gaze.

THE GOVERNOR SENT TWO OFFICERS TO MEET THE TRAVELERS.

VII.

THE DHAULAGIRI.

THE travelers were three days in reaching the eastern frontiers above the lakes and the English station of Naini-Tál. Toward the 25th of March they had passed Chakráta, and cleared the pass of Niti-Liti, at a height of more than five thousand meters. It only remained to them to cross the two arms of the Çogra and the peak of the goddess Manda, before entering Nepál.

The major had not ceased grumbling during the entire ascent.

"How much better off are we," he said; "what have we gained by this journey? We are already in the midst of glaciers and snows, and we have managed to stretch our itinerary to nearly double its length. If we had started from Dárjiling we should already be at the foot of Mt. Everest, and we should have had some admirable hunting."

"*Morbleu!*" cried the doctor, who was fond of French oaths, "haven't you hunted all you want to thus far? You have forgotten the tigers, and the buffaloes of Garhwâl?"

And Plumptre sighed with genuine sadness:

"It is precisely because I remember . them that I regret them. What beautiful shots we are losing!"

Goulab the shikâri, who, his rites being accomplished, had rejoined the travelers above Gangotri, somewhat reassured the insatiable hunter by informing him that the Himâlayan chain is the most capricious in the world; that after reaching a height of seven thousand meters, one frequently has to descend again to below three thousand, and even to two thousand; and that at each of these descents game is found again in abundance, more especially the wild elephant, and the *suilliens*; among them the *babiroussa*, that wild and curious animal, provided with four long and broad tusks, giving it a most terrible aspect, but which is less formidable, as a matter of fact, than the wild boar of Europe.

He added, to give him a final bit of consolation:

"As to the tiger, he pushes his way to incredible heights, and we can never be certain that we shall not have to defend ourselves against him, even at three thousand meters' altitude. Be prepared for the chance of a surprise."

With this hope, the brave Scotchman took his way over the mountains. For the rest, incidents of quite another order were not long in furnishing the explorers with emotions that they were not expecting. When they were about to enter upon the Taklagar road, one of the two ways the gates of which had been opened to them by the Nepalisian permits accorded them by request of the Calcutta government, the travelers thought they ought themselves to draw up a map of their explorations.

They therefore assembled in council in a village of the western frontier, about the thirtieth degree north latitude, and devoted an entire day to resting, in order to recover their strength, already somewhat tried, and to make out their itinerary with the most rigorous exactitude. All were compelled to contribute, and each one brought to the task, in addition to his own intelligence and his personal opinions, the experience acquired by previous efforts and courageous investigation.

Dr. MacGregor was, under these circumstances, able to furnish the best advice, having already had occasion upon a previous expedition to penetrate as far as Khátmandú. He revealed to his friends the result of his personal observations, which, united to notes made by Merrien of the statements of previous explorers, sufficed for the elaboration of a common plan.

"Gentlemen," said the physician, "you are not ignorant of the fact that Nepál is an independent state, very shut in, very wild, of which we ourselves know very little, in spite of the presence of our minister in the very capital of this state. It is counted among the number of regions reported unknown, and its frontier, which is very indefinite, has no fixity except on the Indian side, and this in consequence of the wars which the British Government has victoriously sustained against the wild and independent peoples of the region—notably against the Gúrkhas, who, dispossessed by us, after bloody combats, have ended by adopting our hegemony, and furnishing us to-day with the best foot-soldiers of our Indian army.

"These limits, often moved back, make of Nepál a long quadrilateral, backed, or rather inclosed, by the double chain of the Himálayas and the Trans-Himálayas. This quadrilateral measures about seven hundred kilometers, or four hundred miles in length by a hundred and twenty-five kilometers, or seventy-two miles in breadth. The sum of the population contained within these boundaries has never been ascertained exactly, and it is quite at hazard, relying upon the declarations made by the native authorities, that our geographers estimate it sometimes at three, sometimes at five millions of inhabitants. Such statistics are evidently fanciful."

"Doctor," interrupted Plumptre abruptly, "how does that interest us? What we need to know, in order to carry out our enterprise, is the road that we are going to follow, together with the dangers or the difficulties that it may offer, and the means that we shall have at our disposal to escape these dangers and overcome these difficulties."

It goes without saying that in this respect MacGregor knew no more than the common run of mortals. The silence that he maintained, in place of responding to the officer's question, gave Merrien a chance to intervene.

"My dear major, we have for our enlightenment only the reports of these travelers who have preceded us. And these are very incomplete, since none of them, not one of them, I say, has been able to penetrate to the heart of the mountains; and thus far it has been necessary to hold to the angular measurements of the highest summits as made from the plains of Hindustan. The mission that we have voluntarily assigned ourselves is all the more glorious for that. We shall be the first among Europeans, perhaps even among Indians, to force the gates of Nepál, and approach, according to our ability, the majestic summits that such men as Adolph and Hermann Schlagintweit, and the Pandit Nain-Sing, have been able to contemplate only from a distance."

The Scotchman responded in a friendly manner and with a gracious smile :

" I understand that very well, my dear Merrien, since my intention has been to accompany you in your bold project. Yet it would appear to me wise and prudent should we be advised of the nature of the obstacles that we shall encounter."

"They will be of various kinds," replied the Frenchman. "But the most obstinate ones will very certainly be presented by the people of these unknown countries. God grant that we shall have to come into as little contact with them as possible !"

Then they took the final census of the expedition and the inventory of things indispensable to the journey.

Each man, and Cicely Weldon figured as one, carried with him a double-barreled rifle, one of the "chokebore" barrels of which answered for either shot or bullets ; three hundred cartridges divided between the knapsack, the cartridge box, and the belt, a six-barreled revolver of the same caliber, a hunting knife, tent-stakes or supports, a reserve of blasting powder, some ropes of hemp and copper thread, a pike, and twelve steel climbing spurs. That made enough of a burden in itself. They had to add food supplies in the smallest possible compass : two boxes of pemmican and of Liebig, one of kola powder, a bottle of essence of coffee, and a gourd of rum.

Thus provided, the explorers arranged for their halts. The march through the mountain region could not be estimated in figures based on the average day's journeys over the plains. They decided, therefore, to make twenty kilometers a day the desideratum, and twelve the minimum, which allowed of their reaching Dhaulágirí toward the 10th or the 15th of April at the latest.

They also inspected their foot-gear. This plays an important part in the life of mountain climbers. The travelers were provided with strong leather gaiters, *passe montagnes* of heavy wool, jerseys of tricot, and hunting jackets, soft woolen gloves, a loose cloak, which could, however, be held close to the body by means of a belt ; these completed the equipment of the valiant comrades.

Finally, as they could not carry everything upon their shoulders, they took pains to place all the supplementary baggage on light litters which they were obliged to carry, two and two, by means of straps passed over the neck of each bearer. It was decided that they should relieve one another from hour to hour of the drudgery of this carriage.

Through a sentiment of gallantry that was altogether French, Merrien proposed to exempt Miss Weldon from all drudgery, and all especially heavy burdens. The plucky young girl refused to accept this indulgence, which humiliated her. She did not in the least consent to leave to her friends all that concerned the material cares of existence.

Each day, at each halt, they took counsel as to their next proceedings. This foresight was indispensable for the avoidance of events that were to be feared. The worthy Goulab, for whom there were now no secrets, had confided to the travelers the information obtained at the sanctuary of Gangotri. Some fifty Siváites had passed that way in advance of him, and from the details that he had gathered, the shikari had recognized that the Rájput guide, Ramu, was among them. He then summed up his impressions in a counsel of caution that was very skillfully defined.

He was convinced that the Dogra had been able to lead a certain number of fanatics on the mountains for the sole purpose of laying a snare for the white travelers.

They would before long find them on their road, and then, far from the eyes of English authority, the wretches would not hesitate to attempt an attack. It would then be necessary to give battle, and perhaps under disadvantageous conditions.

All the maps were unfolded, all those, at least, that related to the expedition. They were unfortunately very incomplete, none of the preceding explorers since Montgomery, Baille, and the Pundit Nain-Sing, having succeeded in passing the elevation of the Niti Pass. Adolph Schlagintweit himself had not been further than Nanda-Devi.

Nevertheless, not one of the daring excursionists had a moment's hesitation in facing the dangers of the route. All responded with a vigorous exclamation to the little discourse that Merrien thought it his duty to address to them.

"My dear colleagues and rivals, whom I am happy to call my friends, the moment has come to examine your resolution afresh. There is yet time to retrace your steps. The excursion that has led us to the foot of the Káila mountains, to the very 'Mouth of the Cow,' is a very pretty one to have acccomplished. The fame of it is sufficient, and I believe that you have already your names upon the rocks of the Himálayas, and upon history."

Major Plumptre was not pleased with this speech, which seemed to him to be inspired by disdain.

"Mr. Frenchman," he cried, with some ill-humor, "is it your intention to beat a retreat yourself?"

"Never," declared Merrien, laughing. "Even if I were about to die, I should implore some Bothia to carry my bones to the summit."

"In that case, I find you very inconsiderate in daring to propose a retreat to Englishmen. Where you go, we go."

"I agree with Major Plumptre," said Cicely Weldon on her part.

"I didn't leave Srínagar to stop at the seventy-ninth meridian from Paris. Go ahead, then, Mr. Merrien, and we will follow, that is, unless we go ahead of you."

There was nothing more to say after such replies. They set out with no delay, and in three days they had traversed eighty kilometers; they had not only done more than the proposed average, but they had "skipped" certain stopping places, such as Niti-Liti, and the plateaus of Milam. The evening of the fourth day they had reached Taklagar, and penetrated into Nepál without having had their progress interrupted by any prohibition or any frontier broils. This result had been obtained thanks to the resolution and wisdom of Merrien, who was unanimously proclaimed the leader of the expedition. The Frenchman had decided that it would be best to follow as long as possible the line of the summit at a mean altitude of five and six

thousand meters, where one would hardly encounter
anyone other than the Bhután shepherds, and need
not dread the unexpected appearance of Hindu or
Nepalese zealots. The event had proved him entirely
right, and, what was entirely unlooked for, but a very
agreeable surprise to the travelers, they had been
enabled to ascertain that at this level, by a strange
freak of nature, the summit line that they were following formed a veritable flat causeway across the
groups of the chain. Thus they were able to gain
ground while avoiding the dangerous valleys of the
south.

"Yes," said Jean, laughing, "we are here in a region
which only Europeans can approach with impunity.
The sharp cold of the nights renders access to it well-
nigh impossible to men of the southern regions, and
that is what has kept our enemies from following us
upon these heights. God grant that we may thus
continue our way until we reach Dhaulágiri."

Unhappily, this hope was promptly to be crushed.
Taklagar is a sort of fortress fastened between the high
buttresses of the chain. It was impossible to proceed
beyond it, the authorities of the country exercising
their surveillance very actively at this point, which
touches the Tibet frontiers.

Dr. MacGregor could not repress a sigh as he
contemplated the white line of the summits of the
Trans-Himálayas.

And as the major asked the reason of this apparent
grief, he replied very frankly :

"It is truly too bad that we should not be able
to profit by the proximity to descend upon the other
side of the chain into the valleys that separate the

Himálayas from Kuenlun.   It is in this part of Tibet
that the sources of that unknown river are found, the
one called Tsang-bo in French geographies, and confused
with the Brahmaputra on a number of English maps."

He spread out a rather ancient map, on which the
mysterious stream of water figured under the name of
" Burrampooter."

"Well !" exclaimed the Scotchman, "why shouldn't.
we do it ? Perhaps we shall never be so well situated
as we are to-day to settle a question which constitutes a
geographical problem of the highest interest. After all,
to scale Gaurisankar offers glory for ourselves alone, but
to reconnoiter the Tsang-bo renders a service to the
cosmographic science of all nations. The doctor's idea is
a good one. Hurrah for the doctor's idea ! Moreover,
Merrien himself had entertained the same dream !"

The sudden and contagious enthusiasm of the major
came near leading the entire troop into a complete
overthrow of the programme that they had made out
together, and with which the press of the whole world
was presently to concern itself, as well as the scholars
of all countries.

But Jean Merrien showed himself inflexible. He
harangued his companions with a vehemence which the
circumstances justified.

"Truly, gentlemen, has the mountain wind turned
your heads ? Must it be I, a Frenchman, a man of that
race that you call crazy-headed, who recalls you to a
remembrance of honor pledged, of reason, of a plan that
we have adopted after common deliberation ? As for the
rest, do as you please. Go and seek the Tsang-bo or
the Brahmaputra if that seem good to you ! I shall pursue my way to Gaurisankar by way of Dhaulágiri. We

THE GOVERNOR GAVE THEM AN AUDIENCE.

shall have a chance later to return to the Tsang-bo or the Brahmaputra."

This discourse would have sufficed to keep the enthusiasts in "the straight path," if an incident of a different order had not occurred to render palpable the almost insurmountable obstacles to an enterprise that they had applauded without due reflection.

The governor of Taklagar sent two of his officers to meet the travelers. These officers belonged to a manifestly Tartar race. Their angular features, their prominent cheek-bones, their perceptibly flattened noses, attested their origin. Moreover, their accouterments bore marks of the proximity of China, at the same time that the woolen stuffs of which their clothing was made revealed the habit of sojourning in inclement zones. The two envoys of the governor expressed very courteously the desire of the latter to himself see and question the explorers. They found no difficulty in deferring to this request, and, conducted by their guides, they set out upon the rugged and tortuous path that leads from the city to the "palace" of the eminent personage, a formless structure like a stone balcony suspended on the projection of an isolated hill.

They had not to wait at all. The governor gave them an audience at once, in the presence of a third officer whom Merrien and his friends esteemed it great good fortune to find in these regions. He was a Gúrkha, who had served nearly twenty years in the Indian army, where he had won the rank of *soubadhar*, or adjutant, which the general-in-chief had converted into that of lieutenant the moment that Rannah Garry, the name of the ex-subaltern, had been retired.

Very proud of this title, and of the honors which it

had gained for him and his country, the Gúrkha had kept a very genuine attachment for his old superiors, and a profound respect for "Old England." Now, Major Plumptre had known the soubadhar while in garrison at Delhi, and although the latter had never been under the orders of the cavalry officer, he was none the less pleased to present himself to the Scotchman with the language and martial bearing of an old soldier.

"God save you, major!" he greeted him, as soon as Plumptre, Merrien, Miss Weldon, and their suite had entered the audience chamber. Much surprised to hear himself addressed in his mother tongue, the officer was still more agreeably surprised to learn from the lips of the ex-adjutant himself the story of his life and the good will that he felt toward the travelers.

These latter, prompted in a few words, were able to reply suitably to the species of examination to which they were subjected by the official personage with whom they had to do. They produced the safe-conducts countersigned by the president of Calcutta, and delivered by the sovereign of Khátmandú. But they at once perceived the pretensions to independence set up by the singular functionaries of this strange kingdom composed of twenty different peoples.

Rannah gave them to understand that a present of some rupees would completely soften the governor, and the latter found that very day upon a Kashmir rug a very beautiful Sheffield knife with a handle of horn decorated in silver, and five good guineas.

Easily satisfied, the potentate of Taklagar invited all his visitors to a sort of banquet, where they ate a succulent curry made of the meat of the kid, which

was followed by an evening of dancing by some
Tibetan Nautch girls of remarkable ugliness, munching
nuts, while the major alone of all the troop consented to
smoke three pipes of opium in company with the lord
governor.

Thanks to this exchange of civilities, Merrien, the
doctor, and Cicely were enabled to take valuable notes
upon the manners and customs of the region, and
upon the precautions that it would be necessary to
observe during the remainder of the journey. They
learned in this way that the road to the north was
positively closed against them, and that the mystic
barriers of Tibet would be lowered only for shepherds
and traders. But what annoyed them most was the
necessity of descending again into the southern valleys
on account of the impossibility of crossing the Gogra
near its source.

This river, which furnishes the Ganges with one of
its principal affluents, comes out from the Himálayas in
two branches some forty miles distant from one another. They both, however, bear the same name, or
rather the same names, for nothing is more varied
than the denominations of this stream of water. After
having borne in turn upon its western as well as upon
its eastern branch the appellations of Rizab, of Káli, of
Sarju, of Gogra, of Dewa, fused in one only after
leaving Srinagar, that of Dogra, it ends by adopting
the name of Dewah in India, the name under which
it waters Fáizabad, and Sultanpúr, and throws itself
into the Ganges above Azimgar, after having received
the limpid waters of the poetic Rápti.

Now, each of these two sources of the Gogra pro-
ceeds from the dense mass of the Himálayas, through

frightful gorges, between the walls of defiles four or
five hundred meters in height, separated by precipices
two hundred meters wide, across which human industry has not yet had time to throw bridges.

It was the absence of these bridges that obliged
the Europeans to go down into the south. Possibly the
fuming major would have been headstrong enough to
descend into the frightful gorges, if the Gúrkha, Rannah, had not cautioned him to use strategy rather than
open force.

He even held forth to them upon this subject in very
explicit language.

"Get it well into your mind that the sovereign of
Khátmándú exercises only a nominal authority over
the diverse and fragmentary populations whose cohesion
is due only to their hatred of Europeans. It is from
Tibet that the real influence comes, counterbalanced by
the fear of England. But here in the mountains the
hatred of the white men often overbears the fear that
they inspire, and nothing is easier than to hinder them
with obstacles ; to lay snares for them, the least de-
plorable effect of which is to constrain them to turn
back in their path. For the rest," added the old Indian
soldier, "I will give you a guide who is personally
devoted to me. He will conduct you by the shortest
road to Chinachin, and from there to the falls of Kanar,
where he will procure you a new guide."

They were obliged to resign themselves to the enormous loss of time which this detour occasioned. The
travelers descended the eastern arm of the Gogra as
far as the terrible cataracts, and again found themselves within the boundaries of the Tarái toward the
middle of April. The great heat was about commenc-

ing. They had lost an entire month in useless journey-
ing, and it became absolutely necessary to cross Nepál
obliquely along its greatest width.

This first disappointment threw some discouragement
over the little group, but the indomitable energy of
Merrien did not fail. Moreover, the substitute provided by the guide spoke of the remainder of the
journey with so much faith in its success that everyone accepted his opinion, and it was decided that they
take the northern road again as soon as possible.

The guide performed his duty very conscientiously.
On the 17th of April they had passed the Nagal-
pani, one of the sources of the Rápti. On the 25th
the travelers, after great hardships, found themselves at
the center of the high valleys watered by the Gandak.

The explorers did not allow themselves to be dis-
mayed by the difficulties. The guide had warned them
that this part of the journey was not the most arduous
or the most dangerous. The ground, in spite of its frequent variations in level, nevertheless maintained an
uninterrupted elevation. The plateau of Malebun, situated
between the gorges of Bargá, and the Mayandi-Kola,
finally permitted them a reassuring sight of the northern
horizon.

About thirty kilometers away, dominating the great
mass of the "Son of Man," or Náráyana, appeared
Dwalágiri, or more exactly Dhaulágiri, which means
White Mountain.

The prodigious peak rose straight upward in the tender
blue vault of the sky, and its mantle of snow was crossed
here and there by drifts of trailing clouds. At its right,
scarcely less high, secondary peaks were seen resplendent under the rays of the sun, Yassa, Barathor, and

Morchiadi ; at its left Dáyábang and Deorali rose above the dark line of the horizon.

The travelers all paused, filled with religious emotion. The four Hindus, among whom were Goulab and the guide, prostrated themselves, obeying different sentiments. Erect, with shining eyes and heaving chest, Cicely Weldon broke out in admiration :

"There it is at last, the Dwalágiri ! We have seen it ! How beautiful it is !"

"Nothing remains but to climb it !" cried Plumptre. "The eighteen miles which separate us from it is no distance at all."

Merrien intervened, recalling the general plan. He reminded them that it was not Dhaulágiri that they proposed to climb, but Gaurisankar ; which is higher by six hundred meters. The "Mt. Blanc" of Nepál figured on the programme only with the simple title of "visite," the picturesque expression used by the Frenchman.

After the difficulties which had been encountered up to this time, one must assume · that obstacles would not be lacking on the rest of the journey. Now, in order to attain Gaurisankar by following the valleys of the Gandak and the Koci, or along the flanks of the Lama-Dogra which follow the Chiriya-ghátis, it was necessary to estimate the distance as at least forty miles in a straight line.

"Gentlemen," he concluded, with much logic, "besides what is due to our programme, we must not forget that we are in the second half of April, that the heats have commenced, and that our strength will have to be economized. The same reasons which made us renounce the exploration of the Tsang-bo

ought still to keep us upon the slope on which we
are at present; that is to say, upon the southern
slope of Dhaulágiri. Let us then content ourselves with
a glance, and leave the younger for the elder."

But this time Major Plumptre protested against this
sensible language. His arguments were specious.

"My dear Merrien," he replied, "permit me to
oppose to your very correct reasons other good reasons.
Scarcely thirty kilometers separate us from Náráyana.
We shall never be nearer that goal than at this moment.
Why not profit by the opportunity? What is six hun-
dred meters more or less?"

Merrien was not at a loss to refute this argument.
The sentiment of the greater number was against him.
Dr. MacGregor himself passed over to the opposition,
and in order to satisfy his traveling companions, the
Frenchman consented that they should approach nearer
the glorious summit. They took the advice of the
guide, who declared that the best road was that which
skirted valleys of the Bargá as far as Deorali. From
there they would be able to rise progressively along a
gentle slope to the farthest level attainable by man.

This advice they followed, and Merrien, somewhat
disturbed, took his place with the rest. From that day
they again resumed the road to the north.

THE TRAITOR HAD DROPPED UPON HIS KNEES.

VIII.

THE AMBUSCADE.

NEPÁL, as Dr. MacGregor had said, is a country in which you are met by all sorts of surprises. Completely covered by mountains, it is composed of valleys and high plateaus, so that the geographers long mistook the nature of its soil and its boundaries. Numerous English maps make it commence at Siwalik at the Chiriya-ghâti or the Lama-Dogra chain, to terminate at the true Himálayas.

Upon these maps the giants of India belong only to the frontier of Tibet. A manifest error, and one that is to-day universally recognized.

Central Asia, in fact, contains two chains of unequal dimensions, the lesser of which forms the rugged plateaus of Afghánistán to the west of India, while the greater is distributed in two gigantic groups, in two divisions running one from the southeast to the north-west under the name of the Kara-Koram Mountains, the other from the northwest to the southeast, the Himálayas.

This in its turn is divided into two great masses separated by the valley of the Dingri-Maidan, which has caused them to be designated by the titles of Himá-layas and Trans-Himálayas. Beyond the Trans-Himálayas commence the plateaus of Tibet, themselves crossed by the deep valley of the Tsang-bo, and narrowly closed in between the double Himálayan chain and the mountains of Kuenlun which belong to the Kara-Koram system and are almost unknown. Now, Nepál is situated between the Himálayas and the Trans-Himálayas, and the mountains of Dhaulágirí, Gaurísankar, Kinchin-jinga, and Chumalari are found in the center not on the northern frontier of the kingdom.

Thus the travelers were mistaken when, according to Merrien's advice, they adopted the northern summit line in order to redescend toward the Náráyana. Their shortest road was, beyond all possible question, that from Fáizabad to Jamla, across the Chiriya-ghátí, but leaving Jamla upon their left to pass through the frontier cities of Pérthan, of Kebrachi, and of Durkhót. Unhappily, the permits granted by the sovereign of Nepál only left them the choice of two routes, and they had thought it well to avoid that which would subject them to the most annoyance on the part of the worrying authorities of the region. It was for these reasons that they had lost nearly a month, and had use-lessly traversed a thousand kilometers. But it was not worth while to dwell on past mistakes, since they were nearing the goal. They must avoid making others in the future, and prepare for the obstacles which might rise in the path of the little column.

The peoples of Nepál, in spite of their diversity, are generally hospitable and loyal. With the exception of the nomadic tribes, who nearly all belong to the Mongolian type, and are connected by their very visible origin with the Chinese or Manchoo families, the mountaineers of the Himálayas belong to the Aryan race. Tall, well-built, with noble features marked by a warlike pride, the men of these high regions are conscious of their worth, and seem to hold to their independence 'before any other advantage of life. Thanks to the astonishing variety of the climates that succeed one another in accordance with the gradual elevation of the crests, there are found in the Himálayas now the products of the tropical zones, and again the vegetation of the temperate zones.

The same slope gives in the spring a harvest of wheat ; in the autumn, a harvest of rice. While the palm tree, the mango tree, the pineapple, and the banana mingle and ripen in the sinuous depths of the chain, the bread tree, the European cereals, even the fruits of our climes, rejoice the agricultural population of the higher levels, and this at heights which belong to the domain of perpetual snow in our European mountains.

At three thousand meters' altitude crops flourish, at five thousand the resinous trees, the teak, the pine, the fir, the cypress, the larch abound in thick forests ; by means of the warm temperature maintained by their shelter infinitely less robust species are preserved, such as the maple, the aspen, the plane tree, the poplar. The Himálayas present in this respect the appearance of an immense experimental garden. Further up, desolation reigns supreme. No mountain system offers in so great a degree the appearance of death. Bare rocks with sharp crests blend together the entire hierarchy of minerals and earthy sediments. The crust in its upheaval had cracked in places, and the rigid granite rose almost to the skies.

Around about gneiss, mica schist, limestones of multiple origin extend and mingle in gradations that disconcert geological science. And over this chaos of deposited stones and upheaved pyrites the snow lies like a carpet of silver, continually frozen by the north wind, and continually attacked by the sun up to those deadly levels where the rarity of the atmosphere renders life impossible. The travelers had to cross these various stages, and submit to these differences of surroundings, these variations of temperature. The necessity of anticipating them, and of fortifying themselves against them, had constrained them to provide themselves with clothing appropriate to the climatic conditions to which they would be subjected. Together with cotton or flannel stuffs, they had been obliged to carry thicker and tougher materials. Their baggage was overloaded by just that much, and the ascent rendered more difficult. Furthermore, on the litters that necessitated the presence of two carriers, there had been placed certain carefully closed metal boxes, which belonged to Jean Merrien, and concerning which he maintained an obstinate silence.

The shikári Goulab showed himself no less obstinately taciturn. Two or three times Merrien had seen the pensive and searching eyes of the Indian fixed upon his own with an odd expression, as though he desired to confide to him something which he repressed just at the moment of speaking.

At other times the faithful companion's glances rested upon the new guide. This latter was also a taciturn fellow, who was rarely intrusive. They had every reason to be satisfied with his services, moreover, and there had not been the slightest sign to arouse suspicion against him.

It was evident, however, that Goulab was uneasy, that Goulab was distrustful.

Now, if Goulab were distrustful, everyone ought to be on his guard. Was not the Indian as reserved as he was prudent? When the ascent by way of Deorali had been decided upon, the calm anxiety of the shikari was abruptly transformed into agitation.

He did not care to keep his doubts to himself, and this time he went to Merrien of his own accord.

"Sahib," said he, "perhaps you have failed to pay sufficient attention to the itinerary that we are following?"

"No," replied the Frenchman, "but I have, I know not why, an inexplicable repugnance for it. I should have preferred approaching Dwalágiri by its own slopes at the foot of its first terraces. This Deorali route seems to me good for nothing."

"Your repugnance would be explained if you knew that the mountain of Náyárana is the only one exclusively dedicated to Vishnu, while the peaks that flank it are consecrated to Sivá and to Káli, whose chosen seats are Deorali and Barathor."

"Ah!" exclaimed Merrien, "and you who know religious distinctions to the core do not feel very much confidence in the vicinity of mountains over which the Deva of death is the uncontested sovereign; isn't that so?"

"More than that," replied Goulab; "not only do I feel no confidence in them, but I have all kinds of good reasons for altogether distrusting the votaries of Sivá. Remember that the Dogra was one of them."

Merrien did not wish to remain in uncertainty. Doing violence, in some sort, to the Indian's reserve, he asked:

"And you suspect, do you not, that this is a second Ramu? Speak frankly, and without disguise. Have I understood you?"

So speaking, he indicated by a gesture the guide who was walking without a word at the head of the column.

Goulab bent his head in sign of assent. Then, after some final hesitation, he added:

"The man has never been questioned. You should do it in my presence. I can inform you at once, if he lies to you."

They had come to the entrance of a prodigiously narrow and somber gorge.

Sidewalls of three hundred or four hundred meters in height rise like dizzy cliffs on either side of a torrent whose troubled bed and foaming waters they incased.

They were about to enter this gorge without knowing either its extent or its breadth.

It was natural that they should inform themselves before plunging into it, for everything was to be feared in that frightful passage. Beside the danger of an attack, which would be a veritable ambuscade, there was to be dreaded one of those avalanches that are so frequent in the Himálayas, and which displace such quantities of ice and snow, that streams scarcely two meters in breadth have been seen to be transformed in less than an hour into frightful torrents, whose sudden increase inundates the entire valley and raises the water level from fifteen to twenty meters above the ordinary high-water mark.

Merrien made a sign to his companions. The Breton placed himself at the opening of the gorge, watching the least movement on the part of the guide. Then, when they had gone a hundred paces into the valley, the column stopped abruptly   Dr. MacGregor, who spoke a dozen Indian dialects, addressed the guide quickly :

"Boy," he commenced, "we have trusted you, without asking who you are. It is right that we should have fuller information."

The man gave a start. The physician had addressed him in Kashmir dialect with the intonation of the Paháris. He had aimed true. The man must be a native of Punjab, and of Dudputra. How came he to be here, in the mountains of Nepál, so far from his native country ? The Paháris pass in general for very sedentary people and industrious workmen. This peculiarity had been for some time the subject of the doctor's reflections, and he had compared it with the nationality of the first guide, Ramu, a Rájput Dogra ; that is to say, almost a compatriot of the Pahári.

Nevertheless, the Hindu kept his countenance and replied clearly to MacGregor's very definite questioning :

"Who are you ?"

"Pandari."

"Your country—I mean the last city you lived in ?"

"Srínagar, in Kashmir."

The physician kept silence for a moment : he appeared

to consider. Then, suddenly raising his head, he looked the guide full in the face.

"You are a professional guide?"

The man was troubled. To reply in the affirmative was to give his interlocutor the right to ask him for his guide's license.

Now the Pandari, coming from Srinagar by way of Drás, Dehra, Almora, and Rolpah, could not, and for good reason, show such a license.

"No," he said, "I am only an occasional guide. I have crossed the passes many times, and I know the country."

"Do you also know a Dogra, who is called Ramu, and who was our guide as far as Gangotri?"

The man was not disconcerted. He replied boldly, "No," without taking his eyes from those of his interlocutor. All present at this scene kept silence, not taking their eyes from the group, and not knowing what MacGregor was getting at.

The latter was preparing his effects. Suddenly, and with apparent indifference, he let drop this very suggestive phrase:

"Since you come from Srínagar, you must certainly know two of my professional friends—Dr. Lall-Sing Catterjee and his pupil Madar-Goun."

In speaking these words, the Englishman fixed so sharp a gaze upon the guide that, in spite of all his power of dissimulation, the latter could not hide his confusion. He stammered something, and finally confessed that he knew the two native physicians.

MacGregor turned toward Merrien and his companion, and fearing that the Pahári would understand English, he spoke in French:

"I know now what I wanted to know," he said.
"Dr. Madar-Goun has long been known to me. He
is one of the worst enemies of Europeans in general,
and of the British influence in particular. He is strongly
suspected of having connection with the secret societies
of India and elsewhere. I am now very exactly informed on his score; and if we return from our expedition, I shall be able to furnish proofs to the Supreme
Court of Calcutta."

"If we return?" cried Major Plumptre. "Why do
you speak thus, doctor?"

"I feel absolutely certain that we have fallen into
a trap, and that we shall presently be attacked."

"Ho! ho!" cried the officer, "that is not at all
reassuring. On what grounds do you found that suppo-
sition?"

MacGregor rapidly explained. His entirely plausible
inferences rested on the double occurrence of a Siváite
guide succeeding another guide of the same religion. He
did not conclude that all Siváites pushed the worship of
the God of Death as far as the offering up of human
sacrifices, but the three attempts which had already been
made upon the column, two of which attempts had been
followed by the death of the victims, and the third of
which might have had the same termination, since they
had lost all trace of the little Christian Madrasi, were
more than sufficient to justify the inferences of the
physician.

He then added, designating Pandari, who had retired
into his fatalist silence:

"The simplest prudence commands us to shoot this
man at once. Nevertheless, since we cannot commit
homicide on mere suppositions, however probable they

appear, I recommend that one or another of us keep
him constantly in sight.   At the first alarm we will
blow his brains out."

"So be it!" said Merrien; "but meanwhile, what
are we going to do, gentlemen?"   The alternative was
embarrassing.   To beat a retreat was to recoil before a
menace not yet actual; to go forward was to throw
one's self into the unknown, consequently to face peril.

Merrien, always wise, was the first to give counsel:

"Gentlemen, I have opposed the project of ascend-
ing Dwalágirí for reasons that you know.   At present, on
the contrary, I am of the opinion that we should continue
our route for several reasons, chief among them the fact
that, in gaining the heights, we shall escape the pursuit of adversaries, whom the cold in itself will suffice to
check."

"Hurrah for Merrien!" cried Plumptre.   "All right!
Let us climb the cliffs by the shortest way, and we
shall avoid a surprise in this infernal passageway."

"But will everyone be able to follow us?" questioned the doctor.   He indicated Miss Weldon, Goulab,
and the two faithful Hindus.   Cicely responded, with a
charming gesture of indifference:

"So far as I am concerned, doctor, you know that
I am an American."

The shikári on his part unfolded a large shawl brought
from Srínagar, and with a smile that was full of pride
he added:

"I know what cold is, doctor.   In fact, we are old
acquaintances.   With this I shall be able to face it
without fear."

The two Indians, who were devoted to their masters, made similar replies.

"Then," concluded Merrien, "there is no need for hesitation. Let us retrace our steps, and try to scale the cliff."

At the first sign of retreat the Pahári showed by a gesture the annoyance he felt. Seeing which, the major had seized his rifle and rapidly pointed its muzzle at the guide. But Euzen Graec'h caught hold of it, saying to the Scotchman peaceably :

"Bah! that's useless! don't lose your powder. I will take care of this bird. He shan't fly away from me, I swear to you."

Then, with the same placidity, he walked up to the Indian, and with a hand like a pair of pincers gripped Pandari's shoulder. Held in that frightful clutch, the traitor dropped upon his knees, and a hoarse cry sprang from his throat.

"Come, come!" joked the ex-sailor, "don't cry yet. I don't want to kill you so soon. Later on we'll see about it. But for the moment, I only intend to spare you the hardships of the journey. You ought to thank me for that. Come now—whoop!" So speaking, the Breton forced the guide's arms violently backward until the wrists crossed. By the aid of a slender cord he bound them in such a way that the man was incapable of making the least use of them. Then, lifting him as a marketman would lift a bag of meal, he threw him over his left shoulder.

"It is astonishing how little these Hindus weigh!" exclaimed the Hercules, with a *naiveté* that, in spite of the gravity of the situation, made them all laugh.

"Are we ready?" then asked Merrien's vibrating voice, as the explorer sent his glance over his troop in review. He saw that all were arrayed for the march.

He himself took the lead, in company with the sailor and his burden.

They put Miss Weldon in the center of the column, flanked by her two Yankee body-guards. Goulab, the Hindus, Plumptre, and the doctor brought up the rear.

They were not more than ten minutes in regaining the entrance of the gorge. Nothing occurred along the dangerous defile.

"Zounds!" said the doctor. "The Pahári has had no time to warn his accomplices. Otherwise, it is not credible that we should have been permitted to come out alive from the infernal passage. Two or three rocks detached from the overhanging cliff would have been enough to lay us all out."

And the doctor pointed with his fingers to the frightful height of the walls that were as smooth as walls of glass or ice.

He had not finished his sentence before Merrien, who was some fifty meters ahead of the troop, gave an abrupt command:

"Halt!" he cried. "To arms!"

Euzen Graec'h quickly threw down the human bundle with which he was encumbered. His left foot on the chest of the prostrate Pandari, he had put his rifle to his shoulder at the same time that Merrien did his. In the twinkling of an eye the other travelers had spread to the right and left, ready for skirmishing. They were more than a mile from any town, on a sharp and exposed crest that commanded the steep cliff under which they had just passed. As far as the eye could reach there was nothing to be seen but the northern chain, and, to the south, the wooded slopes they had climbed the day before. It was a bad place to

give battle, for it was precisely by way of the cliff that
the enemy was approaching. The assailants, to the
number of fifty or thereabouts, ran at the top of their
speed, to open a downward fire upon the little troop.
It was evident that they had expected to wait for the
column in the middle of the defile in order to crush
it, just as the doctor had foreseen.

But seeing no one coming, and warned, doubtless,
by scouts posted along the route, they did not wish
to let their prey escape.

One of them, the first to arrive at the edge of the
precipice, aimed rapidly at the sailor standing erect
upon Pandari.

He had not time to press the trigger. His arms
opened, letting the rifle drop into space, whither it was
immediately followed by the man.

The latter could be seen to turn over several times before
he came crashing down at the foot of the granite wall.

"That's one!" cried Plumptre, reloading his weapon.
"You were right just now, Graec'h. There was a better
use for the powder."

He pointed to the guide turned on his face under
the ex-sailor's foot, and asked: "Well, what are you
going to do with that one? I think it is time to get rid
of him by sending him to his god."

"I think so, too," replied the Breton.

He stooped, placed his rifle on the ground, and gathering up the miserable Pahári by the nape of the neck
and the thighs, he bent him over his titanic knee. This
he did with marvelous ease. Literally broken in two, the
traitor uttered a dreadful death cry. A single blow from
the butt-end of a rifle closed this frightful wail, crushing
the scoundrel's skull.

It was answered by two shots from the top of the cliffs. They hit no one.

"Bunglers!" cried Euzen, who, together with Merrien, Goulab, and the doctor, had taken aim.

Ten of the assailants were now at the edge of the abyss. Four of them fell as the first had fallen.

Jean Merrien turned toward his companions. He had had time to inspect the line of the heights.

"Gentlemen," he commanded, "we have time to reach the wooded slopes, and then we shall be under shelter. I will cover the retreat with the major, the doctor, and Goulab. Let all the others file down the side of the slope. Euzen, you take charge of the heaviest of the baggage. Save the boxes. You know how important they are."

That was the order of the commanding officer. Everyone obeyed. In the twinkling of an eye the body of the troop had cleared the crest of the plateau, gaining the shelter of the forest of teaks and pines which fringed the slope. Meanwhile, the four men who remained behind swept the line of the cliff with their unerring fire.

That done, they in their turn followed their comrades' retreat, joining them under the trees.

The skirmish had ended well, since they had sustained no loss and had killed a dozen of their adversaries.

But they could no longer think of continuing the ascent of Dhaulágiri, especially by the Deorali road. The most elementary prudence, even, urged them to regain the valleys of the Bargá as soon as possible, where they would find an asylum by the firesides of worthy and hospitable mountaineer families. They would, moreover, have to keep the closest watch, not

THE ASSAILANT COULD BE SEEN TO TURN OVER SEVERAL TIMES.

relaxing it in the smallest particular, especially while
crossing the forests. If the trees furnished a provisional
shelter for the explorers, they would be of equal aid
to their assailants. It was a terribly difficult retreat.
Even though they were safe from the great flesh-
eating animals, and from serpents who never attain to
such elevations, they had still to dread buffaloes,
yaks, boars, and even wild elephants.

Moreover, they were obliged to find their relation to
the points of the compass every moment, in order not to
lose themselves in the depths of the woods. Frequently
the descent sloped suddenly at a tremendously sharp
angle, and there was nothing for the travelers to do but
to let themselves slide down on their backs ; catching
with their hands and feet, at the tree-trunks, at tufts of
brake, at anything in fact that would break their fall.
Sometimes the slope would cut perpendicularly across a
deep ravine, over a yawning gulf that did not reveal
itself until they had reached its dizzy rim ; many times
they had good reason to tremble, for it happened that
Morley, one of Miss Weldon's servants, descended one
of these treacherous banks more rapidly than he would
have desired. The unfortunate fellow rolled for two
hundred meters over the slippery grass and damp moss
to the very edge of a precipice giving upon a valley
four hundred meters below. He owed his safety entirely to his providential encounter with an enormous
stump that sprang up at the point mentioned to check
the poor boy at the very mouth of the abyss.

Thus they were nearly eighteen hours in regaining
the plateau of Malebun, which they had left the evening
previous to their adventure in the Deorali gorges. This
made five more days lost, without counting the hardships

they had undergone and the dangers they had run. Twice, in the course of the stages of their progress, which were cruel in spite of their shortness, they had been obliged to bivouac in the midst of the trees. The anticipation of possible ambuscades had prevented their lighting a fire, and they had suffered severely from the terrible cold of the night.

In all these trials the bold adventurers, now united by a friendship that was rendered firmer and closer by community of suffering, were equal to the circumstances and to the mission that they had undertaken. They all showed a touching devotion to the courageous young girl who shared their perils. They united to keep her from the most severe extremities, before everything else, and Cicely Weldon, moved to tears by such disinterested affection, vowed to her friends that she would never forget the days of Himalayan hardships. She appeared no less distressed at being in some sort a hindrance to her companions, reproaching herself for having imposed further toil and anxiety upon them by her presence.

They finally reached the little town of Takam on the Mayandi-Kola. A complete day of rest was indispensable. The travelers allowed themselves this respite.

They could but congratulate themselves upon the reception that had been given them.

Lodged in the house of the officer in charge of the region, they found dry and clean mats to sleep on, and healthful and abundant food at the open-air markets. They had, indeed, to content themselves with the same meat at every meal—that of lambs, left there by the nomadic shepherds who come down from Tibet with innumerable herds, the wool of which they sell at Agra, at Delhi, at Gwalior, at Srinagar, and at Lahore, and which they lead, transformed into beasts of burden, laden with the products of the Anglo-Indian peninsula, to supply the markets of Tibet and China.

Merrien, who had not opened his lips since the beginning of the descent, except to give his orders for the march, profited by the circumstances to interview one of these shepherds, and to obtain from him at a cost of sixty rupees the promise that he would abandon the passes of the northwest for those of the northeast.

The travelers gained from this bargain the assurance of permanent supplies, and an easy and cheap means of transport for the baggage that they had, up to that time, carried themselves. The nomads agreed to escort them as far as the Kerang pass at the entrance to the mountain of Chingo-pa-mari.

MISS WELDON GAVE THE CHIEF AN AMERICAN DOLL.

IX.

A CLOUD.

From Thàkur to Gaurisankar the travelers had nearly three hundred kilometers to traverse. They were obliged to proceed by such stages as suited the shepherds who accompanied them, twenty kilometers a day, which gave them fifteen good days of marching. And at the end of the time they would only have reached the foot of the mountain. It was still to be climbed. Would they be any better off than before for the ascent of Dhaulàgiri?

Up to this time, apart from the attack by the zealots on the slopes of Deorali, they had had nothing to complain of on the part of either the population or the authorities. The former had shown themselves at all times cordial and compliant, the latter had been conspicuous by their absence, and no village chief had renewed the inquisitorial pretensions of the "governor" of Taklagar. But they must hold themselves ready for any

event. The territory that they were entering upon was
almost entirely peopled by independent Gúrkhas, and it
was to be feared that these wild natives, refugees from
Garhwál and from Kumáun, would not share the sentiments of respect and affection felt for the English by
their reconciled brethren.

They were soon made acquainted with the disposition of the inhabitants. They encountered no hostility.
The preceding year, in fact, the governor of Calcutta
had sent to Dárjíling a strong detachment of Anglo-
Indian troops, about three thousand men with two
field batteries. This was at once a skillful demonstration, a useful exercise for the soldiers, and a most appropriate hygienic measure.

They had chosen three battalions of the finest regiments of India ; Sikhs, Máharatis, and Gúrkhas. These
last had been sent apparently in order that they might
breathe their native air, in reality in order that in the
course of their mountain maneuvers they might easily
put themselves in touch with the populations on the
other side of the frontier.

Now the latter had swarmed to contemplate and admire the fine deportment, the martial attitude, and the
superb uniforms of these chosen troops during the re-
views and evolutions. The officers who commanded
them were also picked men, and if Plumptre was not of
their number, it was only because it is difficult to make
use of a cavalry officer at from three thousand to six
thousand meters' altitude. The good major had been
greatly annoyed about it, and was forever storming
against regulations that prevent a man from being at
once cavalryman and infantryman. He now abundantly
proved the absurdity of such regulations.

The travelers could not but be satisfied with the reception that they met with. Furthermore they passed to the north of the capital, higher than the valley in which Khátmándú is situated upon the two rivers Baghmati and Vishnumati. The commissions with which they were provided did not permit them to descend into the sacred city, but from the summit line which they followed they could discern in the distance innumerable pagodas, like those of the towns of Pátan and of Bhatgáon, situated in the beautiful valley of the Newa, at the foot of the mountain of Nagarjun and Omhasf.

While wondering at the diversity of the races, admiring the vigor and warlike spirit of the Gúrkhas, the original elegance and literary feeling of the Newárs, the most ancient of the Aryans of Nepál, the explorers could not restrain a pained surprise in noticing the infirmity with which a considerable number of the inhabitants are afflicted. In these mountainous regions, in fact, as in the Alps and the Pyrenees, the goiter, that hideous deformity, has spread to such a degree that it is even found among certain races of animals, such as cattle, sheep, goats, even swine—animals that are very well treated by the more or less fervent Buddhists of the country. Of the three assistants of the shepherd with whom the explorers had made their contract, two were abominably goitrous.

When Cicely Weldon questioned the shepherd as to the cause of this affliction, the latter responded that the Pundits and the Gúrkhas attributed it to the bad quality of the water, which was heavily charged with lime. He added that an additional cause might be found in the fact that the natives carry upon their heads, or hung over their shoulders by means of a strap fastened in front, the heaviest kind of burdens.

Dr. MacGregor shook his head at this last allegation.

"No," said he, "that is not the cause of this deformity. The water certainly has a great deal to do with it, but one must also consider the variations of temperature, and especially the humid exhalations of the ground under the scalding sun."

Another malady produced a still worse effect upon the travelers.

They encountered, in bands and itinerant groups, men, women, and even children, with faces corroded by that horrible disease, that tuberculosis of the cutaneous tissue, which receives in Europe the name of "lupus." The contrast was a frightful one between these unfortunate beings devoured by cancer and their surroundings, these lovely valleys, these wooded and grassy slopes, the marvels of the flora that belongs to the temperate and torrid zones, the exquisite perfumes exhaled by open corollas and fruit still hanging to the branch.

Above Bhatgáon, in a settlement occupied by the magnificent Magyar race—ancestors, so certain ethnologists say, of the modern Hungarians, who claim their founder Arpad from Asia—the travelers could not contemplate without agreeable surprise the successive terraces, admirably arranged by the inhabitants upon the mountain sides. And upon these terraces, in imitation of the high cultivation of Dárjiling and Masúri, fields of wheat alternate with flourishing vines.

The shepherds who served as convoys to the little column, after having shown a somewhat shy distrust, now let themselves go in exuberant confidence. They had never crossed Nepal under such profitable conditions. The white men did, indeed, pay them generously. The leader of the troop confided laughingly to Goulab that, with the money earned on this trip, he would buy a hundred more sheep upon his arrival in Tibet. Besides which, the smaller favors distributed by the Europeans found them appreciative and grateful. Thus Merrien gave the chief herdsman a marine glass which the latter had long admired. Plumptre gave his son a six-barreled English revolver with fifty cartridges ; the doctor divided between the two subordinates two solid Sheffield knives, and two sealed boxes of kola with which to refresh themselves after the fatigues of the journey. Finally, Miss Weldon gave them for their wives some rings, some bracelets, some earrings, and she gave the chief an American doll with which to amuse his children—a veritable masterpiece of mechanism which would long command the admiration of the whole tribe, and the works of which she taught the man to wind up with delicacy and desirable precaution.

This Cicely Weldon was a strange and charming girl.

Tall, and admirably proportioned, like nearly all her compatriots ; fair, but a little "burned" by her travels and the open air ; with tawny golden hair, cut short ; a small mischievous mouth, beautiful blue eyes that expressed both goodness and intelligence, she wore the masculine dress with an ease that took from her none of the womanly graces.

Up to that time her presence in the ranks of the little company had only tightened the bonds that united the different members of the expedition. Even the mystery with which she was surrounded, and concerning which she had made them her confidants, contributed to make this union closer.

Nevertheless, a little jealousy seemed to be springing up among the members, owing to the rivalry between the French habit of command of Jean Merrien, and the pretensions of British pride, of which Plumptre was the incarnation. The natural preference of the young American "miss" for the leader of the expedition—whatever pains she might take to divert attention from it, even to dissimulate it—must needs give occasion for differences between the two men, but only such as could occur between gentlemen and warm-hearted men.

Fortunately, besides her truly superior intelligence, Cicely was provided in the highest degree with that almost infallible instinct of women, that sagacity which permits them to read souls, and that delicate art which allows them to pour healing balm upon the wounds of love. She was pained at the idea of possible rivalry between two men whose high qualities and chivalric loyalty she could appreciate in one as in the other.

But it had not taken her long to establish the difference between the two characters. In contradiction to the reputation given our countrymen by foreigners, Merrien was very little of a talker. He expressed himself, on the contrary, with a terseness equal to that of Graec'h the Breton, who only spoke on great occasions. On the other hand, the major possessed exuberant loquacity, which afforded a striking contrast to the sober, measured language of his fellow-countryman, Dr. Mac-Gregor, and which had given the latter occasion to administer many a reproof:

"My dear fellow, you are very garrulous in words, but, happily, your actions have the eloquence of silence."

Cicely could not help noticing that, since the beginning of the campaign, Jean Merrien had become more and more reserved, while, by an opposite phenomenon, the Scotchman became more and more wordy and intemperate in his language.

Furthermore, he had upon different occasions allowed ironical remarks to escape him, unpleasant criticisms of the direction given by Merrien to the expedition.

This tendency to bitterness between the two men must then be averted at any cost.

Knowing them as she did, the young girl could easily foresee that the Frenchman's patience would finally give way, and that one unfortunate word would be enough forever to envenom a quarrel that up to this time had had no serious grounds. Already, she had several times seen Jean's brows knit quickly, and a gleam cross his black eyes.

Discord came near breaking out upon a very slight pretext.

They had just halted at the little town of Dudkunda, on the banks of the Tomba-Kosi, after having crossed the second slope of Dáyábang. Nepál, in fact, possesses three mountains known by the name of Deorali, and two by that of Dáyábang.

These are, besides, mythological designations which are common to India. The halt had been requested by the herdsmen in order to let the sheep rest a day, and also because the question had come up whether the herdsmen should separate at this point from their companions.

The travelers found themselves together again in a sort of bungalow, wretched enough, having for furniture only a table and some stools upon some old mats that covered the ground. They discussed the different hypotheses relative to their separation from the shepherds.

"It is here that we really ought to separate," said Jean Merrien. "The Kerong pass is twenty kilometers to the north of the place we are in, by eighty-three degrees, five minutes. That is the most direct route to Thákur-guba, the residence of the Saimprupra Lama."

"We have still another," cried Plumptre, consulting the map ; "that is the Lonkour pass.

"There is a third one," said MacGregor, " the Ibey-Dong pass in the gorges of Anun."

"That one, gentlemen," resumed Merrien, " is forbidden to caravans. Goulab has just informed me that, by a common decision of the Lamas and the Chinese Empire, that route is exclusively reserved to pilgrims who only stop at Ib'Lassa."

"Eh ! what does that matter to us !" replied the major crossly. "We do not have to concern ourselves with the preferences of the Buddhists. If we pay our people a few more rupees, they will not hesitate to accompany us to the end."

"Major," intervened Cicely, "do not forget that the end for us is the mountain of Máyanama."

"All the more reason why our shepherds should accompany us. They will only be all the nearer to the Ibey-Dong pass. Besides, if they are refused passage, they can retrace their steps. The season is propitious, the weather superb, and the shorn sheep can fatten themselves on the fresh grass of the heights."

"I warn you, major," said Merrien, "that they have already refused this service to me, although I offered them a hundred more rupees."

The officer shrugged his shoulders, and replied in a mocking tone :

"Because you did not know how to approach them, my dear sir. The French are miserable diplomats. I will take the responsibility of deciding these people."

They separated upon this bitter-sweet remark ; Plumptre going straightway to win the herdsmen over to his side.

When he was seen returning, however, with a lengthened face and discomfited air, no one thought of making fun of his failure.

"Zounds!" he cried violently, "it is your fault, Merrien. You should have warned me that they had already concluded a bargain with you. At my first overture they immediately replied that all the money in the world could not make them go as far as Ibatia, that is to say, as far as the Ibey-Dong pass, because all the money in the world would avail them nothing if the Chinese should impale them. They added that they had, moreover, promised Sahib Merrien to carry our baggage to the passes of Lonkour or Tinki-la."

"My dear major," replied the Frenchman, without bitterness, "you did not give me time to tell you. You seemed so sure of your negotiations that I should have shown a very bad grace to try to turn you from them."

"It is a service that you should have rendered me, my dear sir," said the irascible Scotchman. "I do not like to be ridiculous."

"Nor to be contradicted, it appears. So much the worse for you. It is easier to direct one's self than others."

So saying, the Frenchman turned his back impatiently upon his interlocutor, who suddenly became very re l.

Miss Weldon saw the impending menace, just ready to break forth.

She rose, and in a voice that was moved with sorrow, she said :

"Come, gentlemen, we have been nothing but friends up to to-day. Shall such a puerile incident bring trouble among us ?"

The two men bowed respectfully before the young girl, but drew apart from one another, without saying a word.

Cicely comprehended that the situation was too strained. She went and shut herself up in the room that had been reserved for her in the center of the wretched caravansary. She passed the rest of the day in making up her notes, and in writing.

The night passed without incident. But on the morrow there was profound astonishment among the travelers at the disappearance of Cicely and her two Yankees.

A letter which the girl had left enlightened them as to her unexpected absence.

Miss Weldon had taken the thing lightly. She chaffed her traveling companions gayly :

My Dear Friends :

Your trifling difference of yesterday came just in time to remind me that you are at the same time my rivals. As I know that you would not let me leave you, on account of apprehensions of a feminine victory over your manly strength, I am playing you the trick of being the first to remind myself of your wager.

Consequently I am leaving you to take the trouble of having my baggage carried by these good shepherds. I abandon it to you, if necessary, and I take the lead on the road to Gaurisankar. The American flag will there precede all others, and there you will be welcomed by it. But while warning you that I shall have four or five leagues the start of you at the time that you will read this epistle, I do not wish to be treacherous to you, and will inform you that I shall go directly by the Dudkunda road to Pangmo.

Your devoted,

CICELY WELDON.

She had done as she said. Convinced that the only way to restore concord between the two men was to remove from them all pretext for rivalry, even courteous rivalry, the brave young girl had resolved to hasten her march toward the desired summit.

She had warned her two American body-guards to hold themselves in readiness to set out that very night. All three had rapidly sorted out the things most necessary to their immediate needs, and had put them in three knapsacks. Then, provided with their rifles and necessary ammunition, they plunged resolutely into the darkness and the perils of an unknown mountain road.

On receiving this singular missive, the Frenchman and the Englishman looked at one another with embarrassment, almost with consternation.

"These women! They're all alike!" cried MacGregor, with a significant shrug of the shoulders: "creatures of nerves and emotions. One never knows what they are thinking; one can never foresee what they will do. Here we are all upset on account of this crazy girl."

The major appeared deeply moved. He approached Merrien, and extended his hand spontaneously.

"My dear friend," he said, "I was wrong yesterday, and at other times, as well. I can but excuse myself. I feel great affection for Miss Weldon, and I was jealous of you. There, my confession is made! At present, I think the most important thing is to rejoin her, and bring her aid and succor."

The Frenchman responded warmly to the pressure of
his noble rival's hand. He said :

"I agree with you, Major Plumptre, and I think that
you are the most loyal and generous man that I know."

"Well !" said the Englishman. "then let us lose no
time in advancing upon the Pangmo road."

Without being able to explain it the two men felt
simultaneously a sinister presentiment. The recollection
of the dangers they had run since the commencement
of the expedition, and just recently in the abortive attempt to scale Dhaulágiri, justified them in their dread
of new ambuscades. They were, no doubt, reassured
by the thought that this time they were no longer at
the mercy of a guide bought or acquired by the ferocious worshipers of Sivá : there was no doubt that the
herdsmen to whom they had intrusted the. care of
their baggage, to whom they had confided the task of
piloting them across this mountain-covered country, had
merited all their confidence. But, after all, they were in
an unknown region, they frequently crossed enormous
desert places, ten and fifteen miles square, with no sign
of habitation or cultivation ; they could make no profes-
sion of Christian faith among natives belonging to all
the sects of India, especially to Buddhism and Brah-
manism.

They had been able, in spite of the proverbial hos-
pitality of the mountaineers, to estimate correctly the
repulsion with which the white men inspired nearly
all the peoples of Nepál. At Naokot, to the west of
Khátmándú, they had come very near being obliged
by the governor of the place, more annoying than the
one at Taklagar, to descend again to the south ; perhaps even to have the permits vested with the seal of

THE MAJOR EXTENDED HIS HAND TO MERRIEN.

the Bengal Presidency indorsed at the capital. The major was obliged to show his teeth, which were very sharp, and to express himself in forcibly concise language on the subject of the rights due to the boundless power of England. This haughty, almost threatening attitude finally compelled respect on the part of the functionary for the privileges of Great Britain.

There was no room for doubt that at Pangmo, the young American would find herself confronted by just as difficult, and perhaps even more vexatious exactions. And what redoubled the anxiety of the travelers was the discovery that Cicely had forgotten to take with her her personal commission, which also covered her two attendants. They, therefore, hastened their progress along a route as difficult as one can conceive a road to be that is no wider than a footpath, and that rises and falls with the ridges; thus rendering the journey very fatiguing, and lengthening it to a disheartening degree. They had left their baggage in the hands of the shepherds. knowing very well that if the Nepalese and Tibetan mountaineers had been able to accomplish the trick of utilizing the sheep as beasts of burden, they had not, on the other hand, been able to learn the discipline which would keep them from wandering in every direction, nor to rid themselves of that strange spirit of imitation that Panurge observed in them.

In order to secure the safety of the transports, they left the guardianship of them to Dr. MacGregor and the two Hindus, while Merrien, Plumptre, Graec'h the Breton, and Goulab, hastened, at forced march, to seek the young girl.

From time to time, worn with fatigue, the little troop called a halt at some propitious spot. The country had a somewhat wild but singularly rich beauty. Fixing his eyes upon the double chain of moderately high summits that separate Dud-Kosi from Tomba-Kosi, Merrien could not but regret that this fertile region should lie fallow, literally abandoned by the colonists.

"Verily, Plumptre," said he, "this country is a perfect paradise. We are marching across an enchanted landscape, intoxicated by the fragrance of flowers and fruits. Nevertheless, there is no cultivation to make the ground fruitful, and its products are owing only to the lavishness with which Providence has endowed it."

The Scotchman shook his head, then replied very gravely :

"It is somewhat the custom in France to decry England. Nevertheless, by what you have already seen, by what you are still seeing, you must acknowledge to yourself the service that England renders to humanity. If the south of Nepál is repopulated, if agriculture again flourishes, if the mountaineers are growing gentler, if the Gúrkhas are crossing the frontier to enlist in India, and, their time once up, bring back to their country the idea of civilization, is it not to contact with England that all this progress is due ? It must be remembered that the mountains which are a barrier between us and the stationary world of China have nevertheless afforded passage to the Chinese troops, and if the region that we are passing through astonishes you by its solitude, it is only because it has been the scene of bloody wars, and terrible devastation. A hundred years ago the Gúrkhas were vanquished by the Tibetans and the Chinese combined, who took possession of Kerong, of Dudkunda, and of Naokot. Since that time the valleys of the seven Kosi

have been almost abandoned.   If England takes possession
of Nepál, richness and joy will again spring up in these
districts."

"To the great profit of Old England, is it not?" retorted Merrien gayly; "and you will create sanitariums
on the slopes of Yassa, of Goussainthan, of Máyanama,
and of Mergui, while the Russians, weary of Siberian
cold, will come to take a sun bath, facing you upon the
southern slopes of the Kara-Koram, and Kuenlun ranges."

"The Russians!" exclaimed the officer, with equal
gayety. "I hold them of no more account than a European gean [choke-cherry] compared to a Khátmándú
cherry."

They were chatting thus on terms of the most jovial
cordiality when suddenly piercing cries attracted their
attention.

They had traveled a dozen kilometers from the point
of departure. The road, although in disrepair, was now
straight and fine, continually swept by the mountain
winds. It now extended in a natural embankment
between the two valleys, covered to the north by the
enormous mass of Goussainthan, rising imperceptibly at
the east toward Máyanama, across the snows from which
no human eye has yet been able to discern that king of
giants, the Chingo-pa-mari of the Tibetans, the Gaurisankar of the Nepalese, the Everest of the English. From
the center of a confused mass of monstrous excres-
cences, some rounded like a dome, others cut horizontally
across like Table Mountain of the Cape of Good Hope,
rise a dozen white heads in such a way as to appear
welded all together.

There was the unknown one—the goal toward which
they tended; the mysterious mountain that scholars have

measured from the Indian plains, but whose exact position no white man, no Hindu pundit, has been able to determine in the chaos of eruptive rocks, in the midst of the giants that surround it as if they would hide it from sacrilegious gaze.

Now, on the road, about two kilometers down, a human figure was moving, running toward the travelers. The wind which blew from the east had carried its cries across the majestic silence of the peaks. As yet, neither the features nor the ethnological characteristics of the person could be distinguished, but, thanks to the marvelous clearness of the atmosphere he was recognized to be an Indian. Who was this man, and what did he want? They were soon to be informed.

The man continuing to run, and the explorers hastening toward him, it was not more than ten minutes before they met. The newcomer had torn garments, a body covered with scars, and bloody feet. He was exhausted by a long run, and his lips had scarcely uttered the word, "Sahibs," when he gave out, and fell unconscious into the arms of Euzen Graec'h.

"Thunder!" cried the sailor, in the utmost surprise. "I know that face. It is Miss Weldon's little Madrasi. So! the little fellow isn't dead, then!"

THE THREE RIFLES THREATENED THE ASSAILANTS.

X.

BLOCKADED.

THE first moment of stupefaction having passed, and each having convinced himself that the Breton was not the victim of an hallucination, they hastened to lavish their care on the poor child. There was the utmost need to revive him, to restore him, and to hear the communications he was about to make to the travelers.

Energetic rubbing, and some drops of rum poured with difficulty between his teeth, brought him to his senses. But it was some time yet before the little Madrasi could recover the use of his tongue. Although his face was drawn with pain, his eyes filled with tears at his sense of powerlessness to express himself, and his gestures, more eloquent than explicit, urged the Europeans on to the northward. Finally, disconnected words sprang from his oppressed bosom.

"Living! Ramu! Weldon! Quick to his rescue! Attacked in the mountain!"

That was enough to reveal to the four men the general import of what he had to say. But in order to avoid a misdirected course, and fresh loss of time, Merrien imposed silence upon Christi's confused demonstrations, and questioned him methodically:

"You were Ramu's prisoner, weren't you?"

"Yes."

"You met Weldon and his two companions?"

"Yes."

"But, at the same time, Ramu and his men have attacked them?"

"Yes."

"And you, you escaped to warn us?"

"Yes."

"Very well," concluded the Frenchman. "We have not an instant to lose. But we must know where to find our imprudent companion."

The little Madrasi comprehended the question put to him by the eyes of the explorer. He extended his hand toward the road, and said in English:

"Three miles—three miles—about five and a half kilometers!"

Then Plumptre reached him his gourd, and two or three biscuits, also a leaf of his memorandum book on which he had hastily scribbled some words. Laying him down on the slope of the road in the shade of a bunch of cypress trees, he told him to await the passing of the troop, which would not be long delayed. He would find Dr. MacGregor, in company with his two Hindus and the herdsmen. The child moved his head in assent. He smiled to reassure his friends as to his condition, and commenced to bite vigorously into the biscuit. The three Europeans and Goulab, loaded rifle in hand, were already climbing the slope with athletic step.

This is what had happened.

Enchanted with her bright idea, which was an amusing piece of mischief, Cicely Weldon had meant to carry out her escapade, and put as great a distance as possible between herself and her companions.

The night was superb, lighted by a moon which sent into strong relief the slightest projections of the rocks. No surprise, no ambush, was to be feared under this marvelous radiance.

So the little group rapidly gained ground in the direction of Pangmo, a most wretched village, where they arrived at daybreak.

Pangmo contained barely two or three hundred inhabitants, living in the depths of wretched hovels. It was a degraded, ferocious, but cowardly population, which did not attempt any attack upon resolute people, unless the assailants were in the proportion of twenty to one.

The perpetual raids of the Gúrkhas and other warrior tribes of Nepál have gradually decimated and reduced this degenerate Metch branch, formerly celebrated for the beauty of its women, in whom they now carry on a business, selling them as servants or odalisks in all the markets of Tibet. and northern India.

Fortune favored Weldon and her men : entirely ignorant of this peculiarity, they passed through the larger part of the settlement under cover of an obscurity dense enough to disguise their costumes and their personality. Moreover, very few of the women who are the slaves, or rather the beasts of burden of their husbands, had commenced household labor at that early hour.

A mile further up, the travelers met some ragged children, who fled at their approach, uttering loud cries.

Then, from the hollow of a valley, they saw first some heads emerge which hastened to conceal themselves. But further on the heads showed themselves in greater numbers, making a hostile clamor.

Disconcerted for a moment, Cicely at once comprehended that she must let nothing appear of her anxiety, and that the best way to force respect from the evil-disposed was boldly to pursue her onward march.

Unfortunately, the light in the sky was spreading, and it was impossible for the three companions to disguise the smallness of their number.

Suddenly, at a turn in the road, a herd of furious people sprang up, brandishing rifles and sabers, and threw themselves in front of the three travelers with such evidently threatening intentions that Cicely stopped and took aim with her carbine.

"Ah!" said she, speaking to her nearest neighbor, the Yankee of German descent, "these are not people of this country. I recognize our Deorali assassins. And they even have with them our old acquaintance, that rascal Ramu."

The two Americans had imitated their companion's action. The three extended guns threatened the assailants.

But what could two men and a woman—three men, in the eyes of their adversaries—do against fifty fanatics animated by the worst possible intentions! With their

backs to a perpendicular wall, they were exposed to the
fire of their enemies, however little these might make use
of their arms.

One circumstance was a protection to them: They
had to do with the worshipers of the Fire God, with
religious murderers, with the sect of the Thugs, or
stranglers; in whose eyes the act of slaying a human
being had no true merit unless it were accomplished
without bloodshed, or at least without blood being spilled
at their hands. Thus were explained the previous
crimes accomplished by Ramu: the death of Gourap-Sing,
thrust by him between the teeth of the daboias; that
of the Mussulman saved by Dr. MacGregor's care, and
succumbing, when they believed him to be healed, to
the poisoning of his wounds with the juice of euphorbia, or upas.

With such adversaries they could defend themselves, if they could keep them at a distance. Still there
was reason to fear that rather than let their victims live,
and moved by the spirit of self-preservation, the odious
bandits would not hesitate to have recourse to the
blade and the bullet.

In a few moments the restless eye of the American
Morley, examining the smooth walls which rose behind
him, had discovered a sort of fissure between the
rocks. About this fissure one could see a heap of
rocks forming a rough staircase, and there was a precious
shelter for people in such a critical situation. He rapidly
pointed it out to Cicely, saying:

"Miss Weldon, let us try to reach that corner. There
we shall be covered, and shall be able to fire from there
at our ease."

The young girl acquiesced in this project; marching

in single file the length of the wall, without taking their eyes from their enemies, all three endeavored to reach this protecting cliff. As if they had guessed their intentions, the Thugs scattered to the sides of the road, not quickly enough, however, for three among them, struck by avenging balls, fell prostrate in the road.

Some sixty meters separated the fissure from the three. With quiet devotion the two men both at once declared to Cicely their intention of saving her first. The latter then ran to the fissure, while her acolytes, watching the line of the ridge, used their arms with effect, bringing down two new assailants. None of them had been able to foresee the trap that was set for them, for while they were trying to gain the shelter, the infernal scoundrel of a Ramu had been laying new plans. Quicker than lightning, two of the Durga-Kali, entirely naked and anointed with that kind of grease which renders them as slippery as serpents, had scaled the wall, rounded the fissure, and squatted down, silk handkerchief in hand, gag between the teeth, crouched like tigers ready to spring.

Just as Miss Weldon, looking straight ahead of her, took refuge in the protecting cranny, two nervous arms suddenly encircled her. A hand was placed upon her mouth, stifling her cries, and a running noose tightened about her neck.

Cicely felt herself lost. One moment of prayer in her heart and upon her lips, and she fell swooning. One of the assassins, leaning over her, laughed in triumph, and taking the ends of the handkerchief passed between them a fine steel bar, designed to act as a lever to break the cervical vertebræ, which renders death inevitable. But at the same moment something unexpected happened — miraculous succor intervened.

While the two Hindus, leaning over their victim, prepared to consummate their crime, a third Indian glided from behind them. This one seemed to fall from the perpendicular wall. He held in his hand something brilliant and sharp, a Malay kris with a flat blade grooved on the under side.

The newcomer gave one bound. His knees rested on the back and shoulders of the Thug, and his kris buried itself in the bandit's neck. The man fell dead upon the body of the unconscious Cicely. His accomplice, surprised by this attack, and seeing the kris raised above his head, evaded the blow and leaped in terror out from the cranny upon the road. He had, however, only jumped out of the frying-pan into the fire. He had literally thrown himself into Knebel's arms. With a single blow of the butt-end of his rifle, the sturdy American crushed the bandit's skull, and wild with rage over the unconscious body of his young mistress, he was also about to kill her savior, but the latter sprang in front of him and seized his upraised arm, crying :

"Knebel, no kill me! Me, Christi, no dead. *No* dead, Sahib Weldon. *Me* kill Thug. He living."

The Yankee gave a cry of joy, and embraced the brave little Madrasi. Then, aided by his companion, who had just reached the shelter, they carried Cicely to a cleft in the rocks, where the young girl, already freed from her bonds by Christi, finally recovered her breath and her consciousness.

As soon as she arose she warmly thanked the brave child whose intervention had just snatched her from death.

CICELY FELT THAT SHE WAS LOST.

But Christi was uneasy. With a brevity necessitated
by the circumstances he explained himself to his companions.

Some twenty meters above them there was a terrace
backed by the mountain. It was reached by the staircase
of rocks. Once there, the travelers would be for the
moment sheltered. They would command and be able
to watch all the movements of their adversaries. As for
him, he would go back to the road by a detour in order
to notify the rest of the column to come as quickly as
possible. He would explain to them later the miracle
of this resurrection when they should have time for
explanations.

Every bit of him moved. His eyes, his mouth, his
gestures, all spoke at once.

The Americans saw that his advice was excellent, and,
letting themselves be guided by him, they reached the
bluff referred to. He, then, without waiting for details,
ran along the ridge, and the next moment his three companions could see him running at the top of his speed
beyond the most distant huts of Pangmo.

As the child had said, they were provisionally out of
danger. Behind them the mountain rose in a perpendicular wall of gneiss and mica schist, to a height of about
three hundred meters, a single peak beyond which dipped
the valley of the Tomba-Kosi. At their feet the road
unfurled itself like a ribbon. Beyond were the wooded
banks of the Dud-Kosi. What was going to become of
them upon this shelf twenty meters in height? If they
could see their enemies, and anticipate treachery, they
were none the less spied upon themselves. From time
to time a brown head, a white spot of drapery, was
seen between the rocks and trees. There was no possi-

bility of doubt that the aggressors would not risk an attack in broad daylight, and even by night such an attempt on their part would be extremely perilous.

But if they were insured against the malignity of men, they were by no means so much so against the different danger of a siege.

For it was a veritable siege that they were about to undergo, and with no resources against the most terrible of possibilities, the point of death by hunger and thirst.

Cicely and her two companions, counting on the speedy arrival of Merrien and Plumptre, had brought nothing in their knapsacks but some biscuits, some chocolate tablets and kola wafers. If they were not promptly supplied with rations, they were condemned to die there on that bracket of stone, after suffering the most atrocious torture, unless they ventured a desperate sortie through the ranks of assassins. Now, by this time the Siväites were no longer alone. They had seen their number rapidly increase with all the contrasts furnished by the savage Buddhists of Pangmo. These wild Metchmen, without professing the murderous creed of the worshipers of the God of Death, had, nevertheless a way of their own of eluding the precepts of Kakya-Muni, who forbids the spilling of blood.

Like the Burmanese of Akyab and of Mandalay, they neither crushed spiders nor venomous flies; they drove the cobra di capello and the "Belougas" of their gardens into those of their neighbors in order not to violate the sacred prohibition; but they killed their fellow-men with blows of club or sandbag; they buried them alive up to the neck, smearing their faces with honey.

A hundred of these brutes had just joined Ramu's desperados, and it was possible that they, relying upon their number, would together attempt an assault upon the intrenchment. For three mortal hours the besieged endured that frightful suspense. Each of them approached the crest in turn, and looked over the border of rocks the better to perceive the disposition of the enemy.

Gun in hand, ready to bring down the first venturesome spirit that should attempt the stairway, Cicely and her attendants maintained an immobility that rendered them safe from discovery, while they were preserved from the possible fire of the assailants by the broken rocks which formed a rampart for them.

Suddenly a murmur, proceeding from the foot of the terrace, warned them that an assault was about to commence.

They ran to the wall of rocks, and could see twenty Metch leaping like monkeys along the projections of the abyss. A dozen had sprung upon the outthrow of rock, and were running rapidly.

"Attention!" cried Morley. "We have not a ball to lose. Aim well, and, as far as possible, in the midst of them."

"Yes," added his comrade, "but let the first of them pass, we can dispose of them later."

He was right. In the fury of the attack the bandits got in one another's way. Four of them took the lead. Six others piled on to the short ladder, mutually helping each other.

It was the second group that was made a target of. The discharge produced an astonishing effect.

All were struck by the terrible Remington balls; four fell dead on the spot.

The two men who brought up the rear fled precipitately, and the besieged had only to shoot at short range the four bold leaders who had so imprudently advanced. Unhappily two balls missed their aim, and one of the robust Yankees was obliged to throw himself upon the ladder in order to beat one of the two fugitives to death with the butt of his rifle.

"Three and four, seven, and two are nine," counted the Irish-American philosophically. "Three apiece. That is a fine beginning. If they continue in this way we shall massacre them in detail down to the last one, provided that——"

"Provided that—what?" asked Cicely, alarmed by her brave companion's anxious intonation.

"Provided that our ammunition does not give out, for there are more than a hundred and thirty of them in all." They went back behind the barrier of fallen rocks, and commenced to count their cartridges.

"I have twenty," said Knebel, "leaving a hundred and ten in round numbers."

"I—forty," seconded Morley, "leaving seventy if there are no hitches. And you, miss?"

"Only twenty-two," said the young girl in a tone of profound discouragement.

"Leaving forty-eight. That is rather too many. Let us say thirty, if we count on our revolvers. That is still too many."

They had not finished their examination, when frightful cries rang out. Seized with a veritable craze for murder, the brigands returned to the charge. But this time they all ran to it, and in a few moments the side of the hill was covered with spots of black and white.

"I believe we are lost," said Cicely, her voice trembling a little.

And turning to her friends, she added with great firmness this time : "Remember your promise. A ball more or less will not alter our fate. And you know that I will not shrink. There," said she, putting her hand back of her head, "there, where the white silk turban does not protect the neck."

"Yes, miss !" said the German, in a sorrowful voice, with a sob contracting his throat.

"Come, now for a volley !" commanded the brave girl. But what was this single fire against such a mass of assailants. Already more than twenty menacing arms were seizing the edges of the rocks, and hideous faces, grinning with joy at the thought of the massacre, were rising above the barrier.

Suddenly four shots coming from the road were repeated with unspeakable power by the echo of the peaks.

"God be praised !" cried Cicely piously. "Here come our friends !"

They ran to their observatory, from which the alarmed assailants were letting themselves drop to the lower rocks, and they were able to contemplate a striking spectacle, well calculated to explain the panic of the copper-faced rascals.

Merrien, Plumptre, Graec'h, and Goulab had not stopped running since the moment of their meeting with little Christi.

It was at this precipitous pace that they had come through the village of Pangmo, from which the men had gone forth to give assistance to the stranglers, or to share in the spoils.

Women alone were left in the village.

At the sight of these armed white men, who wore a terrible aspect in their rage, they hurriedly entered their dwellings, where they barricaded themselves as well as they could.

Certainly none of the four travelers thought of disturbing them; they had too much to do elsewhere in the mountain.

They arrived at the precise moment when the band were rushing to a general assault.

Then it was that from the height of their intrenchment, the besieged heard four rifle-shots, immediately followed by a formidable discharge, of which each shot made frightful ravages among the enemy.

These, terrified, abandoned the attack, and fled in every direction.

"To the rocks!" cried Plumptre, with the voice of command that he knew how to assume at the head of his squadron.

In a few bounds the new arrivals were in the mêlée.

Without reloading, using saber, ax, or rifle-butt, they cleared their way. It was more especially Euzen Graec'h who accomplished this formidable task. His quasi-superhuman strength served to disperse the enemy even more by the fear it caused than by its own performance. He was no longer a man, but a sort of god rushing with full strength upon this herd of brutes, hewing off heads and arms with his ax, from which the blood streamed down his arms, upon his garments, transfigured by that bloody rain, and appearing to the slaughterers, petrified by their terror, only under the aspect with which their imaginations invested their own divinity, the sinister God of Death.

And behind him Goulab, full of admiration for this incomparable power, did not cease crying out to the Siváites crazed by their terror:

"This is Rama, newly incarnated, who is come to punish the crimes of the impious! It is Vishnu, who remembers his enemies!"

In the twinkling of an eye the vicinity of the rocky stairway was cleared, and the four newcomers climbed up to join their companions.

"Ah!" cried Merrien, much moved, pressing Cicely's hands. "Thank God, we arrived in time!"

"And above all," added Plumptre almost gayly, "do not undertake any more escapades to punish us for wrangling in your presence. Such experiences cost too dear! What would have become of us if we had not found you living?"

The first demonstrations over, they began to think of dividing the task of protection and surveillance. The enemy had just received too rough a lesson to dare risk a fresh attack so soon. They had prudently taken refuge on the other side of the road, under shelter of the trees which cover the Dud-Kosi slope. But it was evident that they had not lost all hope of renewing the onslaught with a prospect of success.

"We have, indeed, killed or wounded from twenty-five to thirty men," said Goulab; "that is a fifth of their effective force."

"Even add to that the fourteen that we brought down before your arrival," said Cicley, "and you will see that there are still at least a hundred."

"No matter!" replied the shikári, laughing, "so long as they see Sahib Graec'h they will not dare return." And the brave hunter contemplated in amazement the taciturn and modest Breton, who only complained of one thing—of not having water at hand to wash his arms, his face, and his garments, splashed with the blood of the bandits.

"Those rascals," he grumbled, " are as swollen with venom and as soft as vermin. Their brains burst out like fire-crackers, and as to their arms, it is shameful, they do not stick to their shoulders. At every blow I took one off."

Everyone, in spite of the gravity of the situation, broke out laughing at this sally. Goulab, who had just given himself over to worship of the sailor, suddenly approached him, with an hilarious aspect, and with joy in his eyes. He said to him :

"Sahib Graec'h, you are looking for water. There is certainly some in the rock. It will only be necessary to break it a little, and you will see." And he indicated in the perpendicular wall back of them a sort of vein, grayish red in color, and very glittering.

Putting the hand upon it one felt the humidity in it. There must be under the coating of mica schist and silex an abundant ooze due to the penetration of the snow accumulated on the summit, and descended therefrom as in a Paris or London conduit. "Well!" cried the major, " if we are condemned to die of hunger upon this ledge, at least we shall not die of thirst."

Immediately axes and cutlasses came into play. But only for the purpose of breaking the wall.

The herculean arm of Euzen soon caused the vein to bleed as he had recently made the bodies of the Siväites to bleed. A stream, troubled and yellow at first, soon clear and limpid, of exquisite flavor and coolness, poured out of the hole, and a thread of crystal commenced to run regularly and uninterruptedly.

"Good luck!" said Merrien, in high spirits. "There
are no microbes in that, as in the water of the Seine
that my Parisian countrymen are having."

"Humph!" said Plumptre, in the same tone, "if
the microbes are not in the water, they are not very
far from it; and without speaking of the villainous beasts
who are in the surrounding woods, the sun will take
care to draw bacilli from all the blackguards whom we
have sent to the devil."

This speech, in spite of its gayety, recalled the travelers to the discomforts of their situation. It was not a
cheerful one. There were seven of them, and the supplies that the latest comers had brought with them
would sustain them for two days, or three at most.
Furthermore, they had neither tents nor coverings, nor
utensils of any sort, and after having suffered the intense heat of the sun by day, they would have to
undergo by night the terrible variations of temperature
that render ascents so fatal.

Goulab went to take an observation from the height
of the rampart of rocks, and returned with lowering
brow and saddened eye.

"We are decidedly blockaded!" he said.

THE TROOP APPROACHED.

XI.

THE DHOLES.

DAY was meanwhile advancing, and the sun was rising rapidly to the zenith, increasing the heat to frightful proportions.

A profound anxiety had come over the besieged. Independently of the difficulties of their own position, they were full of apprehensions concerning the fate of the doctor, of the two Hindus, one of whom was the cook Salem-Bun, and of the little Christi.

"What is going to become of our poor friends?" said Miss Weldon, much afflicted. "There is certainly no other road than this, and the shepherds will not be long in appearing; this will be the signal for these fanatics to throw themselves on the doctor; and our poor little Christi, after having served us so generously, will have escaped death only to become again the prey of these monsters."

Goulab shook his head, and answered the young girl as follows :

"Have no anxiety concerning Christi. If they have spared him they have a reason for so doing. He is for them henceforth consecrated. Do you not know that the man who escapes death by the noose is forever covered by the protection of Káli ? A Thug would be flayed alive, and even lose his caste, rather than lay a sacrilegious hand upon the victim that the goddess has reserved to herself."

"Ah !" exclaimed Cicely, "that is a very curious detail, of which I was ignorant ! My dear Goulab, what a singular people you are ! "

The shikári drew himself up proudly, but like an educated and well-bred man, he bowed again, his hand upon his heart.

"Lady," he said, "there are many instances of ignorance among your ' civilized ' peoples ! There is not one race merely, but a thousand, in India. As for me, I am an Aryan like yourself, a Rajpút, one of those who form, ever since Rama, the noblest of the families. But I am a Kashmiri, while that abominable Ramu is a Dogra ; I belong to the order of Vishnu, and he worships Sivá. And besides these differences, how many more could I not point out to you that would still more astonish you ! But," he added, "it is neither the time nor the place for an historical dissertation. The most pressing need is that of providing some way of averting danger from the doctor, Salem-Bun, and the other one. I still hope that the Bathia will have scented danger, and taken precautions for the safety of his companions, unless he has chosen to abandon the Tinki-la road."

Goulab suddenly stopped speaking, and inclined his ear, making a sign to his companions to listen also.

The rays of the sun lighted the entire landscape to a very great distance, and the view was marvelous. With the exception of the northern horizon, which was hidden from them by the enormous wall that rose behind them, the travelers beheld at all three remaining cardinal points an incomparable panorama. Human eye has never contemplated a more beautiful spectacle, and this was only a foretaste of what might be reserved for them upon the crest of Gaurisankar.

No-cloud, no mist, trailed across the broadly lighted planes of the landscape, and it seemed as though, by the stroke of a magic wand, some friendly fairy had suddenly raised the veil which covered these sublime regions, to spread their innumerable beauties before human eyes.

To the south, beyond the valley of Tomba-Kosi, clad with luxuriant vegetation, stretched the cliffs that descend to the plains of the Ganges; at the west was Goussainthan, six thousand or seven thousand meters in height, with the snows of the peaks of Kerong sparkling; to the east, the whole Mayanama group rose above the clouds, and from the center of this prodigious mass a diamond spire sprang up, cleaving the blue heavens. This was the sovereign of the land; the Gaurisankar toward which the untiring efforts of the travelers were directed.

And upon the crest that they had just left a cloud of dust rose from the great road, and from this cloud came a long rattling sound, the bleating of three thousand sheep mingled with barking, and the tinkling of the bells that the herdsman had fastened to the necks of the rams.

"There they are! It is they!" cried Goulab at last, his piercing eye penetrating the horizon. The cloud approached. It could be seen to extend, to separate,

to expand to either side of the road, on the slopes of the
two valleys whose verdure suddenly disappeared under
the invasion of this living stream. The ground vibrated
under the shock of all these little cloven feet running
or bounding in an aggregate that would cause a Pont-
Neuf to give way. Finally with opera glasses and
spyglasses they were able to distinguish objects among
the dense crowd. It could be seen that the flock approached rapidly. It passed Pangmo, and the noise of
the bleating was accompanied by the lowing of the
few oxen and cows which followed the mass of sheep.
Soon the head of the column, preceded by a dozen
dogs, arrived at the very foot of the intrenchment, and
the besieged could not restrain a cry of surprise upon
perceiving that neither the doctor, nor Christi, nor the
two Hindus were among the number.

Nevertheless, they were certainly the same herdsmen
and the same flock. With scrupulous honesty the
herdsmen stopped the animals which bore the baggage,
and soon as they recognized the white men upon the
rocks they placed their cargo upon the road. As there
was no immediate danger to fear, Graec'h and the
two Yankees hastened to go and fetch the things left
on the path. They even exchanged some words with
the leader of the Bhotan nomads. But at the question
they put to them concerning the doctor and his
companions, the Bhotias burst out laughing and replied :

"You haven't seen them, then ? They are already
among you !" And they spoke the truth. A cry of
joy had burst forth from the platform, and when the
Breton and the two Americans had remounted to the
terrace, they were able to join in the heartfelt con-

gratulations that the doctor and his companions were lavishing upon one another.

The explanation was very simple. The wind, coming from the east, had brought to the shepherds, far up the ridge path, the sound of the firing.

"Our friends are having a fight somewhere!" the physician had cried.

And from the information given by the little Madrasi, all concluded that a combat must be going on on the sides of the terrace where Christi had left them. If they succeeded in joining them the besieged would have four more rifles at their service, which was a strong re-enforcement, increasing their number from seven to eleven.

But what was more important, the arrival of the four new combatants would have the immense advantage of bringing the baggage, that is to say, clothing, tents, food, and ammunition, of which they would have the utmost need.

That indeed was their special cause for concern.

Now, would they be able to rejoin their companions?

Was there not reason to fear that the assailants, foreseeing the coming of the flock, might advance to meet it, in order to capture or kill the remainder of the column? This hypothesis had every appearance of probability.

Happily the Bhotán herdsmen, as cunning as they were true to their word, were posted as to the situation. The chief decided it, laughing. With his ordinary gay brevity he informed the four travelers as to the mode of procedure they had best follow. This was a revival of the artifice of Ulysses desiring to escape from the cave of Polyphemus, and certainly the nomadic shepherd had never read the Odyssey. But he had had long training in the niceties of his trade, and was provided with more than one trick to play upon the annoying customhouse officials of Tibet and Nepál.

They led out four zebus from among the other beasts of burden. They placed the doctor and his companions upon their backs—in very uncomfortable positions, by the way. They even added very inconvenient packages, and hid all under the coverings of red or white wool, so frequently used by trading caravans. Thus disguised, the travelers could cross the threatening belt with impunity.

On the road the leader of the flock responded as simply as he could to the first Metch who asked him what had become of the other white travelers:

"They remained at Dud-Kunda. I did not agree to keep them or conduct them."

As soon as the troop reached the foot of the intrench-ment, Christi, who had continually peeped from under his coverings, let himself slide quickly from the hard back of his mount, and ran to the aid of his companions.

Now all were reunited; the staff was quite complete. But they were not at the end of their troubles. They were certainly more numerous, better armed; they certainly had supplies for at least ten days, tents and cov-erings for the night; but they were none the less block-aded, and must anticipate and undergo the pains and fatigues of a siege that might last a long time.

"How lucky those fellows are!" said the major, clenching his fists as he watched the shepherds and their flock go up the road again.

Suddenly, coming to a bend in the road, the Bhotias turned toward the north, descending the Dud-Kosi slopes. They had held faithfully to their bargain. Nothing would prevent them now from proceeding by the shortest way to the Tinki-la pass.

The besieged experienced deep sadness at seeing these half-savages disappear, who had been for ten days their true and tried associates.

It was like the eclipse of a hope for them, especially as their thoughts returned to the bitterness and difficulty of their present position.

The route that the herdsmen followed so lightly was closed to them, friendly travelers far from all support, far from all succor on the part of local authorities, and they could only open it at the cost of a bloody combat such as they had already undergone, of a victory that might be dearly bought.

The day closed with these painful reflections. But all possessed a sturdy spirit, and were confident in their own energy. The goal they had desired to reach was too near, their resolution too firm, for them to hesitate in their decision.

They therefore took counsel at sunset in order to conclude all arrangements for the morrow.

They unanimously decided that at daybreak they would resume their march.

To remain where they were offered no advantage. Besides having no succor to expect, they would lose precious time and uselessly waste their provisions. Goulab very justly remarked that the rocky mass by which they were backed was only a freak, and that it must certainly terminate some kilometers further up ; that the level they had reached was apparently the highest that could be attained by the Hindus or even the Nepális of the valley ; that is to say, by men who were unaccustomed both by temperament and constitution to

the cold of the peaks, and too lightly clad, moreover, to
dare to face it, and they would be under protection as
soon as they touched the snowy region.

Thus all militated in favor of bold decision. Plumptre and Euzen Graec'h even pronounced in favor of
immediate departure. But they were made to realize
that this would be the height of imprudence ; that
they knew nothing at all of the ambushes of the road
and the perils of a nocturnal journey.

There was no attack. The bandits had manifestly
become prudent through counting their losses and esti-
mating the frightful precision of firearms. But this
abstention and silence only appeared the more disquieting to the explorers, and they did not relax their rigid
watchfulness.

Finally day dawned—a radiant day, full of brilliancy.
The Máyanama's bulk first showed black, then white and
red in the pale light of the dawn. Then, as the sun rose
in the firmament, the incomparable giant, the throne
of Sivá and Parváti, appeared in the blue like a snowy
phantom, with shoulders upon which a collar of gold,
rubies, topazes, and opals radiated color under a canopy
of turquoise and sapphire.

The moment had come to launch themselves bravely
toward those heights.

But at this very moment a furious clamor broke
forth, and rising, as they had done the day before, from
the wooded slopes, the brigands, Siváites and Buddhists,
with no distinction of belief, united by a common thirst
for murder and pillage, rushed to the assault, veritable
maniacs who had vowed themselves to Yama, God of
Sacrifice and Voluntary Death, hastening to a paradise
of orgies or to the repose of Nirvana. At the first

glance that he threw upon the convulsed faces of those demoniacs, wild for carnage, Goulab turned toward Merrien, and pointing toward the hideous herd, brandishing all sorts of arms as it ran, uttered the one word:

"Opium!"

Yes, it was opium that had transfigured and transformed these savages; that had given them their mad courage; stripping from them even their respect for their odious religious practices. And it was now that the danger was most terrible, for they had renounced the merits of bloodless murder, and were about to give themselves up to the profane joys of massacre.

A hundred men, at least, threw themselves upon the plateau on which the travelers awaited them.

Divided into three groups, the latter met the attack with a triple discharge.

Eleven of the fanatics fell senseless. But at the same instant, six balls passed over the heads of the besieged. A seventh, rebounding from the wall of gneiss, grazed the naked calf of Goulab's leg, leaving a bleeding furrow. The shikári did not make a moan, but he muttered between his teeth:

"It is nothing, nothing! Barely a scratch! But they shall pay dear for it."

He kept his word. Three times in succession the carbine of the valiant Chatrya was extended, and three Siváites fell.

"Attention!" cried Merrien; "only aim at those who carry rifles. They are at present the most formidable."

These tactics certainly produced excellent results. In a few moments a dozen marksmen were put *hors de combat*, and they had for the most part only to do

with the body of fanatics armed with sabers, poniards,
or nooses. Nevertheless their number was not perceptibly diminished, and there came a moment when
the three groups were forced to form themselves into
a square, in order that they should not be broken up
by the onset of the aggressors.

Suddenly, Euzen Graec'h gave a cry of fury :

"Oh, for once I will not miss thee ! "

He had just perceived Ramu hardly thirty steps away,
exciting his followers to combat. To throw himself upon
the assailants, to crush skulls and spines with the butt of
his clubbed rifle, was mere play to the Breton. For a
single second his iron hand clutched the scoundrel's
shoulder, but it only left the mark of its five fingers upon the
brown skin of the Dogra, who fled at this terrible touch.

At the same time ten of the Thugs rushed together
upon the Hercules.

Merrien, Plumptre, and the doctor at once plunged
forward to extricate their friend. It was unnecessary.
With a titanic movement Graec'h shook off the bunch
of humanity, staved in a chest with a blow from his
heel, broke a jaw with his left fist, and, letting his
carbine drop, seized a third body at hazard, and flung
it full at the band of Thugs, who were overcome with
panic. He himself got clear at slight cost, merely a
scratch or two. Then came something utterly unexpected. Suddenly the assailants turned and fled, letting
themselves roll down the rocks with every sign of
violent terror.

Three among them, who had not time to escape,
flung themselves upon the ground, face downward,
multiplying gestures of supplication, to the great astonishment of the white men.

As they did not rise, one of the Americans asked:

"Shall we crush these vermin? If they think we are going to let them alone——"

But Goulab raised his voice, and his companions were surprised by the terror in his face.

"Sahibs," cried the shikári, "we shall have no more to fear from these scoundrels. At present they are streaming down the mountain at the top of their speed. Unfortunately we are threatened by a much greater danger."

"What do you mean, Goulab?" asked Merrien anxiously.

"I mean that the bandits have fled from something stronger than themselves. Only listen, and you will hear the voice of the dholes."

All paused and listened, without paying any further attention to the three wretches who were still prostrate.

A distant mournful cry came down the flanks of the chain from the east. It was a sort of lugubrious, prolonged howl, and in spite of the distance, which was still great, that separated it from the travelers, the latter could recognize the multitudinous clamor of wild dogs, traveling in troops. They must be innumerable.

The dholes, in fact, belong to the canine race, and, like all the Indian fauna, they represent the most terrible element. Of medium size, thin and lank, dirty, and emitting a pestilential odor, they would be hardly more to be dreaded than an ordinary dog, were not their strange habits and their number truly frightful. They are nomadic, live in families, and are as fitted to endure the most vigorous cold as the most extreme heat; traversing the Indian peninsula from north to south, from east to west. Always famished, necessity makes them brave.

Nothing holds out against them, and certain travelers affirm that they do not even fear the tiger and the elephant. But these are tales that it is impossible to verify, and one may consider fabulous that other assertion that the dhole seems rather to profess sympathy for man.

One may cite, unfortunately, examples of villages besieged and boroughs destroyed by these frightful animals. The energetic measures taken by the English authorities, the use of strychnine in pieces of meat placed in the pathway of the troop, have succeeded in almost entirely banishing them from southern India. But these means are far from being equally efficacious in the north, where dense forests, continuous jungles, and vast uncultivated and desert spaces prevent the trail of the devastating herd from being traced.

Whatever might be the manners and customs of these dangerous neighbors, the explorers, not trusting to hypothesis, resolved to surround themselves with all possible precautions. The plateau on which they were situated was accessible only on the side of the rocky stairway. The remaining sides, almost perpendicularly cut, had lent some aid to the ascent of human assailants. But the dogs certainly could not fare so well. If then they succeeded in sufficiently barricading the one side, they would have nothing to fear from the yelping herd, and they would be able to look down from the terrace in all security upon the canine pariahs as they swept past. It would certainly be a curious sight. Meanwhile, the noise increased and drew nearer. The horrible pack came down the mountain with a sound like rolling thunder. They raised a cloud of dust equal to that raised the day before by the passage of the Bhotán sheep. At the same time the barking of the pack took on a formidable intensity. The air was full of it, and the abominable hubbub obliged the onlookers to put their hands over their ears.

"It is lucky that they are coming with the wind," said Goulab. "Perhaps they will pass without scenting us !"

Everyone had run to the rocks. With desperate haste they commenced to move the blocks, and roll them one on top of the other to obstruct the passageway. Euzen Graec'h, while shaking the biggest one of all, suddenly remembered the three assassins. They had not budged from their place, face to the earth, arms crossed, like dead bodies.

"Heh ! Shammers ! heap of good-for-nothings !" cried the sailor, in a voice that made the travelers burst out laughing in spite of their anxiety.

"Come here for a bit and help us ! We'll pay you whatever suits you, villainous monkeys without a skin."

And, as the Hindus did not appear to hear him, he went up to them and kicked them into rising.

"That is the only way to get ideas into your heads," he said.

The demonstration had, indeed, an immediate effect.

Enlightened by the gestures of the Europeans, further reassured by the words of Goulab, Christi, Salem-Bun, and his comrade, who, in order to make them understand, employed nearly all the dialects of India, they passed from fright to delirious joy, and, laughing and weeping at one and the same time, they devoted themselves with as much docility as energy to the task that the travelers required of them.

"Come ! come !" said the Breton, somewhat softened,

"they are not bad fellows. With some blows from a rope's end, and some kindness, they would do whatever you wanted them to."

"We are fourteen now," said the doctor. "I confess that this addition to our force does not displease me."

But conversation came to an end. There was too much to do to stop up the last crevices of the rocks, and unfortunately no human strength was capable of moving the enormous blocks that overhung the road. There still remained a breach, a meter in width. It was more than sufficient to admit the dogs.

The howling was not more than two miles away, and the eye could behold the first undulating waves of this living sea.

They all looked at one another in consternation.

"May God have mercy on us!" uttered Plumptre gravely. "I know too well what these brutes are. I was once near being devoured by them."

"What are we to do?" asked Miss Weldon.

"Wait!" answered Jean Merrien.

An enormous rock, of at least five thousand kilograms in weight, was hanging to the side of the mountain, attached only at its base.

The explorer went and got from among the baggage a carefully closed iron box. He opened it and drew out a little tube of tin provided with a rather long fuse, and introduced it into a crack in the block. Then he waited, a box of matches in his hand.

Now they could no longer hear one another, the yelping so drowned their voices, filling the air with discordant noises.

The pack arrived, panting, starving, like a tremendous tide.

THE ENTIRE PACK PASSED.

From their position in the shelter of the rocks the travelers saw this barking wave sweep on. They saw the inflamed eyes and mouths, the hanging tongues, the breath giving out steam and vile odor. At the same time the filthy herd seized, tore, and scattered in a thousand shreds the bodies of the Hindus who had been slain by the white men and abandoned on the road by their brethren. This occupied only a few seconds, and the dogs, like the African *termites*, left no trace of the bodies; they passed, swept on by the rapidity of their course.

But behind the first ones the mass was denser, more swarming, blacker. The dholes, jostling and hustling one another, sent out wings to their army. One flank rolled over the slopes of Tomba-Kosi under the trees. The other, thrown against the wall of the mountain, crowding and fighting with teeth and paws, found the cleft in the rocks, as water that has broken its dike fills all the hollows that it finds. They struggled and piled themselves into the narrow passage, and twenty bloody mouths showed their gleaming teeth above the first rocks.

Jean Merrien struck his match. He held it to the fuse. They heard a hollow sound—an ominous cracking. The wall split asunder, and the rock was torn from the trench of gneiss, of which it formed a part, leaving the place as empty and fresh behind it as the stump of a recently amputated limb. It fell exactly across the narrow entrance, crushing a dozen of the wild dogs, while a frightful report shook the layers of ambient air.

This unexpected thunder rendered the travelers good service. Panic-stricken by such a crash as they had never before heard, the dholes hastened their pace, and the entire pack, silent with terror, passed as quickly as a rapid train over the road, fleeing in the direction of Pangmo, and were soon blotted out, buried in the opaque cloud of dust raised by their dizzy flight.

The travelers raised their eyes and their hearts toward heaven. They were saved. After having delivered them from the Thugs, the wild dogs had just given them their liberty.

As a measure of prudence, they waited an hour before setting out. But Goulab pointed out to them that meeting with a second pack was very improbable. Three thousand dogs at least had just passed under their eyes. What other troop would be able to find food, coming after these ?

The day was advanced when they sallied forth. No suspicious sign came to reawaken their anxiety. Toward evening they stopped to sleep in the little town of Khansa, whose governor received them kindly. They had well earned their rest.

THE CARAVAN CROSSED ON THE LARGE STONES.

XII.

THE CHINGO-PA-MARI.

Upon leaving Khansa, the travelers still followed for some time the road on which they had come from Dud-kunda. This road that lay along a ridge commanded a valley upon either side. Through each of these valleys wound a stream, the Tomba-Kosi on the right, the Dud-Kosi on the left, both flowing down from the same mountain. The slope was steep, and seemed entirely unsuited to a descent. They agreed, therefore, to continue, as long as they could do so without delaying their arrival, on the road that they had chosen. When they arrived at Gama, the first village that they came to after leaving Khansa, the information that was given them apprised them of the fact that the road parted abruptly in two directions. In fact, instead of running from west to east according to its first direction, it made a bend and sank toward the south.

"Well, my dear Frenchman," questioned the major gayly, "what are we to decide upon ?"

"Well, major," responded Jean, in the same tone, "it seems to me that we can no longer follow this road."

"At least not without turning our backs upon our goal : that is also my opinion."

"And you, mademoiselle, what do you propose ?" asked the young man, in his turn.

"There is only one reply : we must now resign ourselves to the abandonment of outlined paths and advance directly to our goal."

In uttering these last words the young girl had raised her head. They could read in her eyes that the suggestion she had just made did not terrify her ; that she was, in a word, completely decided to proceed to the end.

Her opinion was unanimously adopted, and henceforth the little band confronted the dangers and delays concealed among the inaccessible mountains. The first difficulty that presented itself was the necessity of crossing the Dud-Kosi.

After much searching, a Hindu finally discovered a path descending toward the valley. This path, which had never been used save by some inhabitants of the opposite side of the river when going to Gama, was barely indicated. The almost perpendicular descent would have been impossible to the Europeans, if some trees scattered along the way had not enabled them, by attaching a cord thereto, to improvise a sort of balustrade, by which Miss Cicely Weldon, Major Plumptre, and Jean Merrien let themselves slide almost to the bottom. And now that the river confronted them, deafening them with

the noise of its current, they questioned anxiously how
they were going to get across it.

From the height at which they had been some moments before, it had seemed to them a little stream, with
its waters flowing gently over a shallow bed; and they
now beheld an impetuous torrent, whose windings of a
moment ago had become roaring rapids.

It was again Miss Weldon who succeeded, by means
of signs, in making her companions understand that a ford
must be somewhere near the path.

They resumed their march, and presently, indeed,
some large flat stones emerging from the waters, and
making a very picturesque bridge, served as a crossing
for the caravan.

The ascent resembled the descent, thanks to the trees
which fringed the slope as on the opposite bank. Above,
the country which stretched before the travelers' vision
was slightly undulating, now hills, now valleys, but
everywhere carefully cultivated. Fields of wheat alternated, when the ground inclined, with fields of rice,
and for a boundary between them, cherry trees and fig
trees arose, breaking the monotony of the landscape.
The travelers entered these plantations resolutely, marching straight ahead without encountering a single habitation. They concluded that this cultivated land must all
belong to one estate, and that they would sooner or
later come to the house of the proprietor.

But what was their surprise when, after having
gone a considerable distance, they found themselves
again upon a road, that was very well kept up for
the region. Their indecision was great. Which direction should they follow? After much deliberation the
little band started on again, following the road, and

hoping to come across some village, or at least some
habitation.

Their expectations were not disappointed, for they
arrived in this way at Lanya. They learned there that
the road led to Ghát, the nearest station of the
Máyanama Mountains, in the midst of which was the
summit of Gaurisankar. They learned besides that the
domain they had come through belonged to an Englishman by a special concession, and on condition of keeping up the road. This caused Merrien some disturbance
of mind, and he could not refrain from making a little
attack upon Major Plumptre.

"Say, now, Plumptre, I have but one dread left."

"What is it, then?" asked the major phlegmatically.

"That I may find an Englishwoman on Gaurisankar."

This sally made everyone laugh, the major most
heartily of all.

"In truth," he replied, "if I were sure of it, I
would cease my efforts here and now, and patiently
await your return at the house of my fellow-countryman."

"Why, major!" asked Cicely, "are you already tired
of your trip?"

"No, Miss Weldon, no! I was simply replying to
Mr. Merrien, who always finds a joke on me in order."

Some hours later the travelers came in sight of
Ghát, situated at the foot of an almost isolated peak.
They followed the road a little longer, and finally
abandoned it definitely, and plunged into the chain
which contained their goal. From this time on they
kept always to the north. But their march became more
and more laborious because of the unprecedented heights
that they were obliged to scale, or the rapid descents

they were forced to make. The great humidity of the climate does not admit of travelers venturing far into these regions, or at all events, it renders any excursion very dangerous. The rain softens the soil, and forms a sort of glutinous mud, on account of the argillaceous nature of the rocks. The dense fogs that close abruptly in about the mountain prevent the tourist from ascertaining his position, and hide from him the precipices that yawn at his feet. This danger, which the caravan had up to this time always avoided, either by taking refuge in caves or going into camp on some sheltered plateau, put them at one time in very great peril. It was, perhaps, three o'clock in the afternoon. The travelers were chatting gayly as they followed a very narrow ledge bounded on one side by a stretch of vertical wall, and on the other by a precipice some hundred meters in depth. Goulab had seemed anxious all day.

"Come now, Goulab, my friend, what a funereal countenance! Tell us what is troubling you," asked MacGregor.

"The road is long!" the shikári replied laconically.

"Well, my friend; more so than any other? And then it has the advantage of being flat."

"Flat, but narrow," replied Goulab, again. "And then," he continued, "do we know where it ends?"

"The deuce! We'll soon see, Goulab. We are not yet blind," Merrien interposed brusquely.

"If we do not become so, sahib!"

Jean had not time to respond, when the whole troop stopped, dumb with terror. A mist was slowly rising, and the neighboring summits had already disappeared. They all understood, and a single cry broke from their full hearts:

" The fog ! "

They comprehended the horrible position in which they were placed, on a ledge where they could barely walk four abreast, with no possibility of raising their tents.

What would become of them, not daring to stir, not able to see a meter ahead of them ?

Goulab's grave voice was again heard.

" Well, sahíb ; are we not blind ? This is what I anticipated."

"Why didn't you say so sooner, Goulab ? And now what are you going to do ? " the young man questioned anxiously.

"I am going to take the lead and show you the road," replied the shikári quietly.

"No, no, Goulab ! I do not wish it. It is exposing yourself uselessly."

"I risk nothing, sahíb," replied the Kashmiri, with emotion. "Let us now march in single file, and keep our left hands against the wall."

In this way, without a word, Goulab leading, Merrien, Cicely, Plumptre, Christi, MacGregor, and the rest of the troop slowly advanced ; starting at the least projection of the rocks. It made them dizzy to think that the road might grow narrower ; that they had only room for their two feet ; that a movement might fling them into space.

Suddenly a terrible cry pierced the fog. They all stopped, gasping.

" What is it ? " asked Goulab.

" I do not know," replied Merrien. " Let each one speak his name in turn." And they heard successively the names of Cicely, Plumptre, MacGregor, Euzen

Graec'h, and the Hindus. One name only was missing from the roll, that of Christi.

"The poor child, he has fallen," murmured Cicely faintly. "And to think that we can do nothing, nothing!"

"It is useless to go on, my friends," continued Jean Merrien. "We must wait here until the fog breaks. Possibly Christi is not dead. It would be inhuman to abandon him."

"Yes, yes; let us wait!" the troop, who were all attached to the little Madrasi, responded as with one voice.

And they all gathered together. They wished to be near one another in this common danger. It is impossible to describe the night that followed. Standing upright with their backs to the mountain, and an abyss in front of them, unable to relax themselves, the unfortunate group awaited the daylight. Morning came, bringing no change, and then broken with weariness, despairing, having had no nourishment since the day before, the travelers felt that they were giving out. Complaints were heard.

"I am too tired," murmured Cicely; "I must lie down. I can stand up no longer."

"Mademoiselle, Miss Cicely, courage!" broke in the major and Jean at the same time.

"I cannot bear it any longer; no, I cannot," the young girl repeated.

"Hold on, Miss Cicely, the fog is breaking at last." It was Euzen Graec'h who spoke.

It was the truth. The opaque mass of vapor grew more translucent, after the fashion of the gauze curtains of the theater that are raised one after another and reveal the background by degrees. The web grew thinner, separated in slabs, in shreds, which drifted off like thin smoke.

Soon the heads, then the shoulders of the travelers emerged from this smoke. It sank lower still, to their waists, to their feet. Then above their heads they saw the incandescent disk of the sun, and the incommensurable point of Everest, three thousand meters up in the heavens, while below them the fog unfurled, undulating like an ocean on the submerged peaks and valleys.

Thus must the survivors of the Ark, stranded on the Armenian height, have beheld the spectacle of the globe emerging from the waters of the deluge.

At the same time that hope re-entered their hearts, the imposing vision of these gigantic mountains dazzled their eyes. They had never yet contemplated such a panorama. Their ecstasy had lasted a long time without their even recalling their situation when Euzen Graec'h suddenly cried out :

" Christi ! I see Christi ! "

They started as from out of a dream. The anguish of the night had caused them to forget the little Madrasi. Their eyes were simultaneously lowered, and in place of the abyss which, the evening before, had bounded the ledge, they saw only a gentle declivity sloping down to a sort of broad esplanade. Upon this esplanade, stretched out among the ferns, lay Christi, who seemed to give no sign of life. Then, without a word spoken, they all ran rapidly down the slope, and grouped themselves anxiously about Christi, impatiently awaiting the opinion of Dr. MacGregor, who was kneeling at the child's side.

"This will amount to nothing," he said finally ; "a prolonged swoon that I shall bring him out of."

And taking a bottle out of his little traveling case, he poured a few drops of its contents between the boy's teeth.

The effect of the cordial was soon seen. After one or two starts Christi opened his eyes, astonished to find himself thus surrounded by his friends. He tried to move, but a sharp pain suddenly contracted his features, and he fell back again.

"Dear me, doctor! If only the fall has caused no grave injury!" exclaimed Cicely, in an anxious voice.

"Reassure yourself, Miss Weldon," replied MacGregor, "he is only suffering now from the general numbness caused by this damp night, like the rest of us; and we shall do well to look for a more propitious place for a little repose."

At these words Jean Merrien and Euzen Graec'h took the lead, while Major Plumptre offered his arm to Cicely, and the two Hindus with infinite care lifted Christi, whom everyone had believed to be dead.

They had not taken fifty steps when Merrien and Euzen turned back, wearing an hilarious aspect.

"Come, come, quickly; I have just discovered a palace!" cried Jean gayly. At this puzzling remark, the little band forgot its fatigue and quickened its pace, soon joining the young man, who guided it toward a mass of verdure, an oasis in the midst of these mountains They paused, filled with admiration. In a recess of the rocky wall, a little open space appeared. And growing at hazard, but in a most charming disorder. were palm trees, banana trees, rhododendrons, and epiphytal orchids attached to the branches of a majestic oak.

This occurrence, which is not so very rare, is explained by the transportation of tropical flora by the south winds.

Jean Merrien let them admire this little enchanted nook at their leisure, then, in a solemn voice, he cried out :

"Ladies and gentlemen, I have promised you a palace : I am going to keep my promise. This is only the garden.' Be kind enough to follow me."

And this time, hastening to Miss Weldon's side, he gracefully offered his arm, on which she placed her little hand, laughing as she did so. Then the two, at the head of the caravan which followed, curious and impatient, advanced toward an opening, which was reached by means of two steps placed one above the other, and hollowed out in the rock as though by the hand of man. This opening had escaped their notice at first, masked as it was by the more luxuriant vegetation of this place. Merrien brushed aside the growth and led in the young girl, who, struck with admiration, stopped abruptly, while all the others of the party followed her example as one man. Jean and his faithful Breton enjoyed their surprise.

In truth the spectacle was positively marvelous. The travelers found themselves in a circular grotto, the rocky walls of which were of a blood-red color. In the center stalactites and stalagmites, meeting each other, formed columns elegant in shape, which seemed to support the roof. This latter, at the center of this circle, rose suddenly, and, from the height of the cupola thus formed fell a cascade, the waters of which were scattered in mist by the time they reached the ground. The daylight came through round, regular fissures. The ardent rays of the sun, streaming in through these, broke on every drop of water, and lit a thousand fires in the crystals of the columns. The entire grotto was illumined by the incessant flashing. And the dazzled eye seemed to see in this richness of light the fires of a myriad of diamonds.

The first moment of surprise past, exclamations rose to the lips of all.

"How beautiful it is! How did you discover this marvel? Ah, M. Merrien, you are a veritable enchanter!"

This last sentence came from Cicely Weldon, who was already running about the grotto like a child, calling her companions to share in her enthusiastic admiration.

It was decided that they should remain at least two days in the "Fairy Palace," as the young American poetically named it. Christi, who had been comfortably settled, found himself completely restored the following morning. He was able to join the others in exploring the thousand nooks and crannies of this incomparable place.

The third day finally dawned, and it was with regret that the little group abandoned the refuge filled with the coolness they had had so little chance to enjoy. They found themselves once more upon the mountain, with its wearisome ascents and perilous descents.

As they advanced into the Máyanama range, the peaks rose steadily higher and more arid. They sometimes marched for a number of days without a sign of human habitation. The narrow valleys are veritable funnels in which are gathered the waters of the showers, so that cabins cannot be put up for fear of inundations, and the best sites for the erection of villages are the high promontories from which the water runs rapidly in all directions.

Twenty times they were obliged to flee, abandon their camp, and climb the side of a cliff in haste, to avoid the sudden flooding of a torrent swollen by the rain. In this way, forced to long detours and unexpected tacking, they arrived at the Thung-Lung pass. Since crossing the Dud-Kosi they had described a semicircle about Chingo-pa-mari, and it was by such turnings, but continually narrowing the circles as in a monstrous labyrinth, that they must reach the foot of Gaurisankar.

In the midst of the Thung-Lung pass a new peril awaited them. It was decreed that they should escape none of the dangers with which these mountains abounded. One evening, when they had camped in the cleft of a rock, a dark mass interposed suddenly between the road they had just left and the retreat they had chosen. The opening was obstructed by an elephant of gigantic size, and with long, black hair. The travelers were safe in their little cave, for the elephant could not enter its mouth, which was large enough for the passage of a man, but much too narrow for such a colossal creature. But if the pachyderm could not altogether enter, he could without difficulty seize the things which had been spread out by the Hindus in preparation for the supper and the night's rest. Already his enormous trunk had carried off a cake of rice and two bottles of wine. The rest was quickly taken to the back of the grotto, but the elephant, furious at finding nothing more, commenced to puff into the travelers' faces a fetid breath that filled the entire cavity. It was impossible to remain longer in such a place, and Jean Merrien, Major Plumptre, MacGregor, Euzen Graec'h started to attack the dangerous proboscidean, when Christi cried out :

"An exit ! I have found an exit !"

And with nervous hands he cleared an opening in the rock large enough for a man to slip through. One by one they went out by way of this passage, and joined each other on a platform which was in reality the roof of the cavern they had just been in, and from which they now looked down upon the elephant.

The latter, furious at seeing his prey escape him, started to make an attempt to reach them. His weight dragging him down for one thing, the very steep slope for another, caused him continually to fall back to the point he started from.

The travelers, recovered from their first fright, now were laughing heartily at the fruitless efforts of their formidable adversary, when suddenly the scene changed. The elephant had finally hoisted himself on to a lower ridge ; a moment more, and he would reach them. Mac-Gregor raised his rifle, took an instant's aim ; then fired, but only wounded the animal. Excited by the shot, the elephant concentrated his entire force upon one supreme attempt, and with a single bound stood beside his enemies.

" Fly ! fly ! " cried Christi. " Here is a path which leads to the road we were just now on."

And taking the lead he ran rapidly down, followed closely by the Hindus and the rest of the company. Cicely Weldon, Jean Merrien, and Plumptre came last of all. The two men took the young girl's hands and dragged her rapidly along, while the pachyderm, undecided in his mind, finally concluded to pursue them, giving them a few moments' headway. It was then a mad race, no one daring to stop to attack the animal who, moment by moment, gained upon the rear fugitives. Cicely felt him at her heels, and from time to time

CICELY FELT THE ELEPHANT AT HER HEELS.

his hot and nauseating breath struck her neck and those of her companions.

With extended trunk the elephant was about to catch the girl's floating blouse, and then all effort on the part of Jean and the major would be in vain : the unfortunate girl would be crushed by the formidable tusks, when suddenly Plumptre dropped Cicely's hand. She looked anxiously at him, without pausing in her running. An atrocious suspicion gnawed at her heart. Did he wish to relinquish her and thus be freer to escape ? At this thought her courage left her, her strength failed her.

Merrien felt her pace slacken. He also had seen the major's movement.

"One more effort, mademoiselle, just one little effort. *I* want to save you," he murmured in the young American's ear.

But what could he do ? A double cry was heard. The elephant had just seized the girl, who clung desperately to the Frenchman's arm. And while all stopped, dumb with horror, a shot rang out, the trunk relaxed its hold, the colossal brute wavered and fell in a heap, a stream of blood trickling down between his eyes.

All this happened in much less time than it takes to tell it. And it was not until they saw their terrible adversary lying at their feet, that they thought to find out who had been Miss Weldon's brave and skillful savior.

Cicely, still trembling with emotion, scarcely able to support herself, and unconscious of what was going on around her, fixed her eyes mechanically on the still smoking rifle of the Englishman. She comprehended everything ; a great thankfulness and a great remorse filled her heart.

She advanced smiling, held out her hand to the major, and said to him so low that no one heard her :

"Thanks, thanks, and pardon!"

They all approached to congratulate the brave officer, while he, distraught, heard the congratulations, unheeding.

Why had she asked his pardon ? Yes, pardon ; he had certainly heard correctly. What could she have done to say such a thing as that? He decided to think no more of it. He was never to know what had inspired Cicely Weldon to such strange thanks.

The Hindus had thrown themselves upon the elephant's body and were cutting him to pieces with incomparable skill. Plumptre's ball had not only delivered them from great danger, but had also furnished them with very delicate food. And that evening, feasting upon some bits of the trunk, feet, and sides the travelers laughingly declared that it's an ill wind that blows nobody good.

After having traversed the Thung-Lung pass, in which this tragic event had taken place, the caravan again ascended to the north, and so arrived in the Tingri-Maidan plain, through the entire length of which flowed the Tingri-Chu river.

But they could go no further to the northward, being stopped at the Tibetan customhouse. From this time their course swerved completely to the eastward, thus passing around the central mass in which is situated Gaurisankar. Most of the rivers which flow down from Tibet pass through the wall presented by the Himálayas by gorges of such depth and such abruptness that it was impossible for the travelers to enter them. It was only by scaling the neighboring cliffs, by a succession of passes more than four thousand meters in height, that they could continue on their way. They were even obliged to avoid certain gaps in the chain by detours of more than fifty kilometers. Time was passing, the food was giving out, and the calculations that they made with great regularity each day showed them that they had traveled enormous distances without making much headway. They were still at the foot of Chingo-pa-mari.

"Ah, bah!" cried Plumptre one morning, no longer recognizing his way, "has the earth turned upside down?"

What had drawn from him this exclamation was the strange phenomenon of the mirage, which on account of the refraction of the rarefied layers of air, renders it difficult to locate one's self, and causes the sun to appear almost motionless at one point of the heavens.

GRAEC'H FLOURISHED THE ROPE.

XIII.

THE AVALANCHE.

SINCE leaving Dud-Kunda the travelers had marched at the rate of fifteen kilometers a day, and eight days had passed. They could do no better, and it was the maximum effort that could be made by human energy at such levels and against such obstacles. They were now in the midst of their definite ascent, six thousand meters up, already feeling the divers troubles that afflict mountain climbers; vertigo, weight upon the stomach, impeded circulation, difficulty in breathing—in a word, they were threatened with all those ills that physicians group under the generic name of mountain sickness. None of them, however, wished to abandon the party. When the goal is so near, one is rarely discouraged.

So near! They knew very little about it. Like the

Hindu pundit who was the first to attempt this tremendous ascent, they passed around the mountain
without seeing it. The level they had reached gave
them a view of all the inferior or surrounding summits.
Nowhere could they discover the mysterious Gaurisankar. The nearer they came, the more closely it
concealed itself. It was a regular game of hide-and-
seek in which the one who escaped the pursuit of the
seekers was the giant *par excellence*, the king of the
Himálayas.

Now the travelers took all possible pains to keep
their way. They were in a labyrinth, as it were, and
the sun alone could guide them, furnishing them with
a point of comparison.

From Dudkunda to Khansa, from Khansa to Gaura,
from Gaura to Ghát, they had sometimes gone up and
sometimes down. They had not apparently gained a
meter.

Now, far from any designated road, they had no path
other than they made for themselves. But with each
ascent came a fresh disappointment. Did they climb one
peak, from its summit they discovered ten, twenty others,
to the north, to the east, to the west, to the south.
Then they had to descend again, and try to measure the
heights, and recommence the ascent with no more chance
of success. Meanwhile all had remarked one thing, and
this common observation had permitted them to com-
pare their estimates with more certainty. It was to the
north that the landscape kept the most unvarying
aspect, and one could perceive in that direction a succession of giant summits, from among which one in particular detached itself with noticeable clearness.

"Can we be mistaken?" asked Miss Weldon, one

morning, on whom all these goings and comings had slowly begun to tell. "Are we indeed in the neighborhood of Gaurisankar? Perhaps we have been victims, in our ignorance, to some effect of the mirage, and are still a great way from the mountain. The savages whom we have questioned would not be likely to inform us as to that."

Merrien responded. His eyes were fixed upon a map, and he and the doctor came to show it to her.

"No, mademoiselle. There can be no error, we are eighty-four degrees, thirty minutes east of the meridian of Paris, and twenty-seven degrees, fifty minutes north latitude. The range on which we now are is certainly that of Máyanama, in the center of which rises Chingopa-mari or Gaurisankar, called Mt. Everest by the English. The two rivers that we have crossed are certainly the Tomba-Kosi, and the Dud-Kosi, and if we succeed in finding the course of the two streams Árun and Bárun, we shall have found Gaurisankar."

That was not the only anxiety that the travelers experienced. There were others, of a different gravity; the first and most pressing of which was the question of food.

At a height of six thousand meters, indeed, the travelers had no dread of dangerous or even intrusive neighbors. They decided, indeed, that there were not enough of these. What would they not have given to meet some of those wild goats in these valleys beside these Himálayan rivers; some of these broad-horned elans, whose flesh is found so delectable by the hunters of the country ! And it was not to satisfy a mere gourmand's caprice, but to insure their very existence, that they gave themselves up to the pleasures of the chase.

In default of these innocent animals they would have found acceptable an attack by one of the great ruminants of the forest, one of the yaks or woolly oxen which are still found on the plateaus of Tibet and of Central Asia.

But nothing appeared. Occasionally, here and there upon the heath, they saw in the distance a white rabbit leaping or a snowy partridge flying; creatures invariably found in the cold regions, perhaps because the law of the struggle for existence has developed the instinct to find shelter for their barren lives upon these bleak summits as well as among the ice of the poles, where the flesh-eaters of all kinds may not seek them. Nevertheless the travelers could still see now and then white-headed eagles, griffins, and vultures start up with hoarse cries above the rocky spires where they had hung their eyries.

Now, during the six days that they had been in the mountain the travelers had greatly reduced their supplies. Up to this time they had eaten almost as usual. Game had not been lacking, which had continued to provide them with fresh meat. Bread itself had been found, thanks to the cleverness of Salem-Bun, who had bought a full supply of corn-meal of the peasants of Ghát; a simple and hospitable people, whose good offices had been very much prized by the explorers.

But everything had given out at once, flour and rice, meat and vegetables. They had to content themselves with biscuit which had been brought in their knapsacks and occasional cups of tea or coffee; but it was absolutely necessary to hasten the ascent, if the supplies were to hold out until they returned.

Since their entrance by the Thung-Lung pass, their march had been nearly circular. They kept continually going around the peak, and, strange to say, it seemed as though the entire mountain turned in a contrary direction. A sort of despair seized them.

The evening of the eighth day they halted on one of the rocky ledges with which they were too well acquainted, since they were all alike.

A gloomy silence reigned while they occupied themselves with cooking their last meal of meat. Salem-Bun had set up in a cranny of the granite wall the tripod on which he did his cooking in the open air, after having announced to his companions that he was going to make them a curry with the last bits of salted kid left to them.

The platform on which they were was a projection half a kilometer in width and length, overhanging dark perpendicular gorges, at the bottom of which through pines, cypresses, rhododendrons, and wild laurel trees could be heard the roaring of torrents. Above them the naked slippery wall rose to the height of three or four hundred meters, except at the northeast, where a frightfully steep slope occurred, itself overhung by a glacier, the surface of which could be seen sparkling in the sun.

The glacier appeared at a distance to inclose a lake. It was probable that the waters coming from the melting snow had collected in this species of reservoir; a very slow trickling stream carried it in dazzling falls into the shadowy valleys of the east, and one could often see the spray of this water, reduced to mist, rise to the crest of the mountain.

"It is strange," suddenly cried MacGregor; "the more I consider this landscape, the more I fear being the victim of an optical illusion."

"What do you mean, doctor?" asked Cicely Weldon.

The doctor had put his hand upon his eyes; seeing which, his companions had imitated him.

"Strange, strange!" repeated the Scotchman. "My sight must be deranged, for everything on the glacier seems to be trembling."

"Bah! A phenomenon of mirage, doubtless, nothing more," corrected Major Plumptre, but the officer had not quitted his place by the fire which the baburdji had lighted, and upon which the pot of curry was exhaling its fragrant steam.

"Come and look yourself, Plumptre," cried Merrien; "your testimony would confirm ours."

The major rose carelessly, as if reluctant. He picked up his spy-glass, which he had let fall at the entrance of the little grotto in which they had taken shelter, and advanced toward his friends, grumbling:

"What a bore to disturb me for nothing! One sees that sort of thing ten times a day."

But he had hardly placed the glass to his eyes when he gave a cry:

"By Jove!" he cried. "That is not a mirage, it is a reality. The glacier is moving, it is coming upon us!"

Everyone sprang for his glass, and the next moment the entire troop had fastened their gaze upon the phenomenon.

"Gentlemen," said Merrien, "this is serious. It is an avalanche, but a diluvial one. I am not mistaken; I have seen plenty of them, on Mt. Blanc, the Pyrenees, and the Caucasus, but nothing which was comparable to the one we now behold. This goes beyond everything, surpassing all conception. May God protect us!"

Then, in sickening stupor mingled with admiration, they all contemplated the terrifying marvel which nature had put before their eyes. It was indeed an avalanche which was descending the slope of the mountains. The entire glacier was moving with a motion very slow at first because of the slight incline, and also, doubtless, because of the first obstacles which it found in its path. But it was evident that these obstacles once overcome, the descent once under way, the advance would be fearfully rapid. Already hollow sounds, rumblings heard faintly in the distance, betrayed that this had been accomplished. The pressure of the enormous snowy mass was splitting the dam of rocks that girdled it. These broke loose under the immense impulse, and from where they stood, the travelers could see them fly out or roll down the slope. Some of the most tremendous blocks fell into the waters of the lake, and then the cascades, increasing in volumes, became torrents. Finally a thunderous noise wakened the echoes of the mountain. The glacier had found an outlet, it had forced the stone rampart : and the avalanche, eating away the walls of the passage, crowded the granite masses to right and left, filled the little lake in the twinkling of an eye, sending its waters wildly out of their basin, and rushed down the side of the mountain, with, henceforth, no possible check.

"I understand now," said Merrien, "why these mountains are a veritable labyrinth, and why the Nepális speak with absolute terror of the Himálayan avalanches. They are daily changing the faces of the peaks, effacing the path of yesterday, and making that of the morrow only to efface it afresh. Either I am very much mistaken, or the phenomenon that we now behold

will in the end help to open the way to us, and tear the
veil from the mysterious Gaurisankar."

"If it does not carry us away!" cried Miss Weldon,
in deep anxiety.

Jean Merrien reassured her.

"No," he said, "that fear should be dismissed. The
platform on which we stand is cut at right angles,
and the torrent descending from the chain cannot sub-
merge us. But it will indeed be better not to venture on
the other slope, for——"

He did not finish. A frightful commotion shook the
atmosphere. A column of air displaced by the cataclysm
sped with the swiftness and force of a waterspout. The
first eddy had cut short the explorer's words.

"To the grotto! to the grotto!" he cried, shouting
at the top of his voice.

All fled to the shelter, and crouched there in terror.
They were able from there to watch all the splendid horror of the scene.

All? no, alas! One was missing; poor Knebel, one of
the Americans.

The imprudent fellow had left the ledge an hour
before and had ventured upon the slopes situated on
the other side of the cleft. The powerless spectators of
the scene, with broken hearts and brows contracted by a
horrible dread, could see the unfortunate man running,
tumbling heels over head, to reach them. Sometimes the
earth slipped from under his feet, and he fell on his back.
Sometimes he clutched desperately at the trunk of a tree
and succeeded in gaining some few feet of ground. But
it was obvious that he would not arrive in time at the
species of isthmus that connected the two slopes. The
avalanche would be ahead of him.

The catastrophe was inevitable. It came. A deluge of stones, of mud, of bits of ice, of powdery snow passed over the levels of the foreground. At the same time the waters of the lake, driven from their basin, poured out in torrents. A sheet of water occupying many thousand cubic meters of space, like an instantaneous Niagara, but of ten times greater volume than the famous falls of Lake Erie, spread like a liquid veil over the side of the mountain, followed immediately by the snowy and rocky mass of the glacier.

It was prodigious, terrifying, and sublime. Trees, bushes, grasses, and turf; the scant vegetation of the wind-swept regions; the dense and bushy mosses of the valley, all disappeared in the twinkling of an eye, all were swept away by the gigantic, supernatural wave. A deafening noise, as of the bursting of a planet, made up of thunder-claps, of the wail of winds started by this sudden displacement, the cracking of tree trunks and rocks, filled the air as with cries of agony. And in the intervals of this cataclysm the explorers, petrified with terror, perceived the unfortunate Knebel at the very edge of the crevasse that separated the plateau on which they had taken refuge from the declivity of the neighboring slope.

The poor fellow's voice came to them between two roars of the avalanche.

"Help!" he cried, in desperation, "help!"

He was clinging to a strong root overhanging the precipice, his feet resting on a sort of bracket of stone. He looked about him with eyes crazed by fright. It was a terrible sight that the travelers were forced to behold.

"Come, then!" cried Merrien. "We must do what

we can to help him. The avalanche has not yet broken over this side. Perhaps it will not do so. Couldn't we try and throw him a rope?"

"Yes, yes," begged Cicely. "Try that, friends. We cannot leave him to perish unaided."

She was about to dart forth at once. The Frenchman gently detained her, saying:

"No, mademoiselle, you would be of no use. The vortices of air are still too violent, and, besides, we will do all that can be done."

Aided by Plumptre and Euzen Graec'h, after they had rapidly tied themselves together, Merrien ventured outside the cleft in the rocks.

The undertaking was an extremely perilous one. It was blowing a whirlwind, and the wind followed all the fluctuations of the meteor. Seized by its gusts as by an invisible and gigantic hand, the trees snapped. Some were torn out by the roots and sent flying into space, with their branches torn, their roots hanging clogged with enormous clods of earth. Blocks weighing many hundredweight, flung as from a monstrous sling, struck the smooth and rigid wall of the precipice, and broke into innumerable fragments. The *arête* of the abyss was heaped with this débris, and the courageous travelers might easily be caught in one of these showers before they could accomplish their generous attempt.

Nevertheless, they did not draw back. Arrived at the brink of the precipice, Graec'h, whose sailor's education made him more skillful than the others, flourished the rope which was coiled in two or three rings. He whirled it about his head and let it fly. The end touched the tree, and Knebel was able to grasp it.

All was not yet done, however. The American must

now, regardless of vertigo, and without hesitating at the terrible shock, trusting himself to the rope, leap the three or four meters between him and the opposite wall, at the risk of being crushed against the granite.

For an instant the explorers considered him saved. Abandoning his miserable refuge, the unfortunate man had leaped, clinging to the rope.

But at the same moment the wind rose furiously. A mass of snow, driven by the tempest, flew over the edge of the cliff. The impulse was so unexpected, so violent, that the Breton was thrown headlong upon the brink, and half buried under a shroud of *névé* * while the rope was cut on the sharp edge of the cliff, and the unfortunate Knebel was plunged two hundred meters into the abyss by the avalanche.

A cry of despair went up from the ledge. The catastrophe was complete. The American was dead, without suffering, doubtless ; crushed by one hundred cubic meters of earth, snow, and rocks.

They were fortunate if they had not two accidents to deplore ! They were promptly reassured upon this point. Euzen Graec'h rose, safe, but pretty badly bruised.

This terrible event cast a gloom over them all, and a profound sadness weighed upon the hearts of the little company.

Knebel was the first European to succumb in this expedition.

Cicely Weldon, to whom he had been a devoted servant and faithful guardian, was cruelly stricken by this loss. Sobs choked her, and a broken moan rose to her lips, through her tears.

" How many misfortunes we have had upon our

* Névé is snow in the condition preceding the glacial

journey!" she groaned. "How many deaths! Is it not
a punishment for our pride, our vain curiosity? Do we
not tempt God by trying to penetrate the mysteries of
the globe, the approaches to which are so guarded by
nature?"

Her companions lavished attentions upon her and
revived her courage. No, their enterprise was not contrary to the will of God, and, sad as the accident was,
it was only too naturally explained by the imprudence of
the unfortunate Knebel himself. If he had not separated
himself from the camp, he would not have been surprised
by the avalanche, and would still be safe and sound
among his comrades.

They let grief have its way, until time should somewhat soften it.

Already Merrien, Plumptre, Dr. MacGregor, and Goulab
were inspecting the landscape and seeking to discover a
fresh path.

The prognostications of the Frenchman had been very
exact. The avalanche had cleared the ground and opened
the road to the explorers.

The Himalayas are thus masked and veiled each day
by the grand and terrible phenomena hidden among their
inaccessible heights. And these very phenomena are
what render them inaccessible.

Thence these unforeseen apparitions of walls unsus-
pected the day before, these overturnings of unstable
crests, in the wake of repeated excavations and the mysterious work of the waters: thence these sudden floods
that transform a marsh into a lake, a stream into a river,
a gorge into a roaring and wild current of water, a glacier
into a cataract. But thence also the extreme difficulty
of the journey, the almost absolute impossibility of a

A CRY OF DESPAIR RANG OUT.

man's surmounting the obstacles and finding the marks of
the road, when that road is reduced to the proportions
of a goat- or bear-path.

In this case the avalanche, in spite of the misfortune it had caused them, had rendered a signal service
to the mountain-climbers—all the northwest of the mass
appeared clear before their eyes.

There, where two hours before were stretched a
glacier and a lake, was now nothing to be seen but a
long valley hollowed into a funnel.

A series of superposed terraces indicated the road to
be followed, and above the last of them a cone of
dazzling whiteness showed its profile against a sky of
remarkable purity.

Merrien pointed it out to the little group, and cried
out in a sort of transport :

"There it is! There it is, that Gaurisankar we have
so yearned for! If my calculations are right, we ought
in two days to be at the entrance of the zone that
it dominates. Come, then—forward !—this time without
regret ! We touch our goal !" This encouraging speech
renewed everyone's energy, and all prepared to follow
the road.

But before leaving the scene of the catastrophe, the
travelers wished to make a final effort in behalf of their
poor lost comrade.

Possibly, thanks to some miraculous circumstance,
Knebel had been able, in spite of all appearances, to escape the almost certain death of the abyss. They could
not depart until they had exhausted all means of suc-
coring him if that were yet possible.

At the cost of extraordinary peril, Merrien, Plumptre, Graec'h, and Goulab descended by the aid of ropes

to the bottom of the precipice heaped with débris by
the avalanche. They were obliged to surrender all
hope. There, where some hours before the steep slope
had terminated in a valley carpeted by thick vegetation, was now only a chaos of ruin, as if an earthquake had crumbled the mountain, shaking to pieces
the entire mass of the Máyanamas. Of the trees, recently bushy and green, there remained not a vestige ;
and at the bottom of the gorge there lay a pool of yellowish water, which ran slowly into the prodigiously
enlarged bed of a stream. Upon the side of the seared
slope an enormous rent, a gaping wound, two hundred
meters long and more than five hundred meters wide, was
still pouring into the abyss the last eddies of rock and
water.

A mound of heaped-up earth alone indicated the huge
tomb under which rested the crushed remains of the poor
American. They had to climb up again more sorrowful
than before they had gone down, and it was with tears
and farewell prayers, after having planted upon this
cyclopean grave a cross made of two pine branches, that
the travelers took leave of their companion, now effaced
from among the number of the living.

The dangerous and fatiguing march began again. But
this time, at least, the explorers had the satisfaction of
feeling that their trouble was not pure loss, and that they
were rising continually toward the peak.

They first crossed the bed of the little lake that
had been dried up by the cataclysm, then the site of
the glacier itself.

Singular to relate, the ground here was as dry as
though it had never borne a wet bed of ice. Stranger
still ! at this level of six thousand meters or there-

abouts, they did not experience the difficulty in breathing from which they had suffered at much lower
altitude.

The doctor explained this anomaly by the displacement of air that had been brought about by the
meteor. According to him, the phenomenon could not
have taken place without freeing a prodigious quantity
of all kinds of gases, bringing a fresh supply of oxygen
to the rarefied atmosphere.

He calculated that, unfortunately, this relative comfort would not last, and the ordinary density of high
altitudes would soon be resumed.

He was only too correct. After passing another
night under tents erected on a plateau seven thousand
meters in altitude, the travelers realized, from the un-
conquerable lassitude of their limbs, the congestion and
vertigo that they experienced, and the overwhelming
oppression for breath, that they had reached regions
fatal to every creature that breathes. The moment had
come to use the most extreme measures against that
greatest of all dangers, the danger of asphyxia.

Then they unpacked with the greatest care the
boxes that had been placed on the litters which the
travelers had transported sometimes on the backs of
mules, sometimes on oxen or sheep, and sometimes on
their own shoulders. Jean Merrien explained their nature
and the part they were to play.

"Here," said he, "is the most recent product of the
inventive genius of man. The copper helmets that we
are going to put on much resemble diving jackets. These
bags that you see contain little steel bottles and little
glass tubes which have in them bi-oxide of manganese,
and the water requisite to the production of oxygen.

Communication is established between the tubes and bottles by means of valve conduits, the cocks of which are ready to each one's hand. In the steel tubes is liquid oxygen, reduced to this state by twelve atmospheres' pressure. The valve projects the oxygen into the interior of the air chamber placed on the left side of the breathing tube in such a way that the gas does not reach the lips entirely pure, which fact regulates its expenditure and also spares the lungs which breathe it. At the same time, the bi-oxide of manganese, until the quantity inclosed in the bag is completely exhausted, permits the oxygen consumed to be replaced by a fresh supply.

"The apparatus that we have here contains the supply requisite for ten days' breathing. Let us then be sparing of it, and finish our ascent within that period."

THEY WERE LYING IN THE SHADE OF THE PINE TREES.

XIV.

FAILURE OF AIR.

BEFORE definitely setting out for the summits the travelers prepared their itinerary, and made all their arrangements with the scrupulous care demanded by prudence.

Their position determined, they decided that they were eighty-four degrees, twenty-six minutes, nineteen seconds, east longitude, and twenty-seven degrees, thirty-two minutes, fifty-four seconds, north latitude, to the east of the peak supposed to be Gaurisankar, to the southwest of Ni-la pass, to the northwest of Ouallangchun. A wide valley, opening at their right, showed them in the distance the course of the Arun, a gorge at their feet, and beyond that of the Barun.

The column at once divided itself into three groups. The first consisted of Merrien, Plumptre, and Miss Weldon ; the second of Dr. MacGregor, Goulab, and Morley ; the third, of Euzen Graec'h, Christi, Salem-Bun, and his Hindu comrade.

It was decided that the ascent should be accomplished under the following conditions:

The first group should begin to climb, taking the lead by an hour's march from the second, which should start according to the same regulations, after having received and transmitted to the third, the telegraphic advices sent back by the first. This communication was to be established by means of an electric wire inclosed in a cable, and surrounded by gutta-percha, about six kilometers in length, which the travelers unrolled behind them as they went.

The ascent became very laborious. At each step they were checked by unforeseen obstacles. They were obliged to climb perpendicular rocks, enter veritable plains of snow in which they sank up to the waist, avoid speaking aloud for fear of provoking a disturbance of air sufficient to bring on a landslide. The lack of provisions was greatly felt, and, whatever their energy might be, the travelers felt their strength was decreasing from hour to hour.

The morning of the twelfth day Merrien, on examining the needle, was able to estimate the altitude by aid of the barometric pressure.

"I believe," said he to Cicely and the major, "that we have reached the highest point that human foot has ever pressed."

"What is the height?" asked the officer.

"Seven thousand five hundred meters."

"That is an error: the Hindus of Gangotri affirm that the Pundit of Milam climbed to the summit of Ibi-Gamin, which is seven thousand nine hundred and thirty-two meters. So one could go higher than this."

"We will do so," said Miss Weldon resolutely.
They persevered two hundred meters further, but at
the cost of what suffering !

At the first halt that they made the travelers took
off their helmets in order to economize, so far as possible, their air reserve. No sooner was the mucous
membrane brought into contact with this extraordinarily
rarefied air than the characteristic troubles appeared with
their usual violence. A sharp cough racked the bron-
chial tubes, the blood spouted from Cicely's nostrils,
and the poor child fell nearly fainting on the ground.

Merrien and Plumptre hastened to replace the apparatus upon her head, but the incident had seriously
impressed them all. They asked themselves if it would
not be impossible henceforth to pursue an enterprise to
which nature opposed such insurmountable barriers
Furthermore, they could no longer subsist on biscuit, and
inflammation of the gums announced the danger of
scurvy.

It was indispensable that they should find fresh vegetables somewhere, and, if possible, a little meat, in order
to restore to the blood the red globules wasted by
anæmia.

Suddenly Plumptre, whose eyes swept the horizon of
the peaks, gesticulated with both arms, and without
waiting for the others, let himself slide rapidly down the
talus which they had just climbed. Without trying to
comprehend him, Merrien and Cicely Weldon followed
him upon his hazardous path. The next instant all three
had taken off their air helmets, and lying in the shade
of the pines and cypress clumps, breathed luxuriously the
air filled with resinous odors that played under the
dark branches.

"Truly, Plumptre," cried Merrien gayly, "this is a priceless discovery which you have just made."

"Zounds! my dear friend," replied the Scotchman, "we have just lost the seven hundred meters we had gained, but it was urgently necessary to refresh our lungs. We will make up our distance this evening or to-morrow morning. Meanwhile, let us notify our friends to join us as soon as possible."

They immediately established telegraphic communication, and minutely indicated to the rest of the company the road they must follow to reach the Valley of Health. For thus it was that the three in their enthusiasm styled the unknown Tempé which they had just discovered at an altitude that usually destroys all efforts at vegetation.

Two hours later the column was reunited, and a little joy played upon the faces clouded by suffering and privation.

"Sahib," said Salem-Bun to Plumptre, with a loud laugh, "would you feel disposed to eat a good curry?"

"Ten, if you say so, my boy," replied the officer, "if you have the wherewithal to make them."

"Very well," replied the baburji; "I have the powder, the rice, the wood, the matches, and casseroles, nothing is lacking but the meat."

"Naturally," grumbled the major, "and you think it is funny to serve up this joke to us in place of a dinner."

Goulab interrupted them. He had had time to explore a part of the valley; he returned, saying:

"Major, this gorge certainly contains game—game the easier to chase since it cannot escape from here, except to descend lower. All that is required is that it should not be too abundant or too large."

"We will take it as it comes, Goulab," said Merrien gayly. "Just now the important thing is to have fresh meat. What do you think, mademoiselle?"

"I am entirely of your opinion, M. Jean, and as I shall not require much urging to take my part of the feast, I ask to join in the hunt."

"Bravo! bravo!" applauded her companions, while Goulab, somewhat more serious, said in a low tone:

"Perhaps that is imprudent, mademoiselle. We do not know what animals we are going to run across."

"Very well, Goulab. It is as dangerous for you as for me," and then she added, somewhat maliciously, "perhaps you doubt my talent as a marksman?"

"Certainly not, Miss Cicely, I have much too keen a remembrance of your good shots to doubt your skill. Very well; since you are determined to be one of us, I ask nothing better, for my part; you will bring us good luck. Now," he added, turning to the hunters already grouped: "forward, march!"

"Forward, march!" repeated the young girl joyously, while she slung to her shoulder the fine carbine reserved for her personal use.

After having explored the neighborhood of the camp, which the Hindus had already set up and were scrupulously guarding, the little company descended somewhat lower toward the bottom of the valley. Not until then did they think of inspecting their surroundings. On every side there were only fresh verdure and straight and vigorous trees to be seen, while over their heads rose the gigantic summits that seemed to overarch the valley, their peaks uniting in a colossal dome.

At their feet sported a little stream, winding like a silver ribbon upon green velvet.

"Come, come, the chef awaits the meat, that he may serve us with a perfect curry, and meanwhile you stand there mute with ecstasy, like any poet. You poor amateurs!" cried MacGregor, in a pathetic tone.

A general laugh greeted this sensible reflection, and their slumbering appetites suddenly awoke with incredible ferocity.

They at once made the necessary arrangements, and after agreeing upon a cry for help, and a place of rendezvous, they disbanded in groups of three, just as they had done several days before, but for an entirely different purpose.

The hunters had been separated hardly a quarter of an hour when a guttural cry, prolonged, repeated by all the echoes of the mountain, reached the ears of Cicely Weldon, Merrien, and the major.

"Did you hear that, gentlemen?" asked Cicely, startled.

"Yes," responded Merrien, while Plumptre nodded in the affirmative. "It is the signal agreed upon, and if I can judge from the sound of the voice, it comes from Goulab."

So speaking, they turned back upon their path. They came out upon a sort of cross-road, where the other hunters were already assembled. Facing the group, by the side of a thicket from out of which he had been driven by Christi, a yak of the very finest species was pawing the earth with his cloven foot.

The yak of the Himálayas, or rather of Tibet, is a sort of long-haired ox, with great horns pointed at the ends. A prominent hump follows the line of the shoulders and gives this curious ruminant the appearance of great strength.

Suddenly the animal, lowering its head, butted with
its horns against the earth it had turned up, and then
straightening itself with an abrupt, proud movement, fixed
its eyes for a moment upon its enemies, and, without
further warning, charged upon them. The latter, who
had followed all its movements attentively, and divined
its intention, separated with one accord into two groups,
between which the yak passed like a streak of
lightning.

The animal, furious at having missed his aim, stopped
after a few paces, and turning square around, prepared to
renew his attack. Major Plumptre .had advanced in
front of his companions, in order to aim the moment
the assailant passed them again. But, surprised by the
yak's sudden stop, disturbed by its abrupt tacking, he
lost the impassibility and *sang-froid* that made him so
remarkable a marksman.

The shot was fired, but only wounded the animal,
who rushed upon him. He could not completely avoid
it, and being struck in the side by the yak's shoulder, he
was upset. The brute, forgetting the hunters, stopped as
soon as it could, carried away as it was by its impetus and the rather steep incline at this place. Just
as it prepared to return to a fresh charge upon the
unfortunate Englishman, a report rang out.

The wild ox fell, biting the dust with its smoking
muzzle. The animal was not dead ; Cicely's ball, for it
was she who had fired, had struck the center of the knee
with perfect accuracy, breaking the cap. But before anyone had budged, except the major, who had risen and
shaken the earth from his clothing with scrupulous
care, Miss Weldon had fired a second time, and struck
the animal just at the shoulder-joint. A quiver ran

THE YAK PASSED LIKE A STREAK OF LIGHT.

through its entire frame, and it moved no more. Then they vied with each other in complimenting the young American. Major Plumptre came forward, much moved, and, bowing before Cicely, he said :

"I owe my life to you, Miss Cicely. I shall never forget it."

"Major, one good turn deserves another. You have already saved mine. Henceforth we are quits."

And turning to Goulab, she added laughingly :

"Do you always find, shikari, that it is imprudent to take me along ? "

"Did I not say also that you brought us good luck ? " the Hindu replied gravely.

"We now have a choice morsel, thanks to Miss Cicely. We had better profit by it at once. We must notify Salem-Bun," cried MacGregor, who had not been made oblivious to his hunger by these incidents.

"I will go," said Christi. And in less than a moment he had climbed the slope.

Some moments later he reappeared, accompanied by the two Hindus, who set to work to cut up the prey with the utmost possible care.

Choice bits are not lacking in the yak. It is, in fact, game of the first quality. whose extraordinarily savory flesh partakes both of the nature of butcher's meat and of venison. Independently of the parts that one usually prefers in its European cousin, the yak furnishes cuts peculiar to itself. Such are the hump, which the gourmets of India and Nepál consider fit for a king, and the tail, which is prepared with sauces, and in ragoûts of all kinds.

The baburdji and his assistant declared that they had never been at such a feast before, and they implored Miss Weldon to be henceforth purveyor for their larder.

Put into good humor by this success, which insured the little company supplies for some time to come, the young girl proposed a fresh "battue" in the thickets of the valley.

"Miss," said Goulab, smiling, "although I hold a good enough rank among hunters, I am a little humiliated not to have better deserved, thus far, my title of shikári. If you wish, I will try to restore my good name, for I have just now seen numerous traces of four-footed and feathered game. It is only a pity that none of us thought of bringing a dog. It would have been a great aid to us in pointing for rabbits and pheasants. But since we have none we will try to do without one."

"I am with you, Goulab," cried the indefatigable major, who never wanted to be left out of any sport.

"And I also," added the Breton. and Morley the American, who were anxious to hear the rifle's voice.

Meanwhile Cicely, Merrien, and the doctor had returned to the camp, where they found the little Madrasi occupied with gathering wood for the dinner.

Salem-Bun had already cut a beefsteak big enough to feed a caravan four times the size of theirs. and put the rest of the meat in pickle in the salted oil in order to have it in readiness for future repasts.

The young girl and her two companions seated themselves under the shade of a little pine wood, and commenced to indulge in all sorts of fancies.

"Truly," cried the enthusiastic Cicely, "this valley is an Eden. The temperature that reigns here is perpetual spring, and just now, on the banks of the stream, I noticed magnificent trees like those of the temperate zones, such as poplars, beeches, the ash, the chestnut, plane and maple trees. I am not even certain that I did not see oaks."

"It would have been nothing astonishing if you had seen them," said MacGregor. "The Himálaya region, as I believe I have already told you, is a world apart, which possesses all the zones and all the latitudes of the globe. The Taráï has given us the climate of the tropics, and we have recently been able, and to-morrow shall be still better able, to judge of the tremendous cold of the peaks."

"But, doctor," resumed Miss Weldon, "how do you explain the abnormal temperature of this valley at this altitude?"

"I can't more than half explain it, and I confess to not being entirely satisfied with even that explanation. Poor as it is, it may nevertheless be right, but we have neither the means nor the leisure to verify it."

"Speak it out, doctor," insisted Merrien, who was greatly interested in the physician's words.

"Such as it is, my theory is justifiable. I imagine that we must face the south, and we may be certain in that particular when the twilight shows us in which direction the shadows fall: for I fancy that here we shall be free from those optical illusions that, when we were up above, showed us the sun continually in the same place. We face the south, then, and in all probability the mountain mass will be opened its entire length by a ladder of valleys which receive the wind from the same direction as ourselves. Now, this wind, observe, comes to us directly from Bengal, over the Sunderbunds, Calcutta, Dárjiling, etc. It thus brings us both humidity

and warmth, seeds from the lowlands and the fertile
growth of the marshes. It is in this way that I explain
the presence of this paradise."

"Nothing could be more logical than this hypothesis, doctor," said Jean Merrien, "and as for me I find
it quite sufficient."

"There is, however, a 'but.' Damp winds are usually very low ones. Now for the south winds to attain
such an altitude, there ought to be, it seems to me,
at the other end of the valley, a sort of flue."

"That is what we must verify."

Just then a succession of reports, borne upon the
echoes of the valley, interrupted their conversation.

"Goulab and Plumptre are having their heart's desire," said Cicely Weldon gayly. "We shall soon know
if they have been lucky."

They knew in half an hour, the friends returning with
that air of proud beatitude that characterizes triumphant
hunters. Plumptre brought back three pheasants and
four hares ; Goulab, six partridges, two pheasants, and two
grouse of the *couroucou* family. Euzen Graec'h, the
least fortunate of all, had, nevertheless, brought down his
three hares. In the presence of these additional supplies,
the enthusiasm of the company knew no bounds.

"Decidedly," said the doctor, "this place is good,
and we might do as did the Apostles on the day of
the Transfiguration—erect here our tents. Suppose we
stop our ascent here ? Aren't we on Gaurisankar, after all ?"

"Suppose, then, that we found a colony," joked Merrien. "At least we shall be sure of having no intrusive neighbors."

Goulab shook his head, and when asked the meaning
of that doubting gesture, he replied :

"Sahibs, nothing could be less certain than your
security in this place. I have, in fact, discovered proof
that this valley is known to travelers. It furnishes one
of the passages between the Ouallangchun pass and that
of Ni-la, as is demonstrated by the existence of a path
over the nearest buttress."

He pointed to the eastern crest overhanging the
valley.

"That absolutely disenchants me!" declared Miss
Weldon, with a gesture of irritation. "Is there not a
corner of the globe that has not been profaned by
man?"

Merrien commenced to laugh at this, and gayly
bantered the young girl.

"What would you say, mademoiselle, if you should
chance to hear that remark from the lips of the man
who shall climb Gaurisankar after us?"

"I should say that he was right, my dear sir,"
replied Cicely, who had the courage of her convictions.

The day ended in the midst of a multiplicity of occu-
pations. The dinner, carefully prepared by Salem-Bun,
was found delicious. It was also plentiful.

Then, as the Hindu cook knew his art to its founda-
tion, having added to his natural gifts the education he
had received from the divers English masters whom he
had served, he was able to lay aside important stores of
cold meat for the rest of the trip.

The next morning they had the satisfaction at last
of seeing the sun rise normally, and they were able
by its light to explore the depths of the valley. The
fog which lay like a fleece over the levels did not
prevent the travelers from sweeping the landscape with
their glance. But they only commenced to enjoy a

comprehensive view after having climbed the opposite ledge. In order better to arrange the plan of their route, they decided that Goulab, Plumptre, and the doctor should follow the path of the caravans, while the rest of the company should go up the valley as far as the rocky mass which made of it a sort of *impasse*.

The result of this strategy was to bring them all to a point of junction forming a terrace. A fresh wall, analogous to those that they had so frequently encountered, closed all egress toward the center of the mountain.

"There is no further doubt of it," cried Merrien, striking the wall with the end of his iron staff. "The peak is concealed there behind this rampart."

"Then we shall not see it," declared MacGregor, in discouragement.

"We shall see it!" exclaimed the Frenchman, with emphasis. "I have vowed to scale Gaurisankar: I shall do so."

"Have you wings?" asked the doctor mockingly.

"No, but I have my hands, my spurs, and my ropes. Besides, at first sight, this wall does not appear to me to be more than one hundred meters high, and if, instead of descending into the valley we had continued our route along the ledge, we should certainly have come out at this terrace."

A very animated discussion then ensued between the different members of the column. MacGregor, for the first time, expressed the opinion that they already had done enough, that to attempt new adventures would be to tempt Providence. He supported this sentiment with very conclusive reasons.

"My dear Merrien," he said, "it is folly. You have

already satisfied yourself as to the impossibility of approaching the highest levels without the aid of our tubes of oxygen. Even here it has taken a veritable caprice of nature to inclose in this fissure of the mountain mass air that can be breathed. I cannot otherwise explain this anomaly. How do you hope to overcome the obstacles born of the interdict of creation itself?"

"Doctor," replied Merrien, "if I only wished to do what everyone can do, I should not have come as far as Gaurísankar."

It was of no use for MacGregor to say anything; he vainly produced his best arguments one after another. Jean Merrien was intractable, and such was the force of his resolution that he won over Plumptre and Cicely Weldon. Each of these declared that nothing should be conceded to a rival.

"Where France goes, there can England go!" cried the Englishman, with spirit.

"And young America will not be behind them!" exclaimed Miss Weldon with the same enthusiasm. They were thus far in the debate, when they saw Christi running rapidly, making almost incomprehensible signs.

When the little Madrasi, breathless with his run, had at last recovered sufficient calm, he explained himself. He had just discovered, in turning the wall, an excavation from which escaped boiling water and vapor, the sulphurous odor of which indicated the presence of a mineral spring. Guided by him the explorers entered a sort of tunnel, the vault of which, at first low-arched, rose into a sort of half-circular hall, terminated by a narrow flue through which the clear blue sky could be seen.

"This conduit must come out upon the upper

platform," said Merrien. "Perhaps we might get out this way and reach it?"

The hypothesis was admissible. It was yet to be verified.

In order not to involve the entire company in this difficult passage, they made an examination of it, and as the temperature of the crypt, in spite of the vapor that filled it, was not insupportable, the doctor, Goulab, and their companions entered it at the furthest possible distance from the hot spring. If necessary, should the heat become too great for them, they would only have to regain the cool grassy slopes of the valley itself.

The three who were going to attempt this ascent, the most difficult that they had yet undertaken, set out with the assistance nature had provided, aided by their own industry.

In the twinkling of an eye hooks and ropes were ready. Euzen Graec'h and Merrien commenced to climb the first loose rocks.

THE COMPANIONS EMERGED, ONE AFTER THE OTHER.

XV.

THE CRATER.

IT was a veritable chimney, caused by the gases of the earth piercing through the enormous rock which rose perpendicularly from the vault of the grotto to the level of the open air a hundred meters higher up, so that Merrien said laughingly to his companions:

"We are to fill the position of chimney sweeps, and we must climb like them. I hope that we shall find foothold." This mode of ascent, though offering considerable difficulties to an ordinary man, was of truly elementary simplicity for the gymnasts accustomed to that sort of exercise.

It was a question of raising one's self after the manner of the little Savoyards, bringing hands and feet, back and knees to one's aid wherever the narrow opening would permit such gymnastics. But as nothing could be more irregular than this tubular conduit, as it now contracted, now widened ; it presented enormous variations in diameter, and other methods were necessary to the overcoming of these formidable difficulties, in order to avoid a fatal fall.

Merrien was provided with several hooks and a hammer. Thé operation, slow as it was difficult, consisted in driving these hooks one after another in the rocky wall, and mounting by their aid, adding one more at each step. Relieved by the Breton and the major in turn, the Frenchman finished this arduous task in less than an hour. And in order to spare the others the fatigue of continually mounting and descending, they slipped a cord through the hooks thus planted, and by the aid of this cord raised the necessary materials after the fashion of masons and painters upon their scaffoldings.

By good luck the wall, in spite of its inequality, was made of a homogeneous limestone, which retained the iron once driven into it. They thus had no breaks to fear, no giving way under the weight of the heavy bodies that would be suspended from the hooks.

These were of very superior temper, and could be firmly inserted in the stone which formed the circumference of the flue. At the end of the seventieth, Merrien, entirely satisfied as to the resistance of the steel and the solidity of the wall, cried from above to his companions that they might in their turn commence the ascent.

He had already reached a sort of entablature forming a cornice, when they perceived that from this cornice started a second flue, cut through obliquely ; the gentle slope of which was made still easier by the presence

of regular steps of rock, placed there by a caprice of
nature.   It might be said that some prehistoric giant
had made this cavern his chosen retreat, and had cut this
strange subterranean stairway for his own use.   Positive,
now, of being able to reach the upper level, the young
man renewed his invitation to his friends to join him, and
extended to them a rope previously fastened to the end
hook, which he took pains to fasten upon the little ledge
that he had reached.

Miss Weldon was the first to venture upon the perilous ladder.

The brave young girl had not been boasting when, at
Srinagar, she had enumerated her previous exploits on the
banks of Niagara and the Zambesi.   Supple and vigorous, she gave proof of extraordinary boldness and strength
in hanging to the floating balustrade furnished by the
rope, and ten minutes later she was by Merrien's side,
followed almost immediately by Plumptre.

The good major, although he was the third to arrive, was proud of the *tour de force* that he had just
accomplished.

The cry that burst spontaneously from his lips was
an altogether surprising bit of homage from an Englishman.

" My dear Merrien, the qualities of your race are justly
boasted of.   Only a Frenchman can set other peoples the
example of conceiving such extravagant feats, and of
carrying them out."

To which the Frenchman replied with gay courtesy :

"Bah, my dear major ! do not congratulate me.
There is every reason to suppose that, if I had had no
competitors, I should not have done what I have done.
But do not let us delay for compliments," he added.

"We shall have time enough to congratulate each other when we come down from Gaurisankar." And all three, fired with fresh enthusiasm, commenced to climb the Cyclopean stairway.

Merrrien was again the first to reach the upper platform. A great cry of joy burst from his lips, followed immediately by a clapping of hands from Cicely, and the enthusiastic hurrahs of the Scotchman. Certainly it had never before been given to human eye to behold so marvelous a spectacle.

The three travelers found themselves on the brink of a gigantic pit, and the panorama which stretched before them embraced an area as great as a third of all France.

The great circular platform surrounded Chingo-pa-mari like a collar, the snowy brow of the mountain rising as much as fifteen hundred meters above the level at which the travelers had arrived.

Below them, as far as the eye could reach, the entire mass of the Máyanama accented itself like a map in relief, and the Himálaya range with its imposing strata, its powerful buttresses, the thousand folds of its arms, extended in all directions before their vision. To the north the continuation of the masses, connected by their passes, maintained an abrupt slope toward the banks of a stream that could be seen shining like a silver ribbon in the narrow Tingri Máidan plain, the stream called the Tingri-Chu. Beyond, the great line of the Trans-Himálaya rivaled the true Himálaya in elevation, and revealed peaks of prodigious height that human activity has never been able to approach. To the east Kinchinjinga, the rival of Everest, seemed close at hand, and its well-defined contours, its powerfully accented outlines, made it appear like an isolated pyramid, while after it came the mighty masses of the Singālilā, Gnarim, and Doukiah Mountains. To the westward rose the succession of heights already scaled by the column—the Thiang-Loang pass, the Gossainthan mass—and away in the background, sparkling through the violet mists, was that Dhaulāgíri that the travelers had vainly tried to climb. Finally, to the southward unfurled the valley of Arun, and the eye could easily follow, with a sense of color perspective, the marvelous gradation of gorges of which the valley they had reached the day before was only the highest step.

The three travelers paused, filled with a sentiment of pious admiration. Cicely Weldon in particular manifested profound emotion.

"Heavens! how beautiful it is!" she exclaimed at intervals.

"Do you regret the ascent, major?" asked Merrien, laughing.

"No, by Jove!" replied the officer, "and I understand why nature should put a high price upon such scenes."

They could not satisfy their gaze, and words failed them to interpret the multitudinous sentiments that agitated them.

"If we could only get our comrades thus far? Eh! What do you think, Plumptre?"

"I think," replied the Scotchman, "that we ought at least to let them know about it. They will come then, if they wish to."

Merrien tore a leaf from his notebook, scribbled some lines upon it, folded this brief epistle in a square of paper, which he fastened to a pebble; then leaning over the edge of the flue, he dropped the stone. This fell

with a noise comparable to that of a succession of fire-
works, exploding one after the other, and the Frenchman
had the satisfaction of seeing it picked up by their
comrades, who ran up, attracted by the noise.

The proposition must have given rise to some discussion, for the echoes of the flue, acting as a means of
communication, brought some of the fragments of conversation to Merrien's ears, some shreds of sentences
that had to be pieced together to make sense. Jean
Merrien interpreted them to his friends.

"There will certainly not be more than three who will
make the ascent : the doctor, Goulab, and Euzen. Salem-
Bun prefers to remain below. Wide horizons do not
tempt him. He is decidedly a *pot-au-feu* man."

This joke had no further success than to elicit from
Miss Weldon the following scathing remark :

"Do not mock, M. Merrien ; he has chosen the
better part. You may soon have occasion to regret that
you did not remain with him."

At this moment the expected comrades emerged one
after the other from the oblique conduit, and the first
comers received them with lively congratulations. The
doctor, after vigorously rubbing his legs and back, exclaimed :

"What a road, my friends, what a road! It is true
that, when one is fairly on the ledge, one doesn't lack for
air."

"Humph!" sneered Plumptre, "we had better not
flatter ourselves too soon. We have no assurance that
we shall long possess that happiness."

"What do you mean, major?" they all asked,
alarmed by this speech.

"I mean that it would be very possible to have

the counterpart of the avalanche here. But in place of
being too cold, and smothered with snow, we shall
be too hot, perhaps. Either I am much mistaken or
we are now over the mouth of a gigantic crater,
forming a circle about the principal peak. You can further assure yourselves of the truth of this by your own
examination."

So speaking, the officer pointed to a kind of basin
hollowed out upon the other side of the rim of this
prodigious pit. They all concentrated their attention
upon it, and at once shared the officer's apprehensions.

There was about a mile between where the travelers stood and the snow-clad rocks which served as a
support to the central peak. By a marvelous effort of
Plutonic forces, these rocks rested one on top of the
other after the fashion of an enormous staircase, and
it was easy to see that these Titanic steps rendered
it possible to climb up to the upper cone.

Merrien kept silence before this picture. As to Cicely
Weldon, she could not repress a picturesque exclamation :

"Truly, might it not be said that God had transported
the materials of the Tower of Babel to this mountain?"

This comparison expressed exactly the impression
made by this phenomenon of the grouping of the
rocks.

The granite blocks had been placed there not in the
pell-mell chaos of an upheaval, but with astonishing
symmetry, with artistic proportions and lines giving them
the aspect of a ladder affording access to higher and
higher levels.

The snow heaped up upon their surfaces, and upon

their *arêtes*, concealed the joints and the lines of division of this unparalleled scaffolding. Exposed to the south winds, this face of the pyramid, in spite of its great height, had felt the beneficent effects of the warmth ; and the continuous action of the solar rays, when the glacial north winds did not blow from the direction of Tibet, had sufficed to maintain at this point a constant evaporation, which was still another argument in favor of Dr. Mac-Gregor's hypothesis. The abnormal vegetation of this slope was thus explained, as well as the presence of an atmosphere dense enough to be easily breathed.

But another cause doubtless intervened to increase the production of oxygen. By stooping, the travelers were able to gather up minerals of argentiferous lead that were scattered in innumerable beds. Manganese was there, a product of the soil, and the heat, arising from invisible chemical action upon the metal, restored to the air the gases necessary to combustion and to life. All these things were in themselves very reassuring. Other things it is true, offered menacing warnings.

The basin was of a hundred meters' continuous depth, which, spread over an extent of less than a mile, gave only a very gentle, hardly perceptible slope. On observation, the bottom of it seemed to be covered with a short growth, of such perfect homogeneity that it resembled an immense velvet carpet—passing through the greatest variation of tint, from apple green to yellowish white, with a light undulating movement something like the soft tremors that, under the summer breezes, curve and lift the downy ends of the greensward on carefully weeded and mown lawns.

"Singular, certainly !" said MacGregor. "The bottom of this circular valley must be covered with mosses and

rare lichens. I shall not go away from this place without
largely increasing my plant collection."

Goulab, who had taken some steps into the interior
of the crater, heard these words, and responded ironically :

"I hardly think, doctor, that that moss will enrich
your collection, for the excellent reason that it will go
off in smoke."

"Come, now !" retorted the physician. "You are
making fun of me, Goulab ?"

"I am not making fun," replied the shikári gravely,
"and if you care to follow my example, you will arrive at the same conclusion, sahib."

He stretched out his hands to the doctor. The bronzed
skin was covered with a yellowish coating, discolored in
the way that the petals of flowers are when exposed
to the blue flame of a chemical match. On the sleeves
of the Hindu's white garment, on his red leather boots,
and his wide linen pajama, there had been deposited in
thin, evenly staining layers an extremely fine dust, oily
to the touch and giving out a characteristic odor.
There was no longer room for doubt.

"Sulphur !" cried the doctor. "What we have taken
for moss is only solid sulphuric acid ; what we have
seen undulating are sulphuric vapors exhaled by the
earth. We are standing on a *solfatara.*"

He spoke the truth.

That whole immense basin, lying like a collar around
the central peak, was nothing but an upturned *prouvette,*
at the bottom of which great natural analyses were
elaborated. Thence came that escape of deleterious gas
with which was, doubtless, mingled a large amount of
carbonic acid ; thence also came the extraordinary heat

GOULAB STRETCHED OUT HIS HANDS TO THE DOCTOR.

which at seven thousand meters' altitude preserved the
valley from glacial influences.

"Well," said Merrien, "we must once more acknowledge that God is the greatest of scientists. I do not know
of any inventor who has ever conceived the idea or
draughted the plan of an air stove of such dimensions."

They had now all gathered together at the edge of
the pit. They deliberated as to what they should do.
It was certain that if there should be nothing but a
simple escape of vapors, these, by reason of their
specific gravity, would not rise very high, and consequently would hardly inconvenience the travelers. But
if the enormous mass of rock were nothing but a
prodigious laboratory, if its sides concealed some supernatural alembic, was it not to be feared that the
compressed gases might, with tremendous force, break
through suddenly, which would mean overwhelming asphyxia for the unfortunates, whether it proceeded from
instantaneous absorption of oxygen by the greedy
metalloids, or was the result of a general poisoning of
the atmosphere? The prospect was not reassuring.

"The wisest way is to beat a retreat," said the
doctor, "and regain the crypt, and from there the
valley."

"And the peak is there, there—under our hand!"
. groaned Merrien, tearing his hair.

Suddenly seized with a violent resolution, he
cried:

"No matter! Whatever happens, it shall not be said
that I have retreated; that I have missed my goal by
a mile."

And before they could restrain him, the bold Frenchman had commenced to run down into the basin. Miss

Weldon and the major rushed after him, carried away
by the same fervor, spurred on by the spirit of emulation.

The doctor stood in astonishment upon the brink.
He called loudly after them, believing it to be only a
joke. But they continued to run. And those who remained on the edge of the pit could see with amazement
the gases displaced by their running visibly increase,
rise about the three rash creatures, envelop them up to
the knees and then to the body. Finally, when they
had reached the base of the central rocks, the blue and
yellow smoke was floating as high as their arm-pits.

Merrien turned, and cried in a voice which took on
frightful sonority from the mountain echoes :

"Go down again, doctor ; go down again ! We are
safe. We will rejoin you to-morrow."

It was the only thing to do. Heart breaking as it was
to him, the physician gathered his people together, called
the Breton, who had wanted to take his turn in crossing the basin, but who had faltered at the first contact
with the pestilential miasma ; and they all re-entered the
path through the flue to the grotto.

Jean Merrien and his two companions had already
climbed the lowest grades of the peak.

"Mademoiselle," he cried, "and you also, major, here
we are at the last stage of the journey. Henceforth we
are each for himself, save in the case of danger for one or
the other of us. The question now is, which will be the
first to arrive."

And he, passing ahead of his friends, leaped from
grade to grade the sooner to reach the top. Below him
the major had found a more practicable path than that
which Cicely Weldon was following ; the young girl
seemed distraught. Suddenly Merrien stopped.

In front of him the superposed terraces were cut across by a glacier some sixty meters in breadth. It was necessary, to cross it, to follow the Cyclopean strata by which the giant stairway was prolonged.

But this was not the obstacle that had interrupted the ascent of the invincible champion. He felt the air to breathe failing him. Vertigo seized him. Everything under his feet swam around him. He could not mistake the cause of this difficulty. It was nature itself which pronounced the interdict, which cried to the desecraters in the voice of command :

"Thou shalt go no further!"

Without losing a second the young man unhooked the helmet that hung upon his back, fastened it upon his head, and put it into communication with the reservoir of oxygen. Then, seizing his staff, he ventured a couple of steps upon the blue and virgin ice.

But short as the pause had been, it had given Plumptre a chance to catch up to his rival. Warned by this example, the Scotchman had already put on his breathing apparatus. Cicely came third, her head appeared over the edge of the grade ; she had also made up the lost time.

Crossing the glacier might offer dangerous surprises. Merrien therefore retraced his steps to meet his fellow-travelers. He expressed his idea by means of gestures ; they approved it.

Tying together the ropes that they carried at their belts, they bound themselves one to another, and pursued the ascent in single file.

At the end of a few steps, they were assured of the glacier's resistance.

This rested on the hard rock, between two firm walls.

If it concealed crevasses, they could not be very deep ones.

The trip was accomplished without great peril, but not without falls and slips that a steeper slope would have rendered fatal.

Arrived at the opposite brink of the fissure, and suffering no longer from lack of air, the three courageous companions recommenced the ascent of the Cyclopean ladder.

It brought them to a sharp peak terminating in a plateau of forty or fifty square meters. Merrien investigated the barometer. It marked an altitude of eight thousand and six meters, the pressure not surpassing seven hundred and thirty-five millimeters. At their left the summit of Gaurisankar shot up solitary and alone from this point, offering neither path nor steps. They were within eight hundred and fifty meters of the central peak. But a hundred feet more permitted the travelers to command a view of the peak on which they paused. It is true that, in order to climb to this furthest point, it was necessary to employ all the resources of art which the gymnasium puts at the disposition of a naturally vigorous man.

Merrien did not hesitate. With the aid of hands and feet over this flying surface, stripped of everything that could offer a hold, over stones that gave way and rolled from under the feet, he succeeded, bleeding and bruised, after incredible efforts in reaching the top.

Then, standing erect upon a pedestal hardly three square meters in area, on the highest point of the globe that human foot had ever trod, he unfurled the French colors at the end of his iron staff, and this improvised flag waved in the mountain breeze, or, to speak more truly, hung almost inert, hardly stirred by the exhausted breath of this exhausted atmosphere.

The traveler had reason to be proud. He had accomplished what no other had accomplished before him. He had climbed three thousand meters higher than Bailey, than Montgomery, than the Schlaginweit brothers ; than Reuillier, Cunningham, Moorcroft, Webb, Vigne, Johnson, Kooker, and many others ; he had seen—seen with his own eyes—the kernel of that Máyanama chain that the bandits themselves had not been able to discover.

And the panorama at that moment before his eyes was the most marvelous in the world, rendered yet more strange by the extraordinary phenomenon that took place at his feet.

The gas which they had just now taken for a carpet of moss, which they had seen increase and rise in clouds about them, was actually in full ebullition. No other word, indeed, could so well render the expanding of the sulphurous and carbonic vapors of the crater. The immense basin resembled those flanged coffee-pots in which the fragrant drink is brewed by the heat of the alcohol lighted around it. It was full of blue and green smoke, across which lines of very pale flame occasionally ran. Suddenly the Frenchman was seized with a fear. Forgetting the magic spectacle, abandoning his improvised standard upon the peak which Major Plumptre was climbing in his turn, he let himself slide or rather fall a dozen meters upon the edge of a rock overhanging the abyss. He had just perceived Cicely Weldon prostrate upon that rock, and giving no sign of life. Torn and bleeding, Merrien flung himself to his companion's aid, and raised her with anguish.

He knew then what had happened. The young American, overcome by vertigo perhaps, or slipping on the round stones of the slope, had met with a terrible fall. It was by a miracle that her clothing caught on the *arête* of the gulf, and kept her from crushing herself some hundred meters further down against the granite steps of the Cyclopean stairway. The shock alone would have sufficed to explain her swoon. But this swoon had another cause. In her fall the young girl had struck against the projections of the rock. Her head had hit against a sharp point which had partly broken the brass helmet, and torn the india-rubber tube that served for the inhalation of the oxygen.

Jean Merrien came just in time ; an instant later, and he would have found only a corpse : Cicely Weldon would have died from lack of air to breathe.

Without losing an instant, at the peril of his own life, the young man unfastened the straps that fixed the helmet upon Miss Weldon's shoulders, and adjusted his own there instead.

Then taking the torn tube between his teeth, he set about repairing the damage so far as was possible.

Coming to her senses, Cicely appreciated the danger she had run. But at the same time realizing her companion's peril, she wished to return to him the apparatus of which he had deprived himself for her sake. There was a struggle of generosity between the two young people.

Finally Merrien made the brave creature understand that this conflict of devotion would be injurious to them both. She then resigned herself to keeping her metal head-dress, and aided the Frenchman as well as she could in repairing the broken helmet and readjusting the ruptured india-rubber tube.   Their efforts, fortunately, were crowned with success, and Merrien, who was bleeding at every pore, could at last resume his life-preserving mask, mended and botched though it were.

THE FLAME ROSE, CLEAR AND BRIGHT.

XVI.

RIVALRY BETWEEN HEROES.

THE dangers that confront mountain explorers are
formidable ones, and the joys of triumph must needs
be great to compensate for the anxieties with which mind
and heart are constantly oppressed.

In the midst of these occurrences night came on.
The three friends had enjoyed a sunset that equaled the
dawn in splendor. They had been obliged to descend
to the lower grade of the peak, in anticipation of the
advancing night. Already the cold was increasing in
severity, and the travelers knew that at such an altitude it might easily become fatal. The necessity of
fortifying themselves against its attacks was therefore
urgent, all the more that they had no heat other than
that of the body to hope for, and the rarefaction of
the air would not permit a fire to be started on these
barren crests.

What, then, was Plumptre's astonishment, when, mchanically striking a match, he saw the flame rise bright and clear among the shadows. The Himàlaya had given them one more of those surprises which had marked each stage of their ascent. For the match to burn thus freely, there must of necessity be some respirable air upon the peak.

In the twinkling of an eye Merrien had unfastened the copper helmet, an example that his companions hastened to follow ; and after taking a long breath of the cool, delicious evening air, all three exchanged their impressions on the singularity of the phenomenon.

"Truly," said Cicely, "we go from marvel to marvel. It is now certain that the Himàlayas resemble no other mountains. All scientists agree in stating that after passing seven thousand meters' altitude, life on the peaks is an impossibility."

"Doubtless," affirmed Merrien, "and the scientists are right. It is an absolute rule. But every rule has its exceptions. It is a possibility ; and what makes it possible for us is that a local elaboration of gas renews the oxygen in the air over a limited space, and prevents its waste in the ambient layers. If the doctor were here, he could explain it to us better."

"We have no need of the doctor to see that you must be right, my dear Merrien," said Plumptre. "We must be in the neighborhood of a great natural pot bubbling under its cover, the steam of which forms a sort of cylindrical tube which preserves us from the surrounding rarefaction. That is my explanation, and I take it to be clear and luminous."

The officer laughed as he spoke, pointing to a sort of milky mist which formed a cylinder about the platform,

like a vast well at the opening of which a round dark
blue spot, picked out with stars, testified to the presence of the firmament.

"Parbleu!" cried the Frenchman gayly, "you are
right, my dear Plumptre; we are on a boiler. It is to be
hoped now that this boiler has safety valves, and will
not explode under our feet." He ran to the edge of
the platform and called loudly to his friends:

"Oh!" said the major, who had most decidedly a gift
for exact metaphors. "Sugar in a punch!"

The sight was at once magnificent and terrifying.
Six hundred meters below them the entire basin was
in flames. The flames, visibly fed by a subterranean
reservoir, rose in delicate spirals to a height of two
hundred or three hundred feet, licking the sides of the
peak with their bluish tongues, and sending their strange
light, which had so struck Plumptre, into the cloud of
smoke.

The snow of the rocks melted at their contact, but
the water, vaporizing immediately, gave to the atmosphere its proper proportion of oxygen. Enormous
paleocrystic blocks were worn away on the upper
strata, and from this perpetual exchange of forces arose
the soft humid temperature by which the travelers were
blessed on their fairy observatory.

Meanwhile they had returned to the center of the
platform and kept silence for a long time, not daring
to communicate their fears to each other. Merrien spoke
first:

"The picture is magnificent," he said, "but it is
not reassuring. I no longer fear an explosion, to tell
the truth; but I dread now one of two equally serious
calamities."

"Explain yourself?" asked the major and Miss Weldon simultaneously.

"Alas!" said Merrien sadly, "one hypothesis is as good as the other: either the phenomenon will quickly come to an end, and without taking into account the lack of air which will again distress us, we shall suffer from terrible cold without the shadow of a hope of succor; or else it will be prolonged, and then we may die of hunger on the summit, for we cannot think for a moment of going down again into that Gehenna."

Silence fell upon the group again more heavily than ever, for everyone comprehended that the situation was critical.

"At least," said the Scotchman, with a nervous gayety, "we shall have the satisfaction of being present at an incomparable sunrise."

"Meanwhile," replied Merrien, "we shall do wisely to utilize such hours of respite as are granted us. Sleep will do us much good, and, if the volcano does break out, we shall be spared the pangs of death."

The advice was approved. They unpacked their knapsacks, wrapped themselves in blankets, and, a little later, were sleeping with their hands gripping the hard and naked rock, protected by the wall of vapor that enveloped them. It might have been three in the morning when they were wakened by the severe cold.

The first of Merrien's hypotheses was realized. The column of mist had been dissipated. The stars were shining in the fathomless depths of the still dusky heavens.

On the southeastern horizon, behind the enormous screen of Kinchinjinga, a growing spot of white announced the distant daybreak.

" B-r-r !" said Cicely, shivering. "This cold is mortal ! What will become of us ?"

Merrien had already consulted the thermometer. The temperature was falling with frightful rapidity. The column of mercury descended moment by moment; it presently indicated twenty-six degrees below zero.

At the same time oppression and vertigo exercised their demoralizing influence. They were obliged to don their metal helmets in haste.

"We must descend at once," said Plumptre.

This was the last word spoken. And as the two men beheld their young companion almost sinking under the intolerable cold, a common impulse of devotion sent them toward her. Merrien reached her first, and threw his cloak over Cicely's shoulders. She was trembling, and unable to support herself.

In every ascent, the dangers multiply in the descent. It seems as though the guardian spirits of these summits, forced from their seclusion, wished to take a malicious revenge, and, ashamed of having been unable to guard the places committed to their care, determine to multiply obstacles and dangers in the pathway of their conquerors.

The three daring pioneers had been two hours in climbing the peak. It took four hours for them to reach, through a thousand difficulties, the rocks at the base, and the first grade of the basin.

Ten times Merrien and Plumptre were obliged to go to the aid of the young American. The poor child had too greatly presumed upon her strength. At last she swooned, and the two friends, filled with anxiety, were obliged to carry their helpless companion across the low ground already filled with rising vapor. On the margin Cicely revived for a moment, and as the use of the breathing tube was no longer indispensable, she could respond to the eager questions of her friends.

Upon seeing the anxiety betrayed in their faces she gave a pale smile, and stretched out her hands to them.

"Oh, my friends!" she said, in a voice full of emotion, "how can I ever express my gratitude to you?"

"By never speaking of it," said the major gayly. "Now that you are out of danger we are satisfied. But are you strong enough to finish the descent by way of the flue?"

Cicely tried to rise. Her strength failed, and a fresh attack of faintness caused her to drop back into the arms of her alarmed companions.

What were they going to do? What could they do before such a grave complication?

While they had only to descend the rocky steps, or cross the glaciers or deep valleys, it had been possible for them to carry their young companion, relieving each other and allowing themselves necessary periods of rest; this task, fatiguing though it was, was not overpowering. But now the difficulty changed its aspect. It became in a way insurmountable.

How could they indeed try to carry the young girl through this narrow passage, so contracted, during a portion of its length, that there was only room for one person to go through? Doubtless the oblique neck of the flue would render it possible for the travelers to enter the crypt. But that was only the first step. How could they afterward descend the vertical flue for a distance of fifty or sixty meters?

For a moment the two men faltered under the dis-

couraging circumstances. Tears rose to their eyes and
ran down their cheeks. Were they then condemned to
die upon that inaccessible platform, forsaken by God and
man ?

Fortunately this failure of energy was of short duration. Merrien rose and ran to the orifice of the first
flue.

He lay on the ground and called with all his strength ;
but, strange to say, instead of noisily vibrating in the interior of the narrow conduit, his voice was driven back
as if by a vast current of air.

Jean Merrien rose in considerable surprise, and sought
the second opening. Then the singular fact was explained. The vertical flue no longer existed. In its place
a frightful gap had appeared. The vault of the crypt had
caved in along its entire length, and an enormous heap
of stones and earth had formed before the entrance of the
cavern. Doubtless the explanation of the vapor which
they had beheld from the top of the peak had been coin-
cident with an earthquake which they had not perceived
during their sleep. Some great outburst of gas under
considerable pressure had staved in the rocky wall of
mica schist and limestone, which offered little resistance.
The young Frenchman returned in despair to his companions. Cicely had recovered consciousness ; the pure
air of the mountains, entering her lungs, had dissipated
the giddiness of the first hour or two, and she commenced to shake off the deadly torpor which had taken
possession of her. She heard and spoke without effort,
but at the news that Merrien brought she was overcome by violent emotion, and wept profusely at the
thought of the fate of their companions.

"Oh, the poor people !" she groaned. "Perhaps they

have been surprised by the catastrophe, and buried under
the wall of the vault."

Fortunately their fears were not to be prolonged.
While, at the height of their grief, the three friends
were lamenting the horrible accident, a cry from the
still intact orifice of the second flue caused them all to
turn simultaneously.

Dr. MacGregor was standing on the brink, with a
hilarious expression, his hands outstretched. It was he
who had called. Behind him the rest of the company,
safe and sound, emerged, one by one, from the tunnel.
Goulab, the Breton, Christi, and the two Hindus advanced in turn.

"You are not dead, then !" cried Plumptre, embracing
all the newcomers with delight.

"Dead ! And why, if you please ?" inquired the astonished physician.

" Heavens !" said Merrien, laughing, " when we saw the
caving in of the flue we were mightily troubled about you."

"As we were troubled about you, by Jove !"

"That proves that we heartily love each other,
blessed be God !"

" But since the vertical flue has fallen in, how did you
get up ? By aid of the new hooks ?"

It was Euzen Graec'h who replied, with the energy of
the true sailor :

"Ah ! ouiche ! They are under at least two thousand meters of earth. It will be a smart fellow who
finds them. No, we were luckier than that. Gaurisankar himself cut our road for us, making a stairway
for us as far as the second landing. We have had
only to mount, putting one foot before the other, and
that is all you will have to do to descend."

EUZEN GRAËC'H PLACED THE YOUNG GIRL ON HIS SHOULDER.

After mutual congratulations, and narrating on both sides the various phases of the cataclysm, they set out to regain the valley as soon as possible. And as Cicely could walk only with extreme difficulty, Euzen Graec'h approached her respectfully :

"Will you permit me?" he asked. "You weigh hardly more than my knapsack." The giant lightly caught up the supple form of the young girl, and with a couple of movements, placed her on his left shoulder.

"When the tunnel becomes too narrow for two," he added gayly, "why, m'amselle, we'll try to find some way to let you slide gently down."

Cicely lent herself laughingly to this mode of transportation, and the Breton got along so well that she arrived without mishap at the entrance of the valley, at the same time as the rest of the column. Once there they resumed the recital of their experiences, and each took his share in dispute or narration. Their appetites were keenly sharpened, and now that they knew that they were safe, they hastened to revive their famished stomachs. Salem-Bun dashed their enthusiasm.

"Sahibs, the dinner will not be all that it ought. Sivá has taken the best of our provisions for himself."

The Mohammedan laughed, pointing to the crumbling wall under which the venison of the day before was buried forever.

"No matter, Salem," cried Plumptre, "we will breakfast on what there is. Afterward we'll see to replenishing your larder."

This meal was the last they took in the high valley In the afternoon Miss Weldon pronounced herself sufficiently restored to take up the march again. It was now the 20th of May. The monsoon of June would bring a great change in the temperature, and it would not be well to be on the mountain under much colder winds. It was urgently necessary, then, to get down to the valleys as soon as possible. By the Ouallangchun pass they could quickly reach the base of Kinchinjinga or of the Singálilá mountains. They would then have crossed the Nepál frontier to find themselves in Sikhim, from whence a fortnight's march would suffice to bring the travelers to Dárjiling. That is to say, at the head of the railway to Calcutta. The descent of the valleys was made without much difficulty, but not without some regret for those charming regions where they had found repose after incredible fatigue. The explorers' last look, when they reached the lowest terrace, embraced the entire central mass of Everest, and there upon the peak which they had scaled the day before, Merrien, Plumptre, and Cicely Weldon could proudly contemplate the three flags which they had planted upon a crest up to that moment believed to be inaccessible. The colors of France floated upon the highest rock. Merrien, Graec'h, and Goulab saluted it with shouts.

"Alas!" exclaimed the Frenchman, "we only reached a height of eight thousand and eighty meters. We were within seven hundred and sixty-five of treading the virgin ice of Chingo-pa-mari."

"Well!" cried the major, "let someone else do better, if he can. For my part, I shall only return when the English Government has established an improved elevator, with inhaling rooms for ascensionists."

They broke out in laughter at this idea. When they came to a narrow gorge at the bottom of which roared

the raging waters of the Bárun, the doctor pointed out
to his companions the path of a gigantic land-slide, where
uprooted trees, and hanging rocks and earth still men-
aced disaster, while the base and devastated face of
the mountain was still bleeding from the recent wound.
All eyes filled with tears at this picture, and the cruel
remembrance haunted the minds of all.

"It is there that poor Knebel is sleeping his last
sleep," murmured Cicely, kneeling in prayer, while her
companions reverently bared their heads before the
vast tomb made by the avalanche for the unfortunate
American.

Hardly a week had passed since the catastrophe,
but looking back over the exciting events of their
course, it seemed to the travelers that years had rolled
by since the tragedy.

Their trials were not yet at an end.

.   .   .   .

While the courageous comrades, now satisfied with
their experiment, were regaining the level of the valleys, the fanatical hatred of the worshipers of Siva
was preparing new snares for them. Ramu had not
yet laid aside his rage, and some thirty fanatics, who
had sworn to pursue with him his work of ferocious
vengeance, had accompanied him in his course across
the Máyanama mountains.

Since the fruitless attack at Pangmo, and their dis-
persal by the sudden intervention of the wild dogs,
the devotees of the Fire-God had lost track of the explorers. Obliged to flee before the dholes, they had
been forced to let the travelers get much the start of
them, and in spite of their promptness in recovering
the scent, the assassins had found them again for the first

time at the foot of the Thung-lung pass. This was st ll at too high a level for the Hindus to endure the rigors of the icy nights.

Many of them had already succumbed among the precipices of these dizzy regions. Others had been killed by cold and hunger.

But the implacable Ramu held to his promises. This man had the tenacity and the patience of his race. Capable of dissimulating his plans to any extent, he encouraged his savage accomplices in the pursuit of his sanguinary projects by inflammatory utterances and promises of happiness in another life. A truly infernal energy sustained him, and with the scent of a bloodhound tracking his prey, he guided his little troop of bandits to the places where they believed the travelers would be apt to find the best road.

It was useless for the bandits to undertake the climbing of the peak. Now that the sacred mass had been violated by sacrilegious feet, now that Siva and Parvati had received the cruelest insult and inexpiable offense, it mattered little that the desecraters should mount to a greater or less height. The essential thing was to punish them for their abominable crime.

Thus, after having taken all the precautions necessary to avoid missing the chance of meeting again with the odious white men, Ramu finally led his companions toward the Singalila passes, that is to say, into the zones where the average height of the chain permits inhabitants of warmer regions to sojourn without too greatly feeling the difference in the temperature.

He consequently entered one of the narrowest of the gorges that overlooked Darjiling. It was a bold experiment. So near an English town, almost entirely occupied by a white population, it was truly dangerous presumption to attempt an attack against the explorers. But it was the last chance that remained to the fanatics. Their number was considerably reduced. There were not more than a dozen left, and that was few against the number of their adversaries. They were obliged to move by strategy to attack the Europeans singly, and to mark each march of the column by a murder.

When he was very sure of being on the right track, when his emissaries had notified him that the explorers, after crossing the Ouallangchun pass and the Kánki road, were proceeding by way of the gorges which furnished them with quite an easy road to Dárjíling, Ramu addressed his accomplices in a harangue more inflammatory in proportion to the greater amount of resolution and skill required by the circumstances.

The moment was come to give the Mahádeva the most striking proof of their fidelity. Since they had not been able to prevent accursed foreigners from violating the natural sanctuary of Death and of Renewing, it was a sign that Sivá had preserved the culprits for a more complete expiation. The secret of their abominable desecration must die with them, and after having experienced the criminal joy of penetrating to the inaccessible recesses of the mountain, they would have the disappointment of an obscure end, without having shared their discoveries with their fellow-countrymen.

"As for me," cried the fanatic, "I am resolved to undertake anything to give to the divine flame the satisfaction it demands, and I will lay down my life joyfully in this holy enterprise. But nothing will be gained by dying without having perfected our task, and Sivá will be the better pleased with our death, if we offer him first the souls of the victims he has himself chosen."

Having uttered these words, he gave his orders and sent out his satellites into all the passages by which he could anticipate and await the coming of the explorers. Hidden behind rocks, concealed by the trunks of trees and high grasses, the bandits armed with noose and poniard, some even with rifles, crouched like wild beasts on the watch for patiently expected prey. Ramu had warned them.

If the enemy appeared in full force, they were not to hesitate to use firearms. It would suffice to the Mahádeva of Death if the leaders of the troop were offered up to him according to the most acceptable rite, that is to say by strangling. The others might be put to death in the quickest way. Things stood thus when one of the followers, posted on a very high rock, perceived the column advancing through the narrow valley. He went at once to notify Ramu, who hastened to gather his men together in preparation for an immediate attack. The bandits dispersed for sharpshooting to get the advantage of a surprise and the first shots.

"Glory to our gods!" murmured Ramu, who was giving the rifles to the best marksmen of the band. "Glory to our gods who deliver the enemy into our hands without defense! How the mountains profaned by them will be cleansed by the sacrifice that we are about to offer up! Glory be to Sivá the Renewer, glory be to Káli, goddess of strength and beauty, queen of all worlds!"

PLUMPTRE GOT RID OF THE MAN.

XVII.

THE DEATH OF A HERO.

AT this very moment the travelers, almost at their journey's end, were rejoicing over the fortunate outcome of their expedition. Henceforth they had no further obstacles to fear. They were about to receive their reward for their labors, their sufferings, and their losses. And the recompense came to them first in the form of congratulations from their fellow-men, all the English and the foreigners assembled in the Darjiling sanitarium; then the multitudinous voice of fame, extending over the entire globe, would hear their names, forever glorious upon the four winds of heaven.

To insure their return under the most favorable conditions Dr. MacGregor had made the prudent suggestion that they should notify the English posts of Sikhim. Consequently, as soon as the frontier was crossed the travelers had sent one of the Lepcha mountaineers from the Banks of Tistá with a message to the commanding officer of the first detachment that he should come to. In order not to miss a chance of encounter, the little troop resolved to separate into three groups, as it had frequently done before, and to follow along parallel lines the most frequented roads in which they would have the best chance of meeting English soldiers. It was agreed that they should keep as short a distance apart as possible, in order to warn each other by the firing of a gun, either on the hoped for meeting or on the presence of any danger. This last hypothesis was indeed very probable in a region more savage than Nepál itself, the enormous thickets of which might conceal not only bandits, but also dangerous beasts. Sikhim may, in this regard, be likened to the thickest jungles or most somber forests of Tarái, of which Mahánadi, Kánki, and the Tistá, are only the gradually rising prolongation. Fortunately the descent of the Singálilá offered no insurmountable difficulties, and the gorges of Kánki and the Roman had none of those frightful *cluses* which confine and strangle the torrents of the high Himálayas. In proportion as the levels became lower, the chains of buttresses dominating each other, it became relatively easy to keep up communication between the three groups. Moreover, a rule from which they would not depart was to draw together each time that they came to a wood or thicket of any extent. In that way they would always be numerous enough to meet an unexpected danger.

They had marched two days, observing this same order, when Ramu's spy notified his brigand brothers of the approach of the troop. He had not taken time to ascertain the number. It chanced that the advancing group was composed of Major Plumptre and the two Hindus.

At a turn in the road the assistant cook stopped with a gesture of alarm. He had just noticed an unusual noise, something like a modulated whistle in a peculiar rhythm. The ear of an Indian cannot be deceived. That was not a noise born in the throat of any animal whatsoever. It was certainly a signal sent to some band of dacoits ambushed among the rocks and undergrowth.

"Did you hear that?" asked the domestic of Major Plumptre.

"No," said Plumptre, who had suspected nothing, but who, at his servant's warning, put himself at once upon the defensive.

He halted and raised his carbine to his shoulder. Salem-Bun and the assistant cook imitated him.

Another whistle, which was heard this time by all three, sounded a very short distance away, and suddenly the cook gave a cry which was echoed by a report. At the same moment the Hindu reeled, while a stream of blood streaked the brown skin of his left leg. Poor Salem seemed to be suffering cruelly.

"I am wounded, sahíb," he said, with difficulty.

The major supported him in his arms and drew him quickly under the shelter of a high rock. There he made him sit down while he glanced rapidly at the wound. The ball had plowed a deep furrow in the flesh, but having struck obliquely was not buried therein. Plumptre tore up his handkerchief, and hastily bound up the wound.

A second report rang out—a second ball rebounded from the rock.

But a fleck of smoke rising above the path showed the officer from which side the attack came.

Crouching close to the wall, he advanced to the outer corner, and surveyed the opposite line of rocks.

They had reached a sort of crossroads of a wild beauty. In the center foamed a torrent, a tributary of the Roman or the Ranjit with shallow but icy waters. Upturned rocks, enormous bowlders rounded and polished by the centuries, and the long and frequent rains of that humid country, served as arches to a rustic bridge made of an uprooted tree, so worm-eaten that no one would dare to set foot upon it. Trees of all species—oaks, chestnuts, poplars—bordered the impetuous stream, and giant rhododendrons, geraniums four or five yards in breadth, extended their thick full-sapped vegetation in all directions. Heath, ferns of innumerable varieties, saxifrage and giant begonias, and orchids of all kinds and shapes decorated the earth like a flower bed with all the colors of an exuberant flora.

It was plain that they were approaching the low and warm countries; the Tarái was not far off now.

Plumptre made a sign to the assistant cook, who approached.

"Listen," said he, "we do not know the number of our adversaries. We must hold out to the point of death in order to permit our companions to gain the English cantonments as soon as possible. Furthermore, we have been able to send word ahead, and this is certainly not the route that the soldiers have followed."

The Hindu nodded affirmatively. It was not his business to fight, nor was he engaged for such service, but since necessity imposed it, and they were obliged to defend themselves, he would do his best.

Oriental fatalism kept him, moreover, from rebelling against the decrees of destiny. He put his rifle to his shoulder and waited.

Suddenly, on the point of a rock a dark head appeared, soon followed by a bronzed body. The man was naked. He slid like a serpent over the slippery rock, and his manifest intention was to let himself fall into the bed of the stream, the more easily to turn the enemy's flank.

The enemy, represented now by the major himself, covered him with his rifle, watching his every movement.

The Thug looked in all directions. He went on his hands and knees, a poniard between his teeth, a noose thrown around his neck, his head, in the position that he occupied, was lower than his shoulders. He overhung the stream.

Plumptre had only to press the trigger. The target was too beautiful to resist. His ball struck the Indian between the shoulder blades, breaking the vertebræ of the neck. The bandit tumbled over into the foaming waters which covered him. He was dead indeed.

"That makes one," said the major, quickly reloading his gun.

The major had a prejudice in favor of single-ball rifles, and held repeating rifles in but moderate esteem. They were only good, he affirmed, for shooting beasts, whose rapid and irregular movements often failed to give the hunter a chance to reload.

"But," he added, "in all other cases the mere act of removing and replacing the cartridge relaxes the arms sufficiently for the marksman to take a more careful aim."

The death of their comrade exasperated the fanatics. Forgetful of prudence, or perhaps aware of the inferior number of their adversaries, they leaped simultaneously from the crannies and hollows of the road, and rushed to the assault with cries of fury.

In an instant they crowned the crests of the rocks which inclosed both path and river, and looking down upon the little group, fired into it.

"Ah!" said the major, "I am hit."

A ball had just struck his thigh, causing him horrible suffering. He could keep up only by the greatest effort.

Meanwhile Salem-Bun, who had bound up his own wound, was ready, together with his companion, to return the enemy's fire.

"Let us," commanded the officer, "aim first at those who have rifles."

Unfortunately the reverses the Hindus had sustained in their previous engagements had rendered them cautious. They had learned to mistrust the terrible European rifles. The besieged could nowhere behold a head or an arm which could serve as a target.

Absorbed by the surveillance that they exercised over the opposite bank of the stream, the Scotchman and his companions paid little regard to the rocks which surrounded them, thinking them too difficult and too high for the assailants to dare risk an assault from that side.

Suddenly the officer gave a cry. An arm had just seized him by the body, and with lightning rapidity a running noose had encircled his neck.

But Plumptre's strength served him well. With a blow from the shoulder he got rid of the man who hung upon his back, while, kicking backward, he half staved in the stomach of a second assailant.

The latter did not live long. Salem-Bun dealt him a blow back of the ear with his gun-stock and shattered his skull.

But the other one, before falling under a blow from the butt end of the assistant cook's rifle, had time to plunge his kriss between the major's ribs, and even to strike the baburdji between his shoulders.

"Well," said the brave officer, with an effort, " I believe that I have had my last campaign. I shall not come out of this alive."

He added, with emotion, " If only our friends have not fared as badly."

And, taking no further thought for himself, he sprang out from the hiding place which was now nothing but a trap, followed by the uninjured Hindu.

Four of the adversaries attacked him at the same time. The sight of blood running from the officer's wounds encouraged them in this aggression. Behind the first group of bandits, Plumptre could discern a second, and among them he recognized Ramu.

"Ah, demon !" he roared, " it is you, then, who are continually tracking us."

"Yes," sneered the leader of the assassins, " it is I. You see that I am persevering, Major Plumptre. You belong to Sivá, whom you have outraged. The hour has come to pay the price of your crimes."

He spoke in very bad English, but his gesture, and the expression of his face rendered the meaning of his words only too clear.

"Very well," replied the Scotchman. "We will go before God together, my boy."

And, quickly aiming at the Dogra, he fired.

Ramu threw himself to one side. The ball struck a rock behind him. Ferocious cries greeted this awkwardness on the part of the marksman, who was too badly wounded to aim correctly. The bandits rushed *en masse* upon their two opponents.

Plumptre, using his carbine as a club, repulsed the first assault. Then, seizing his revolver, he fired into the group. One man fell, while the assistant cook broke the arm of another.

But the brave Englishman had received two fresh stabs in the struggle. He lost quantities of blood. He was obliged to lean back against a rock to keep from falling. Profiting by this weakening of the enemy, the Thugs threw themselves upon the Hindu. The latter gave a hoarse cry, and fell foaming at the mouth, with eyes fixed in death. Two nervous hands had just tightened the silk noose, devoted to religious murder, about his neck.

The officer was left alone confronting eight opponents. By a prodigious effort of will, he overcame his increasing weakness. He did not wish the bandits to have the satisfaction of taking him alive, for he knew their joy would be at its height, if they could subject him to the same fate as that of his unfortunate domestic.

With his revolver still smoking in his hand, he awaited the near approach of a fresh assault, so that his benumbed hand might aim more truly.

It was Ramu himself who sprang to the attack.

Climbing treacherously along the rocks he flanked the enemy, and while Plumptre with clouded eyes, beheld only the group directly in front of him, the

Dogra leaped suddenly upon him, struck his rifle arm helpless, and took him by the throat with fingers of steel.

The major was lost this time, unless some miracle occurred.

At the same moment an angry shout rang out above everyone's head. Two men who seemed to have fallen from the clouds bounded among the startled Thugs.

With two saber-strokes, Jean Merrien had cleaved a skull in two, and cut off an arm. Euzen, for his part, had run to the major, gripping the shoulder of the Dogra, who gave a howl of rage and pain.

"This time, my lad," said the Breton, "you are going to settle your account."

To bend him across his herculean knee, and bind his arms with the very cord which he employed in his murderous rites, was a matter of a few seconds for Graec'h. Then leaving his captive, whom he kicked into a hollow of the rock, he returned to the swooning major, but already the doctor and Goulab had carried him some distance away, and with the aid of Cicely Weldon, who had become a woman again in this rôle of Sister of Charity, had examined the officer's injuries and dressed his wounds.

The six surviving fanatics had tried to flee. They had not been able to get far. A line of English soldiers had barred their way, and two among them had been killed just as they reached the clumps of rhododendrons. The four others, carefully bound, were reserved for the more inglorious death of the gallows.

What had taken place is easy of explanation. While Major Plumptre and the two Indians entered the narrow defile which had developed into a snare for them, the two other columns pursued their parallel marches, and soon encountered the English detachment which was sent from Dárjiling to serve as an escort of honor. They at once endeavored to rejoin their comrades. Guided by the noise of firing, they had hastened their course, arriving too late, unfortunately, to prevent the catastrophe. The assistant cook was dead, the major dying, and Salem-Bun, who was picked up in the hollow of the rocks, was hardly better off. The poor baburdji had been stabbed under the left shoulder blade by a Malay kriss. After examining the wound, the doctor concluded that none of the vital organs were involved, and that the wounded man would recover, though but slowly.

They laid both the wounded upon hastily constructed litters of branches, and the troop started sadly on. It was a funeral train.

But before quitting the scene of the drama, the soldiers demanded the just punishment of the criminals.

"No," replied the officer in command of the detachment; "these scoundrels belong to the judges. The gallows await them."

Ramu, now standing in chains among his four accomplices, wore a smile of ironical disdain.

"You will deliver me to the Mahádeva, the Renewer. I have fulfilled my destiny in this world. I shall be taken again to the bosom of the gods. I thank you."

The officer stopped, and cast upon the fanatic a glance that made him tremble.

"Yes," he said, "you do not fear death. But how will Sivá receive the dishonored follower who was not able to escape disgrace?"

The five captives had comprehended these terrible words. They lowered their heads, and commenced all at once to tremble.

The officer had made a sign. Five men of the escort approached and made four of the wretches kneel down. One of the soldiers carried upon his person one of the short round razors used by Hindu barbers. He polished the blade.

"Observe what is about to take place," said the Englishman to Ramu. "You will suffer the same disgrace."

The leader of the Thugs turned away, shuddering. It was evident that the punishment in preparation was the most horrible one that such men could conceive of. Their groans and prayers spoke their moral distress.

"Do your duty!" commanded the officer, addressing the soldier.

The latter was a Mohammedan. While two of his comrades held the head of each Thug motionless, he drew the razor from the nape of the neck to the top of the skull, shaving the thick hair in a longitudinal band. Then approaching the corpse of the assistant before depositing it in the grave, he dipped a cloth in the coagulated blood of the wounds and rubbed it over the shaven heads and faces of the four fanatics.

The officer regarded the bandits ironically, murmuring:

"He who appears before Sivá with blood upon his face is banished forever from Káilas. If some days of life are granted him, he must climb the Kedárnáth road upon his knees, and fast thirty days upon the snows of Nanda-Devi."

And with a burst of terrible laughter :

"You will ask the judge at Dárjiling to allow you time to purify yourself."

Then turning toward Ramu, who was raving like a maniac, he said, grinding his teeth :

"Your turn, Dogra. You are a Rájput. For you it is still more serious. You will lose your rank and your caste."

The bandit gave a desperate leap and overturned one of the soldiers who held him, but his foot slipped and he fell into the stream without doing himself any harm.

It was the iron hand of Euzen Graec'h that drew him out. The Breton addressed the English officer :

"Saving your presence, lieutenant, I beg to attend to this pretty scoundrel myself."

And in less than no time he had shaved the wretch, not without pretty well scratching the leathery scalp.

Then, as Ramu writhed in the fierce grasp of the Breton sailor, with hoarse cries trying to escape the ignominy, the colossus subjected him to the same humiliation as the other fanatics.

"Now," exclaimed the Breton, "I have sworn to myself to break this brute's back. I am sorry for the judge and the executioner. They will have to content themselves with the other four."

In less time than it takes to tell it, before the officer and soldiers could interfere, Euzen had seized the Thug by such hair as he had left, and drawing him violently backward broke his spine over his knee.

Then raising the gasping body at arms' length before the eyes of the company, fascinated and stupefied by this Samson feat, he threw him violently into the waters of the torrent.

BUZEN HURLED RAMU INTO THE WATERS OF THE TORRENT.

"Go and die as you have lived, among your brothers, the tigers!"

Such was the funeral oration of the Dogra Rájput Ramu, worshiper of the Fire-God, and friend of the Hindu doctor, Madar-Goun.

The return of the explorers was not the triumph they had hoped for. They came back with heavy hearts and tearful eyes.

Their noble comrade Plumptre re-entered Dárjiling only to die there.

He had at least the satisfaction of living long enough to see around his bed the representatives of all that England and Europe counted as illustrious and worthy.

The Lord Governor came in person to visit him, and to confer upon him in the name of the Queen the title and insignia of knight.

The major, at the very last, called Merrien to him.

"My dear friend," he said, pressing his hand, "you are the most loyal man in the world, and I regret not having known you earlier. Pardon my ill-temper on the journey. I have for Miss Weldon the same feeling as yourself. Marry her! You are worthy of one another, and you will be a perfect couple."

The dying man said the same to Cicely, weeping as he spoke. Then joining the hands of the two young people, he added:

"I hope you will take my poor Salem into your service when he is recovered. MacGregor gives me hope that that will be soon. He well deserves it. As to myself, will you make me one promise?"

"Whatever you desire, my friend, we will do," declared Jean Merrien through his sobs.

A pale smile played about the lips of the dying man.

"It will be very difficult, but you are not people
to stop at difficulties. I have carried with me a delightful memory of the valley that we discovered on
the banks of the Bárun. I have left you in my will
the sum of two thousand pounds, with the request
that you will bear my remains to that enchanting spot.
If necessary, you can buy the valley of the Maharája
of Nepál, and found there some benevolent institution for
the poor Englishmen who do not know where to find
shelter."

"We promise it, my friend," responded Merrien and
Cicely solemnly.

These were the last words of Major Plumptre.

At Dárjiling, then at Calcutta, they gave him an imposing funeral. Then the same company which had followed the brave officer to his last dwelling place went
to congratulate Jean Merrien and Cicely Weldon, whose
marriage was celebrated in the Catholic church of the
capital of India.

Euzen Graec'h was Merrien's best man, and Morley,
the faithful companion of the American, filled the same
office for her.

Dr. MacGregor led her to the altar. Little Christi
figured as a choir boy. While belonging to the sect of
Vishnu, Goulab bore himself with much composure in
the church, and Salem-Bun, who, fortunately, had recovered, forgot that he was a Mussulman in admiring in
bridal dress, and with long fair hair almost grown out
again, her whom he had so long beheld in the masculine costume that she had worn with so much ease
and jauntiness.

Finally, the evening before the explorers with their
attendants took passage for Europe on one of the

steamers of the Messageries Maritimes, the Lord Governor gave a dinner for them.

"Is this the last campaign you wish to make, madame?" he asked gayly of Cicely.

"Milord," replied the young woman, laughing, "Scripture teaches that the wife must follow her husband. Now my husband intends to visit, next year, the Trans-Himálayas, to reach the source of the Tsang-bo, and penetrate as far as Lhassa into the cavern of mysteries."

"Then I may bid you *au-revoir!*" responded the viceroy, gallantly kissing the hand of the brave woman.